Also by Cynthia Kadohata

CHECKED

Cynthia Kadohata

WITH ILLUSTRATIONS BY MAURIZIO ZORAT

atheneum

A CAITLYN DLOUHY BOOK

ATHENEUM BOOKS FOR YOUNG READERS

NEW YORK LONDON TORONTO SYDNEY NEW DELHI

ATHENEUM BOOKS FOR YOUNG READERS • An imprint of Simon & Schuster Children's Publishing Division • 1230 Avenue of the Americas, New York, New York 10020 • This book is a work of fiction. Any references to historical events, real people, or real places are used fictitiously. Other names, characters, places, and events are products of the author's imagination, and any resemblance to actual events or places or persons, living or dead, is entirely coincidental. • Text copyright © 2018 by Cynthia Kadohata • Cover illustrations copyright © 2018 by Klas Fahlén • Interior illustrations copyright © 2018 by Maurizio Zorat • Hockey stick illustration on page 405 copyright © 2018 by Thinkstock/Skarin • All rights reserved, including the right of reproduction in whole or in part in any form. • ATHENEUM BOOKS FOR YOUNG READERS is a registered trademark of Simon & Schuster, Inc. Atheneum logo is a trademark of Simon & Schuster, Inc. • For information about special discounts for bulk purchases, please contact Simon & Schuster Special Sales at 1-866-506-1949 or business@simonandschuster.com. • The Simon & Schuster Speakers Bureau can bring authors to your live event. For more information or to book an event, contact the Simon & Schuster Speakers Bureau at 1-866-248-3049 or visit our website at www.simonspeakers.com. • Also available in an Atheneum Books for Young Readers hardcover edition • Cover design by Russell Gordon; interior design by Mike Rosamilia • The text for this book was set in Neutraface Slab Text. • The illustrations for this book were rendered digitally. • Manufactured in the United States of America • First Atheneum Books for Young Readers paperback edition February 2019 • 10 9 8 7 6 5 4 3 • The Library of Congress has cataloged the hardcover edition as follows: Names: Kadohata, Cynthia, author. • Title: Checked / Cynthia Kadohata. • Description: First edition. | New York : Atheneum, [2018] | A Caitlyn Dlouhy Book. | Summary: To help his dog through cancer treatment, Conor gives up hockey and finds himself considering who he is without the sport that has defined him, and connecting more with his family and best friend. • Identifiers: LCCN 2017025626 | ISBN 9781481446617 (hc) | ISBN 9781481446624 (pbk) • ISBN 9781481446631 (eBook) • Subjects: | CYAC: Hockey—Fiction. | Doberman pinscher—Fiction. | Dogs—Fiction. | Veterinary medicine—Fiction. | Fathers and sons—Fiction. | Single-parent families—Fiction. | Friendship—Fiction. | BISAC: JUVENILE FICTION / Sports & Recreation / Hockey. | JUVENILE FICTION / Animals / Dogs. | JUVENILE FICTION / Family / Parents. • Classification: LCC PZ7.K1166 Che 2018 | DDC [Fic]—dc23 • LC record available at https://lccn.loc.gov/2017025626

To hockey kids all over the globe chasing
their dreams—or just having fun

CHAPTER 1

I GAZE AT the tall stairs and pause, gathering my strength, leaning my head back to stretch my neck. The sky's a little gray 'cause there's a fire near our house—we live in Canyon Country, near the Angeles National Forest, and the forest is on fire. But this morning the smoke still looked far away, so Dad and I decided to drive to the park and do our usual sixty-minute Saturday workout, just 'cause we're workout animals. If you make an excuse not to work out one time, that means you can make an excuse the next time too. We've brought my Doberman, Sinbad, like we always do. There're 280 concrete stairs leading from one level of the park to another. Now Sinbad looks at me eagerly, wagging his stub of a tail, but he never climbs up and down the stairs with us. He just doesn't see the point.

Dad starts running up the stairs, and I follow. "Come on, Sinbad!" I cry out, but even without looking, I know he won't join in. Dad's thirty-five and in amazing shape for an older guy. He's already way ahead of me, so I pick it up. It's eighty degrees, though it's only seven in the morning, and I'm immediately sweating. June in Canyon Country can get pretty hot.

My mind is on how my next week is looking hockey-wise. Tomorrow, three and a half hours of stick time with Shu Zhang. Then dryland muscle work with Shu. Monday, power skating and coaches' time with Aleksei Petrov. Tuesday, pre-tryout clinic with Dusan Nagy. Wednesday, off day. Thursday, lesson with Ivan Bogdanov. He's a figure skater who competed for Bulgaria in the Olympics. I skate with him to help my agility. Friday, pre-tryout clinic with another club in case I don't make my first-choice team in almost two weeks. Saturday, three and a half hours of stick time with Shu. Then dryland with Shu. Plus any scrimmage that I can latch onto during the week. Plus working out a few times with my dad. Oh, and sometimes I do stick time by myself, just to get on the ice.

Hockey is in my soul. I inherited my soul from Dad. He made it to the American Hockey League, which is the main development league for the National Hockey League, which is the premier hockey league in the world. He says that when he was twenty-three years old and briefly the best player on his team, the NHL was so close he could taste it. Then he made it up there—to the NHL!—but got sent back down in three weeks. All together he stayed in the AHL for four years, all in Des Moines, Iowa. That's where I was born, a million miles from here.

We sprint up and down the steps for fifteen minutes, then trudge up and down for another fifteen. Afterward—soaking wet—I lie on the grass to rest by the steps. Sinbad sniffs at me.

"Enough relaxing!" Dad says, but I've only been lying there for maybe *one* minute!

"Seriously? I just laid down!" He looks at me

with zero sympathy. That's the way it is with hockey. Nobody has any sympathy for you, not one person.

We do push-ups—I can do thirty-three perfect ones and a few more half-baked ones. But I'm somehow getting my energy back. Then we rest for thirty seconds and do clap push-ups—I do ten. Usually I only do eight, so I'm suddenly thinking I'm pretty beast.

Squats, several exercises with a ten-pound medicine ball. Frog jumps, one-legged slaloms, scissors, double Dutch. Five hundred crunches. I'm an animal!

We finish with stretching. I'm a flexible kid, but for some reason I hate stretching. I just go through the motions.

Then Dad takes a break with his phone while I walk off with Sinbad. There's hardly anyone in the park. Dad lets me go off by myself with Sinbad 'cause my dog's really muscular and really protective. Dobermans stick to you like superglue. Otherwise I'm not allowed to be out alone. Dad's a cop, so he's seen a lot of bad stuff—he knows what can happen to a kid on his own, even in Canyon Country. Sinbad and Dad are my only family. I mean, I have an aunt and my grandparents, but I don't have a mom or sisters and brothers and cousins. My mom died when I was two. I can't remember her at all, but Dad says I was so close to her that for my first year nobody else could even hold me. Then my dad was married for eight years to another woman, but it didn't work out for a bunch of reasons that I'll get into at some point. One reason was hockey—when a kid plays travel hockey, it takes up a lot of space in your life. Some people don't like that.

When I started playing, it was like Dad was living through me, but not in a bad way. It was more like him and me got so bonded he was out there with me on the ice during games. Even though I play defense, I got the winning goal in one playoff game, and later in the car he was tearing up about it. Getting that goal was pretty much the best moment of my life. Everybody was jumping all over me and pounding my helmet so that my brain was ringing and I was in a total other, like, awareness plane. When I told Dad about that later, his eyes got a faraway look, and he said, "Yeahhhhhhhh . . ."

CHAPTER 2

HEADING HOME, AS the car drives along the 5, I see smoke billowing over a long stretch of hills and rising into the sky, so that it looks like evening—even though it's nine a.m. The sun is red. The fire just started Thursday, but it's already at fifteen thousand acres. Fire's scary, but not totally unexpected—we're in Canyon Country, man. Thing is, I love our house. It's not a nice house or anything compared to the houses of a lot of the other guys in hockey. But I love it. I love seeing the hills in the mornings and walking Sinbad before school on the path just a mile from where we live. I was pretty much born to live here in the middle of all these hills and woods. Even if I make the NHL someday, I'm staying in Canyon Country.

A few streets over from where we live are some fancy-schmancy houses, nothing a cop like my dad would ever be able to afford. But he loves his job. He can't believe anyone pays him to do it. Our house is tan, a thousand square feet with two small bedrooms, a tiny dining room, a living room, and one bathroom. The backyard's just dirt and yellow-green patches of grass. Dad doesn't like to water a lot 'cause water's so expensive. I mean, I feel guilty every time I flush the toilet. I just see dollar signs going down the drain. I go out back every couple of days to clean up dog poop, but otherwise we don't use the yard much.

When we pull onto our street, we see fire trucks at the end of the cul-de-sac. It feels like it's already a hundred degrees. There are no flames, but a lot of smoke rises just over a ridge. It's hard to think at first—the smoke just seems so *big* that all I can do is stare.

"Maybe we should start loading up the truck," Dad says.

We packed up yesterday, just in case the fire got close, so loading won't take long. Dad's a motor cop, and yesterday he took his police motorcycle to a friend's house. We also have a fifteen-year-old Volvo that's our primary car. But we're leaving that behind.

I go in, grab my hockey bag and two sticks, and load them into the truck, Sinbad following me in and out again. I look at my hands a second, not sure why. Maybe just to make sure I'm really here. Like is this all real? Is that big fire really coming?? So. Sleeping bag, hockey gear, hockey and skating trophies and medals, luggage with clothes, dog bed, ten pounds of dog food, and Sinbad's water bowl. I finish loading up. Aunt Mo, who lives all the way in Long Beach, has offered us her place to camp out at. Dad carries boxes of photographs, his old hockey scrapbooks and trophies, and boxes of documents. He squints out at the smoke, and for the first time I see a flame. "Dad!" I say. "Dad!" But I don't move. I can't.

"You better disconnect your computer," my father says calmly. His calmness makes me able to move again.

I rush in and unhook my computer, my fingers shaking a bit. In this area, you always know a fire is possible, what with the drought and living near the tree-covered hills, but somehow when it's here, you just want to panic, even though you know you can't. But the urge to panic is strong—I just want to scream and run away. "Gotta get my stuff," I say out loud. I trust my dad 100 percent, so if he thinks I have time to get my stuff, then I have time to get my stuff, period. I pack my computer, monitor, speakers, and keyboard into a box, then carry it all out. Dad is just placing his own computer into the truck. The flames have expanded into a whole row, and a flame jumps about ten feet, exactly while I'm watching, so that the fire's maybe two short blocks away.

"Dad! Dad, shouldn't we go now?" I ask, my voice sounding squeaky.

A flame jumps another ten feet, and Dad says casually, "Yeah, we better just leave everything else and get going."

Sinbad is upset and starts barking at nothing in particular. The firemen spray at the flames, but suddenly the fire springs down the hill, and Dad and I jump into the truck. Sinbad barks more before hopping in. He snarls from inside.

Dad drives to the end of the block, and we sit in park for a few minutes as the flames grow larger. Dad just wants to stare back at our house. Then a fireman starts yelling at us, and we drive off. I open the window and yell out, "Thank you!" to the fireman, who holds up a hand in acknowledgment.

"Dad! What if we never see the house again?" I ask.

"We've got insurance," Dad says, but I can tell he's worried.

A huge roar fills the air, and a jet passes low over the hills while dropping a load of red chemicals, some of which end up on the houses at the end of the road. That's called Phos-Chek—Dad told me last year when we happened to drive by a big wildfire in San Bernardino. It's colored fertilizer and water, and you drop it on trees. It insulates the trees from the heat, and after the fire's put out, the fertilizer helps the vegetation grow again. Dad knows some stuff about firefighting 'cause he once thought about trying to become a smokejumper or a hotshot after his hockey career ended. Then he had me, and he didn't want to travel away from home, like he'd have to during the fire season, in case I grew up and wanted to play hockey in the summers. A couple of years back, when those nineteen hotshots got killed fighting a fire in Arizona, we went to their 125-mile funeral procession with about a dozen of Dad's cop friends and their kids. Thousands of people lined the roads. It was July—hot as frick—and many people were crying. We all stood at attention as the white hearses passed by, and knowing what was in those hearses, I remember this desperate feeling, like I wished I could go back in time and shout at those hotshots, "The fire's coming! RUN!" We always take Sinbad on nonhockey road trips, so he was at the funeral too, and I swear that dog knew how serious it all was. He stood there at perfect attention, like a show dog. Going to that funeral is why I always say "hi" or "thank you" to firefighters.

Now I notice Mr. Griffin at the end of our street, standing there in his flip-flops like he's taking in some scenery.

"Should I tell Mr. Griffin to leave?" I don't wait

for an answer as I roll down the window and call out, "It's time to evacuate!"

He waves at me like I've only said, *Hi, how are you?*

"Evacuate!" I say again.

He nods, and I keep watching him stand there until we turn the corner. He's a Vietnam vet, so maybe he's not worried about danger? Like he's seen it all? "Why don't you call your aunt?" Dad suggests.

I take out my phone and dial Aunt Mo. She doesn't answer, so I leave a message: "Hi, Aunt Mo. It's Conor. We're evacuating. We're on our way to your house."

The air's gotten so smoky, it's hard to see too far down the street. Dad drives slowly.

"Will we be homeless for a while if the fire burns our house?" I ask.

My dad shoots me a look. "I'm not going to let you be homeless," he says, like maybe he's annoyed I asked. The one thing about my dad is that he can get a little sensitive sometimes about certain things, like his ability to provide for me. So now I can feel he might be annoyed.

I hug Sinbad. Dad's my dad, of course. There's

nobody like your father. But Sinbad's with me every second I have free. There's nobody like your dog, either. We got him in a high-kill shelter in Los Angeles. We went to three shelters that day, but we wanted to make sure we got the right dog.

Sinbad's ninety-five pounds; probably around six years old. He lies across my lap.

When we finally reach the 14, it's closed to traffic, so we have to take surface streets to the 5. We pass plenty of people driving trailers with horses and other animals. I saw on the news that there's a large-animal evacuation center set up nearby. We even see a male lion in a cage on a trailer behind a pickup—there are several animal sanctuaries in the area, and a couple of them house big cats. It's kind of surreal to see a lion like that, practically right in my own neighborhood. It just goes to show what a crazy world it is.

It's sixty miles to Aunt Mo's house, and the traffic sucks, so it takes two hours to get there. The whole time I'm thinking about our house—twenty-four hours from now, it might not be there. Everything depends on the firefighters now.

In Long Beach, we unload and say hello to my aunt. Then I go take out the lawn mower. Most people with yards have gardeners, but Aunt Mo has me about once a month, and if I'm not around, she does it herself. It's cooler in Long Beach 'cause it's near the water, so the heat is bearable as I work. Sinbad just lies in the shade on the porch. After I'm done, I pull out weeds and cut down dead flower stems. When I'm finished, things look pretty good if I say so myself. Could "gardener" be a good backup if I don't make it in hockey?

After the yard's done, I check my phone, see the fire has spread to seventeen thousand acres. One person has tweeted out a picture of a huge cloud of bloodred smoke rising behind some hills. But I can't tell from the picture exactly where it was taken from. Sinbad stands up and paws at the door, so we go in.

Aunt Mo is tall like Dad and looks just like him— they're twins—with pale brown hair and green eyes. I'm half-Japanese, so I have dark hair. When I was younger, a couple of times strangers said to my dad, "He's cute. Where did you get him?" They thought I was adopted.

Aunt Mo is a compulsive movie watcher. She watches three or four hundred movies a year. That would average out to two hours a day, every day. It's like a part-time job. She never actually *goes* to a movie, though.

After I get us all drinks, we sit in front of her huge television.

"All right . . ." She picks up a notebook and flips through it. "Next on my list is *Brooklyn*. It's about a young woman who immigrates to the US from Ireland in the fifties. Okay with you boys?"

That sounds super boring, but I say, "Sounds great."

"Sounds great," echoes Dad.

As we watch the movie, I keep checking my phone, but there are no real updates on the fire except for more tweets with dramatic photographs taken from various areas around Los Angeles, where you can see huge clouds of smoke, and flames that look like the edges of the sun. I think of our little house, sitting there in the middle of all that smoke. In my mind, our home is the size of a Monopoly house, and the fire is as big as it is in real life. Ughhh.

CHAPTER 3

AT FOUR A.M. when my alarm rings, I'm up instantly. Sinbad doesn't move—he usually doesn't get up before nine or ten, 'cause Sinbad needs his rest. That's his way. I mean, if someone was killing me or something, he'd get up and bite their head off, but otherwise, he needs his rest. I'm in my sleeping bag on the living room floor. I go into the kitchen and study the coffeemaker. It's easy to figure out, so I start Dad's coffee, eat some cereal, then go into the guest room. "Dad!" I say. "It's four ten!"

"I'm up!" he says, which is usually the first thing he says. "Did you pack your hockey bag?" he asks, which is usually the second thing he says.

"Yeah, I'm good to go."

He's dressed in about one minute, pours coffee into his thermos cup, and we're off. In the car he turns on the country music station, which plays songs about drinking, falling in love, and losing love. We're both naturally early risers, but today he looks like he got about an hour of sleep. Full-on bags under his eyes. I mean, he's old, but he's not *that* old.

"Dad," I say.

He comes out of a daydream and asks, "What is it, Conor?"

"You okay? You look real tired."

"Just thinking about the house. I remember how cool it was to buy my first house. Do you remember that? But it should be okay. Mr. Griffin is hunkered down—I called him last night after you went to bed. The fire seems to have passed, but it's not far away enough yet for us to go back. The wind could change."

I look at my dad. Something doesn't feel right, so I ask, "Is that it, just the house?"

"Let me tell you something. Divorce kicks your butt. I'm still healing," is what he says.

Dad and Jenny have been divorced for only seven months. I nod, but he doesn't see. "Okay, man, I was just asking. Just making sure you're, you know, okay." I pause, then guilt washes over me. "Are we okay for money? I know all this hockey stuff costs a lot." I ask this 'cause Jenny received a load of money when they got divorced. She was mostly going to school while they were married, but she got half the money Dad earned. She's getting a PhD in English, specializing in Milton, who is some famous writer guy. Dad also pays her alimony, which is money he gives her every month.

"Conor, I've told you this before. If you want to go for this, I'll find the money. I'll work two jobs if I have to, but one way or another, you're going to skate as much as you want. Got that?"

"Got it. But I don't want you to work two jobs."

"I was just saying. I'm not really going to work two jobs. We're okay for money. We just can't buy groceries." He tosses me a look. "That's a joke, Conor. Lighten up."

What can I say? When he's right, he's right: I thought he was serious when he said that about groceries.

I'm pretty sure my stepmom leaving grew out of me playing hockey so much, and now my dad never has money 'cause he got divorced and 'cause I play hockey. So I say it out loud.

"So is it the money that you're crying about?"

He looks at me, confused. "What do you mean?"

"I heard you crying a couple of times at night. And I just mean she never would have left if I didn't play hockey."

He doesn't deny it. Instead he says, "You know what? Jenny was all about going to school, and that's okay. You were her second, or maybe more like her fourth, priority. But you're my first priority. That's just the way it is. I would never cry about money. Never. I don't know what I'm crying about, to be honest."

I can see Dad's getting riled up. He wants me to chase my hockey dreams in the worst way. He spent his childhood playing hockey even more than I do, and it's all he wants me to do—so that I'll be able to compete with kids from cold climates who skate constantly. When he was four, his parents made a rink in their backyard for him to skate in for hours every day during the winter. They wanted us to move to their town in Iowa so they could remake the rink for me, but California has become a hotbed for youth hockey, and Iowa, not so much. There are some California midget and bantam guys who are some of the best youth hockey players in the country. Bantam and midget are the next two older levels after mine. We don't have as many great hockey players as in cold states like Michigan and Minnesota, but teams from my club have gone to the national championships three times. That's one of my dreams. I got lots of dreams.

I actually know there's another reason Dad doesn't want to move to Iowa. It's a pretty safe state, but there were those two Iowa boys who got kidnapped during their paper routes and were never found. It was a long time ago, but I heard Dad talking about it once when his parents were visiting. I could tell something about those two cases just stuck under Dad's skin. That's why he got me Sinbad, so I could go out into the world and grow up, but I could stay safe, too. Dad and his friends always say that the hardest part about being a cop is when something happens to a kid. Basically, you become a cop thinking you're gonna save the world, and then you find out you can't save everyone. Some days you can't even save anyone at all . . . some weeks . . . some months.

When you're a cop's kid, you kind of realize things about people that are maybe darker than what most kids realize. My dad sees a lot of bad stuff at work. I mean, he's seen a seventy-five-year-old woman with her chest sliced open, he's seen a two-year-old who'd drowned, and he's seen five dogs dead in someone's garage. I hear all this stuff listening to him talk with his cop friends when they play poker. I accept what I know—it's just part of my life. Maybe, in a way, that's why I'm so close to Sinbad. I love my dad more than anyone in the world, but sometimes I can feel something kind of emanating out of him. It's a darkness or a sadness or something, and as much as I love him, I just can't be around him sometimes. But then, when I'm with other kids who don't see what I see, that can be hard too. So I just want to be with Sinbad. He's so happy, and he makes me happy.

And see, just like Sinbad gets me away from the darkness, my hockey gets Dad away from his darkness. He even said so one day when he'd had three beers. I see how proud he is of me, and I know the only way to make everything right is to work as hard as I can. It's a lot of responsibility for me, but I don't mind 'cause like I said, hockey is in my soul.

CHAPTER 4

IN HOCKEY I'M what's called a peewee. That's eleven- and twelve-year-olds. I'll be twelve next month, so this is my last year in peewee. I'm trying to make the jump from peewee AA to AAA next season. Tryouts are coming up in less than two weeks. The AAAs are kids who skate fast, pass good, hit the puck hard, and want the puck more than life itself. That's me, I know it. I know it, but I got to prove it to Coach Dusan in the tryouts. Just thinking about this makes my stomach turn. Dad keeps saying, "Don't worry about being worried, worry about getting the puck. Don't think about anything but the puck."

When we get to the rink forty minutes later, Shu, in cargo shorts, is just unlocking the front door. He's sixty, but his calf muscles are still as big as grapefruits. He was on the Chinese national team when he was young.

Shu doesn't say hi. He says, "Last time you lazy, this time work hard."

"I had a stomachache last time."

"I don't care, skate hard or I pinch you." Then he reaches over and pinches my neck, I mean, really pinches HARD.

"Ow! I haven't even done anything yet! How can you pinch me?"

"I forget to pinch you last time," he says, walking away.

Dad heads to the ice, and I head to the dungeon-like locker rooms. Even at this hour, the dungeons are overly warm. I strip and put on my socks, leggings with cup, shirt with built-in neck guard, elbow pads, shin guards, shoulder pads, hockey pants, pants shell, mouth guard, and jersey. Then I focus on my skates. They have to be tied just right, or I'm no good. I pull the laces taut on the bottom eyelets, and then on the top, I wrap the laces twice around my ankles and pull tight but not too tight, then knot them. I stand up and concentrate on my skates. All good.

I'm already sweating as I take off my skate guards and grab my helmet, stick, and water bottle. In the hall I pass Rocko rolling in his hockey bag. "Hey," I say.

"Hey," he says.

That qualifies as a long conversation when it comes to Rocko and me. We used to be good friends—he was in my class in third grade, but he moved to Glendale that summer. Later, by coincidence, we started hockey together, ending up on the same team for two years. Then when I made AAs, and he didn't, he stopped talking to me, even when I said hi. And his mom and dad stopped talking to my stepmom and dad. Some of the kids and parents are like that. Not a lot of them, but some. Maybe we would have drifted apart anyway. He just seems way younger. Like, his dad still ties his skates, even though that's against the rules for peewees. Also, Mr. Rockman likes to complain to the coaches, which doesn't even seem to embarrass Rocko. He complains if he doesn't like the way practice goes, if he doesn't think Rocko played enough in a game, etc. Everybody at the rink knows who the crazy parents are. Some are crazy in a kinda funny way, and some are crazy mad like Mr. Rockman. You gotta have an incredibly talented kid for a coach to take on a parent like that, though some coaches are more tolerant than others of screaming parents. Still, I'm basically cool with Rocko, just don't see the need to try to escalate back into friendship.

Now my dad, even though he knows a lot about hockey, never complains to the coaches. Once in a while, if he has a suggestion, he says he politely shoots the coach an e-mail, but he won't confront a coach like Mr. Rockman does. Dad's main focus is not on the coaches but on me. Dad says you have to work hard to dig every ounce of your talent out of yourself. "You can't be sure how much talent you have until you hit a wall," he told me once. Now and again I think I've hit a wall, and sometimes that gets me so upset I cry, but I push through it and get better.

I stomp down the hall with a bunch of other skaters. Until I step on the ice, I feel like I'm kind of a regular kid. Then I step on the ice, and the world changes. All my working out, all my skating lessons, all my hockey practices, all the time I spend hitting the puck in my driveway—it all comes together and makes me feel like a gladiator or something as I sprint once around the rink with my stick, stopping to slap a puck into the net. I had my skates sharpened yesterday, and they feel great!

A few midget AAAs are among the group here to skate with Shu. Midgets are fifteen to eighteen years old. I've talked to the guys here before. They're seventeen, and they're awesome. They're here 'cause they're reaching for the brass ring. The brass ring is either college or major junior or the pros. Anything, as long as you can keep playing at a high level. Except for Rocko, that's the only type of player who shows up at five in the morning to skate with a sixty-year-old Chinese man who pinches them hard on the neck when he gets mad. I've heard "Don't be lazy, I pinch you" about, I don't know, fifty times. And I've been pinched maybe twenty times, including today.

"Don't be lazy!" I shout for no reason, and skate at top speed halfway around the rink and come to a quick stop, spraying ice into the air.

Fifteen guys and one girl show up. Except for the girl—Ji-Hye—Rocko and I are the only ones who haven't made AAA yet. Ji-Hye plays college hockey, and she's super mean. Me and Rocko usually just try to avoid being in line near her so she doesn't beat up on us.

Shu appears and says, "I time you." He swings his stopwatch around in the air, and we all get in line. I get in front of Ji-Hye, but she pushes me out of the way and says, "Move over, or I'll sit on you." She's serious. She pushes and trips boys who are smaller than her, and then she sits on them. I let her go in front of me, since it's pretty embarrassing when she sits on you. You can't get up. You're only set free when Shu decides to make her get off. She lives in Koreatown near Jae-won, my best friend from last season's team. When I'm over at his house sometimes and she's home from school, we troll her just to get on her nerves, like we go to her parents' place and ring the doorbell. I don't remember if she sat on me first, or if Jae-won and I trolled her first. The funny thing is, at the same time, we all respect each other.

One by one, Shu times us. The fastest guy around

the rink clocks in at 14.45. That's blazing for a seventeen-year-old in full gear. Ji-Hye's lap is 16 flat. Mine is 16.21. I'm fast for a peewee. But I know I still need to learn to get into the hockey zone, like how it happens sometimes when I feel like I can see half the ice at the same time, my peripheral vision as good as my forward vision. Like how it happens when I know what a player is going to do before he does it. "*That's* a hockey player," my dad likes to say.

Shu pinches no one, so we all clocked pretty well for us. Next we zigzag through the cones while touching one of our hands on the ice. Then Shu runs a full-ice scrimmage. I manage some good moves and even dangle a midget before getting off a slap shot. During a break, Shu says approvingly, "You make AAA. You AAA." Really?? I stand there for a moment, letting his words wash over me, inside me. That's the first time he's ever complimented me! I look over to my dad; he's talking to the other parents. I'm pretty much 100 percent certain all they talk about is hockey. Maybe they throw in a few sentences about golf or politics or whatever, but basically they talk about hockey. Then it's like *whoosh*, as soon as I take my mind off the ice, I think about our house. In my mind the fire's huge, and the houses and firefighters are tiny. I see the flames lick at the sky, but I shake the image out of my head and turn to Shu, aware that I'm frowning. *Focus.* There are a million things that can distract you every time you're on the ice. Sometimes big things.

So: *focus.*

After three and a half hours of alternating drills and scrimmages, one of the workers revs up the Zamboni to level the ice. We change and go outside to do muscle work.

Muscle work starts with frog jumps up and down the big garden. The parents are watching, even though it's hot outside. My quads are burning. Rocko collapses, but I keep going. A couple of other kids collapse. I keep going. Ji-Hye hasn't stopped either— she's stronger than some of the boys. Finally it's just me, her, and the midgets. Two more jumps, then with a groan I collapse to the ground and breathe hard. I groan again. Can't move my legs. I don't even watch what's going on, just wait for it to end. After a minute, Shu taps me with a foot, and I just look at him as he skates away. Next is push-ups. I do my thirty-three. Then everybody's counting as the midgets keep going and going and going. The world record for nonstop push-ups was set by a Japanese guy who did more than ten thousand. But Shu tells them to stop at two hundred. So that's about six times more than me—means I need to work harder. Me and Ji-Hye get pinched at the same time. "Lazy, you both lazy." *Ouch*—it feels like he's just torn off a piece of my flesh. In fact, it makes me almost dizzy for a second.

A few more exercises, and thirty minutes later Shu sets us free. When Dad and I walk back through the rink, the figure skaters are on. Ivan's out there working on spins with a girl. I've seen her around, and her skating is as amazing as frick. You concentrate on eight edges when you figure-skate—front left outside, front left inside, etc.—and she works her edges perfectly. She's like a frickin' brain surgeon at ten years old.

I stop and drop my gear, then hop up and down on a bench up to thirty. Then I pick up my gear and continue. Dad doesn't say anything.

I take a moment to transfer my mind from the rink to the rest of the world. The rest of the world where you get in cars and drive around to places that aren't rinks and communicate with people and eat something besides buffalo wings and soggy salad from the rink café. It's hot here in Burbank, and I think about how hot and dry it'll be by our house today.

"Dad, can we drive by the house to see if it's okay?"

"Read my mind," he replies as we walk across the parking lot. "Taco Bell first?"

"Sure," I reply. As far as I'm concerned, someone should declare Taco Bell a national treasure. You know what I'm saying?

CHAPTER 5

WE'RE ABOUT AN hour from home. I eat my tacos over the bag, trying hard not to spill. Weekends, I get to eat junk food one day, and this is the day. But thinking about our house, I don't really enjoy my tacos as much as usual. The lettuce feels like paper in my mouth, and the meat tastes more like clumps of seasoning than actual beef. I eat everything anyway, 'cause I'm food-driven like Sinbad. Half an hour later I can see smoke in the distance. As we get closer, the sky's dark like yesterday. It's unbelievable, actually. I check my phone: the fire's at twenty-two thousand acres, but I can't find anything about houses burning down. I try to search my instincts, to see if our home is within those twenty-two thousand acres. But I come up blank.

The 14 is open, so we get there fast. Our street is silent, empty. There's smoke and flames way in the distance but nothing nearby. All the houses look intact, but there're signs of a fire: a car that looks burned out, a blackened tree, the charred front of a neighbor's house. I spot our little house! I feel like it's so beautiful, it's practically shining. I smile at Dad, and he smiles back. A man in some kind of uniform-like shirt walks up to the window and knocks. Dad lowers the glass, and the man says, "You live on this street? We were just about to lift the evacuation orders. The fire's heading in the opposite direction now."

"Thank you. Appreciate you taking care of our street," my dad says.

"Sure thing. I heard it wasn't so bad on this one. Next street over, there were some problems. Have a nice day."

"Thank you!" I call out, and he raises a couple of fingers in the air in reply.

We go to check out our house. The backyard is blackened, and the outside wall is charred. The avocado tree looks dead, the leaves in a circle on the ground. I push at some crunchy leaves with my foot. No more guacamole for us—we can't afford avocados from the store. "All that guac was fun while it lasted," I say.

Dad just laughs. "We got someplace to stay tonight!" We high-five. We still have a house! I go check my room, and everything is completely, completely normal. *Yes!*

We head back to Long Beach to get our stuff. I zone out—you get expert at that when you play travel hockey, 'cause of all the driving you have to do. When we get to Aunt Mo's place, Sinbad is sitting on the sidewalk as my aunt seems to be trying to entice him back into the house with food. I get out of the car, and he trots over to me.

"He ran out when I opened the door," she says. "I'm sorry! He was upset that you weren't here. He started whining."

"How long has he been out here?" I ask, rubbing his head. He sits extra straight in front of me, like he's some kind of perfectly behaved dog.

"You're going to be mad at me," she says.

"No, I'm not."

"Two hours. Every time I tried to get close to him, he stepped away."

"No prob," I say, 'cause I can see she feels bad. Of course, inside I have to admit I'm kind of upset with her. I know a kid from school whose dog got out the front door, and she never saw the dog again. But Dad flicks a finger on my back, like a warning, so I smile and say, "Thanks for taking care of him."

"The evacuation orders are lifted," Dad tells her. "We went by the house, and it's fine. The avocado tree looks dead, though."

"Oh, I'm sorry," my aunt says. Then she brightens. "But come in and watch a movie before you go home."

So we go and watch the original *Star Wars*. It's her second-favorite movie, so she knows all the words. Honestly, none of the *Star Wars* movies would make my top hundred, but I'm always happy to watch whatever Aunt Mo wants, 'cause she's such a cool person. I'm already over the Sinbad-getting-out thing. Dad says she put her whole life aside when my mom died and he needed someone to babysit me after he quit hockey and got a job with LAPD and Jenny was going to school. Aunt Mo worked weekends and nights so she would be free during the weekdays. Then she did it again for a few months after Jenny left. So Dad and I pretty much watch whatever she wants, even the super-girlie stuff that makes me want to pull out my hair, like all that *Twilight* crap. But her favorite movie is the original *Terminator,* which I'm not allowed to watch yet. Looking forward to it, though. We went to a team dinner once after a game, and Arnold Schwarzenegger was there at the restaurant. He let the whole team take a picture with him, even though he was in the middle of dinner, and then he signed my shirt and wrote *To Aunt Mo. From the Terminator.* When I gave it to her, she said, "Good times!"

CHAPTER 6

AT HOME AGAIN, I water the avocado tree, just in case there's still some life in the roots. I know a little about plants, and you gotta be hopeful about them even when they look dead. 'Cause plants just have this special kind of life force. They want to grow again. That's more important than spending money by using too much water, so I let the hose run a long time before I stop. There's a little Phos-Chek on one of our walls, but Dad says we'll need a professional to remove that. So I go inside, set up my computer, return the trophies to the shelves. Somewhere out there, the fire is still burning, but we're safe now. I think about how nature's bigger than anything. It's the number one thing in the world, really. No matter what's going on in anyone's life, if nature wants you to stop what you're doing, you have to stop what you're doing. Here in Canyon Country, nature can slap some perspective into you whenever it wants. You'd think knowing how much you can lose and how quickly, you would feel like, *Why should I do anything when I could lose it all tomorrow?* But actually, I feel the opposite. I mean, I've known for a long time that you gotta be intense about stuff, since anything can happen in the future. I remember when I was six, I overheard my step-mom telling Dad that she wanted to have a "real child" with my dad, meaning a kid from the two of them, like I wasn't her real kid . . . which I guess I wasn't. So I went to my room and thought about my mother, who I couldn't even remember, and I felt like maybe my dad didn't love me anymore, and maybe all I had left was my mom. And maybe I had to take care of myself. I didn't cry. I just sat there on the floor in my room—the room I have now—and stared straight at a blank wall until my dad came in and asked what I was doing. Then in a few months, my dad kind of asserted himself, plus he got me Sinbad, and things settled down. But I never forgot that sometimes you might end up alone—like what if something had happened to my dad at work and I ended up with my stepmom? So the moral is that family is the most important, but you also gotta have your dog, you gotta have your hockey, you gotta have these super-important things in your life, 'cause it might turn out that you got nothing else.

But. You also gotta do your homework. So I do mine halfheartedly—it's some equations that I grind my teeth while I do. Then Dad and I do our weekly cleanup. I'm responsible for the living room, dining room, and kitchen. It takes a couple of hours, with Sinbad following me from room to room. I give him a rawhide bone, and he lies down and chews while I work, and then when I move to a new room, he follows with his bone. Afterward I usually open all the windows to get the smell of household chemicals out of the house, but the air outside's smoky. I decide it's a bad idea to take Sinbad for a walk with the smoky air. Instead I play tug-of-war with him for an hour. He would go on for five hours if I let him. I pull as hard as I can, and one time he lets go and I fall backward. I can't tell if he did that on purpose, but I laugh.

I sit on the floor and put my arms around him and talk to him like he's a person.

"I know you're wondering why we're not going for a walk, but we can't today. It's been crazy. We coulda lost our house," I tell him. "I'm still processing. But I love living here anyway. It's the perfect place to live, except for the fires. But everywhere has something wrong with it. This place is pretty great, you have to admit. You like it here, right?" He lays his paw on my knee like he does sometimes when I ask him a question. I think that just means *I love you*, and it's his answer to everything—there's literally no question you can ask him that *I love you* isn't the answer to.

I hand Sinbad his bone, and then pretend I'm going to steal it. He lopes toward the door, then turns to look at me to see if I'm serious. When he sees I'm not, he lies down and chews. I play video games for about thirty minutes. I got a used Xbox from eBay that I bought with my own money two years ago. So I play once a week, just 'cause it was a lot of money for me and I really wanted a console. But to tell the truth, I'm kind of *meh* on video games. I just like them 'cause sometimes I need to unwind. Then I remember that I haven't eaten and turn off the game.

Though it's only eight, Dad already seems to be in bed; his door is closed. But as I walk past his room, I hear something strange. He's crying again. Sobbing, in fact. I just stand there, kind of amazed. I've never heard my dad cry this hard before. Is it still the divorce? I want to knock on his door, and my hand hovers near the wood. But do I want to knock on the door for him, or for me? I decide it's for me, and that he wouldn't like me bothering him just now. In fact, it would embarrass him. I finally just return to my room and close the door and switch on the ceiling fan to drown out any noise I might hear from Dad's room. Half an hour passes. I sneak out again, and he's still crying.

So I keep checking his door until he's snoring. I don't even feel like eating anymore. I'm not sure what this crying means. I feel like I should tell someone, like someone who works with him, that maybe he's not entirely okay at the moment. On the other hand, it's none of their business. Or is it? I go back and forth. He's got a lot of pressure out there in the streets, and if he's not in perfect condition, maybe he'll be making the wrong decisions. Is that the way it works? I just don't know. I mean, I'm only a kid.

CHAPTER 7

THE NEXT MORNING in history class, every-
one's slouching in their seats. School's almost out for
the summer, and nobody's taking classes seriously at
all. History is the class I like least. You'd think history
would be super fascinating. I mean, a lot of crazy stuff
must have happened in the past, but the textbook and
my teacher make it seem like nothing interesting has
happened, ever. Whenever it occurs to him, my dad
finds something for me to read, stuff he says is real
history. Maybe from WikiLeaks, maybe from someone smart he agrees with, or maybe from someone
smart he disagrees with. He makes me do this 'cause

he says when he became a cop, he was surprised to find that he didn't know anything at all about the real world. It was all a surprise to him.

The only class I like this year is science. My teacher loves anything to do with science, whether it's astronomy or zoology or biology. She's just amazed at every big and little thing in the world. Once in a while, she'll tell you some crazy fact just to freak you out. Like did you know a cumulus cloud can weigh as much as dozens of elephants? Interesting, right?

When the last class lets out, I stand around with some of the kids as we wait for our parents to pick us up. "'Sup," says a guy I don't even know. He might be from seventh grade—he's from the junior high adjoining my school. We actually share one of the buildings.

"'Sup," I say back.

"You play hockey, right?"

"Yeah."

"My dad wants me to start playing sports. What do you think about hockey?"

"It's a big commitment," I say. Plus he looks older

than me, so that's pretty late to be starting hockey.

"Yeah, I don't want a commitment. If I have to do sports, I just want something that might be fun. Is there even hockey over the summer?"

"Yeah, there's in-house hockey all year."

"Do you have to be good for in-house?"

"It depends on the team. I've been on some awesome in-house teams, and I've been on some bad ones. You skate?"

"Can't I learn?"

"Yeah, sure, it's easy. If you're just thinking about how fun it is, it's the greatest thing in history, actually."

"Cool. I hear you're pretty good."

"I guess so." I kind of flush with pride.

"Cool. There's my dad. See ya. Good luck with your hockey."

"Yeah, thanks." That happens periodically, where someone I don't even know comes up to me and starts talking about hockey. I guess I'm known as the hockey kid. It feels good 'cause they're kind of respectful, and they give off a nice vibe. It's like they want me to do well. It's kind of like when I see that

ten-year-old ice skater that Ivan works with. I hope
she gets to nationals someday. I would be super
happy for her.

My power skating starts at four fifteen, so Dad
picks me up at school with all my gear in the car.
Then we drive to Ice House in Panorama City. My
main rink is Garland Ice Rink in Burbank, but to go
to the best coaches, sometimes you have to travel to
different rinks. I also go to the Ice Palace sometimes
to skate with a guy named Sasha. It's funny that they
named it "Palace," 'cause it's the most truly rinky-
dink rink ever. It looks like it was built in ancient
Egypt. Sometimes if I'm feeling sensitive, I can
hardly breathe in there 'cause it smells so toxic. And
the locker room is even worse than the dungeons at
Garland. You feel like you're in solitary confinement.
I get claustrophobia in there, and I start to worry
about what would happen if the door got locked and
I couldn't get it open. It's irrational, I know, but I feel
it every time.

As we're driving, I remember I've got to do a one-
page paper on something for my writing class, and
right there in the car I decide to write about my dad.

I've known about it for two weeks. The paper's due tomorrow. . . . I like doing papers last-minute. So I have some questions to ask Dad. He seems at peace as he drives, filled with a sense of mission when he takes me to skate.

I tap my fingers on the cup holder, then ask, "Can I ask you some questions about work? Mr. Falco said we have to write a one-page essay about someone in our family. It's due tomorrow. And I'm writing about you."

"Who's Mr. Falco again?"

"My writing teacher. It's this special class they're letting some kids take if they want. Dad, please?"

"It's for school?"

"Yeah, for Mr. Falco." He doesn't answer, and I add, "He's from New York. Queens. He's studying for his master's."

"What's he studying? *What? Are you kidding me?!* Did you see that guy roll through that stop sign?"

He does that all the time, whenever he sees a driver do something dangerous.

"He's studying writing."

We stop at a light, and I see his eyes drift to the

sidewalk, always alert for what's happening on the street. That's just habit with him.

"I want to ask you some questions," I say.

"Sure, you can ask me anything."

I think for a moment as we jump on the freeway. There's some weird, rusting metallic art sculpture off the grass to the side. The idea of it probably seemed better than it turned out.

"So lemme think," I say. "I want to write about police work. So to start, how often do you get attacked?"

"Well, like someone physically ramming into my body or hitting me or pulling out a weapon? I dunno. Maybe once a year. When I was working the streets, I got into more fights, just because I had to arrest people. Believe me, there are some strong guys out there who don't want to be arrested. They try to grab your gun."

"So then if somebody doesn't comply, you have to shoot them?"

"If you shot everybody who didn't comply, you'd shoot a hundred people in your career." He shakes his head. "Nah, I've never shot my gun. The huge, overwhelming majority of cops never shoot their gun in the line of duty."

"So how do you arrest somebody who doesn't want to be arrested?"

"Throw him to the frickin' ground and arrest him. It isn't pretty."

"Oh. And what about people who talk back to you? Do you arrest them?"

He looks at me like I've lost my mind. "If you did that, you'd spend your whole life writing arrest reports. You arrest people for breaking the law. Being rude isn't breaking the law."

"So do people argue with you about getting a ticket?"

"Sometimes. The thing about being a traffic cop is, you have to be the kind of person who knows exactly what you just saw, and you have to project that to the person you stop. Plus, they know in their hearts what they did. Some of them argue. It wastes everybody's time, but I like to let them get it out of their system. Then I give them the ticket. Sometimes they actually thank me for listening to them."

"Cool. But how rude are they?"

"A small number are unbelievably rude." He drums his fingers against the steering wheel. "I don't stop people for unimportant stuff. I stop them when they've presented a danger, like when I think they might be driving impaired or they've gone through a red light. I've been called racist by every race. I've had people tell me I only stopped them because they have a nice car, and other people who tell me I only stopped them because they have a beat-up car. Some of them yell at me, they insult me, they bring up stuff that has nothing to do with me, and nothing to do with the fact that they just sped through a crosswalk with a pedestrian in it. So I let them swear at me, and then they calm down and sign the ticket."

"It doesn't get you mad?"

"Lately it gets me tired. I'm tired. Sometimes I just feel so tired."

"And what about Metro? Did you ever want to join them?" Metro is the elite section of LAPD and is basically their SWAT team.

He slides into the left-turn lane and seems to be thinking. I don't say anything, 'cause I remember how Mr. Falco says that when you're interviewing people, you have to keep your mouth shut and let them ramble and see where they go with it.

"I'm a good cop, and I believe in what I do. I think I make the world a safer place. I mean, there are sixty million police-citizen contacts a year in America. I'm just a bit player. But I think I make a difference."

I deliberately don't say anything.

"For a while being on patrol was rewarding. I felt like I was saving the world—that's a pretty amazing feeling. But some of the things you see, some of the people you meet, I started getting sick of it. That wasn't a side of life I really wanted to see anymore. There was one lady who called over a domestic dispute, and when we got there, she said she was fine. Nice lady. We left, and then later we got a new call to her place. We went there and she was dead.

"Did you feel sad?" I ask.

"Hell, no, I felt like I had to get the guy who killed her. And I did." He pauses, frowns. "But then at night, in bed, I did feel sad. I asked myself, why am I doing this? I have a son, I have a wife, I could have a good life. So I went to traffic. There are still a lot of great officers on patrol, but definitely some of them leave. I have a lot of respect for the good ones who keep at it."

We're pulling into the rink now. The rink's not in the greatest area, so there's a tall iron fence around the whole parking lot. I think about how I can put everything together in a report, weave in some things I already know. I think about Dad not feeling work is so rewarding anymore. I didn't know that about him. I thought he loved his job. He always tells me not to do anything that I don't love. I look at him, see the lines starting by his eyes. Someday, if I make the NHL, I'm going to buy him a big house before I buy one for myself. I'm going to get him a big TV, 'cause he likes to watch so much. I'm going to get him anything he wants. I say it out loud: "I'm going to buy you the biggest TV ever someday."

He looks at me like he doesn't know what that has to do with anything. But we're turning into the parking lot. "Focus," he says.

I grab my bag, get my mind into hockey. Inside the rink, there are two sheets of ice, a smallish one and a regulation-size one. Ice House has the best locker rooms of any of the three rinks I go to regularly.

They're just regular rooms, so you don't feel like you're imprisoned in them or like there might be some pervs lurking about. And they aren't warm and stuffy.

I skate onto the ice where people are doing public skating. Aleksei is waiting and barks, "A minute late!"

"Sorry!" I answer.

All we do for half an hour are really exhausting drills to strengthen my thighs. Aleksei shouts behind me. "Move, move!" That must be something they say in Russia, because whenever I skate with Sasha, he yells almost the same thing, except he says, "Move it! Move it!" Then when there are two minutes left, Aleksei holds on to the back of my pants, and I skate across the rink pulling him. Then when there are about thirty seconds left, I pull him as he holds his skates sideways so that I can hardly move.

When I finally finish, I collapse to the ground. Aleksei doesn't even say "good job," just leaves to get ready for his stick time. I crawl across the ice to my water bottle and push myself up with a grunt. My head is crazy hot, so I take off my helmet and pour water onto my hair, then let water dribble into my mouth. Next I go to the back rink and stretch out flat on one of the benches in the small bleachers, lying there while the Zamboni finishes. Way too soon, it's stick time, and I shove myself up with another grunt.

While Aleksei pushes a goal over to a corner, I take a couple of laps around the rink. Different coaches are using different parts of the ice. We're in the left in front. Dad has found his favorite seat underneath the one heating unit that works. Now Aleksei is setting up some tires and homemade training aids—they're two blocks of wood, with a post attached to the top of them. I call them danglers. They're to teach you puck-handling. You push the puck through them when you're going at fast speeds.

For the next hour, a few other guys and I do a series of fast-moving drills with a puck. Aleksei is a master at keeping everybody moving; you hardly have any downtime with him in charge. He's skating after me while pounding his stick on the ice, screaming, "Skate! Skate, Conor!! Conorrrrrrr!!!" It seems like he's screaming at me for a whole hour.

"WHY AREN'T YOU MOVING YOUR FEET?!! YOUR FEET! YOUR FEET!" Then it's over. And the crazy thing is I had a great hour. Aleksei's stick times are the best! He's the master for sure!

CHAPTER 8

ON THE WAY home, the sky's as blue as it used to be—the fire's still going, but it's down to four thousand acres, and it's way past where we live. You can hardly even smell it in the air anymore. Dad comments on how that's the way life is—something huge happens, and then it passes. Your life turns upside down, and then it rights itself. But after he says this, he's quiet for a moment, then adds, "Usually. I guess some stuff is final. It doesn't pass." He thinks more and says, "Time passes no matter what." He gets like that sometimes, philosophical. He's not like that a lot. He's mostly just interested in sports, but sometimes he likes to think heavy stuff. I wonder what my science teacher would have to say about Dad's comment. I don't know anything about physics, but is it true that time passes no matter what? Every so often, I like having these heavy thoughts too, like just lying around with Sinbad, thinking stuff. I wonder if someone would pay me someday to be a philosopher. Is that a thing?

At home, we eat a bunch of peanut butter sandwiches. I walk Sinbad, take a shower, and then, in the interest of always doing my homework at the last minute, I screw around until almost nine before starting my paper on Dad. I do a little extra research, think about other things my dad has told me over the years, and write my report.

My Dad's a Cop
By Conor MacRae

My dad's a cop. You'd think with all the stuff going on today, like all the anticop sentiment, that he might feel something about all the hate. But I've asked him about it in the past, and he says he just

does his job as well as he can. One of the
things about my dad is he says he's not
a leader-type personality. He's a leader
in situations on the streets, but not like
in offices or like in changing the world
or politics. Most cops are like that. The
officers I've met are good people, not
necessarily nice people. Do you see the
difference? They would die for you, a total
stranger, but they're not always going to
smile at you if they're not in the mood.
So you have police officers, and you have
people who commit actual crimes. And
then you have couples calling 911 because
they're fighting, and one of them is waving
a gun around. You have drunk guys
holing up in houses, claiming they have
a bomb. You have a *really* lot of small
stuff, where people call because their
neighbor trespassed, or just because
they're mad at their neighbor over stuff
you'd think two grown-ups could settle
between themselves. You'd be surprised

how often people get mad at each other.
And every once in a while you get super-
ridiculous stuff. My dad once had to go to
a house because a woman reported that
three days in a row she'd found a random
stuffed-animal shark in her driveway. I
don't think that mystery ever got solved.
So then you go there, and usually it's
routine, though sometimes something
totally insane happens in a situation that
seemed routine ten seconds earlier. Like
you could go on a call because there's
a stuffed shark in somebody's driveway,
and the next thing you know someone's
firing a gun at you. It's that crazy. Other
times you get there, and there's a really
awful person involved, like so awful you
don't even want to know about it. So my
dad had been a cop for seven years and
been shot at, kicked, punched, knifed.
People tried to steal his gun. And like
the huge, big majority of cops, he's never
fired his gun in the line of duty. A lot of

cops like the power of holding a gun, but
they don't like firing it. They know firing
their gun can destroy both someone else's
as well as their own lives. My dad once
said that he thinks if you shoot a suspect
three seconds too soon, it's not justifiable,
but 1.5 seconds is okay. So you basically
have 1.5 seconds to decide if you need
to shoot someone who might kill *you*. At
the same time, he doesn't judge cops who
shoot at that three-second mark. He's just
talking about what he tells himself. But
he got sick of working patrol. Some good
cops stay on patrol, but some quit. Dad
transferred to traffic. He thought he could
have a better life and get away from sad
and bad stuff more if he worked in traffic.
Now it seems like he mostly deals with
rude people, except for maybe once a
year when someone attacks him. I'm glad
he's in traffic now. And that's the story of
my dad the cop.

CHAPTER 9

MR. FALCO SAUNTERS and stomps and paces up and down the front of the classroom, always in motion. "Your family is the key to. Who. You. Are."

A girl raises her hand. "Is that true even though I'm adopted?"

"Absolutely, it's true, but maybe in your case it's a little more complicated. But the family you know, day by day, is the biggest influence on your life. That's why I had you write about them. You write about them to understand them, to express yourself, to know yourself. And, just as importantly, you choose them to write about because some of your most

meaningful work will be about them. Got it? Everyone understand?"

Everyone nods, and he says, "Good. I'll go over
your papers and mail them to you at home in a
couple of weeks. Have a nice summer."

Dad picks me up at four thirty, and we eat chicken
sandwiches he's made before taking off for Garland.
When we get there, I dress in a rush 'cause I'm so
nervous about another pre-tryout clinic.

Coach Dusan, who's going to coach the peewee
AAAs, doesn't even show up for the clinic because
of a family emergency. It turns out I don't play so
good, so Coach not being there works out fine. Three
skaters get past me and score. I hope none of the
assistant coaches tells Dusan, but I doubt they will.
Even if they do, this is still a *pre*-tryout clinic. The
actual tryout is the only thing that matters. Still, my
confidence falls a couple of levels, and when we get
home, all I want to do is hang with Sinbad and hope
he cheers me up.

In my room, Sinbad turns over on his back and
waves his legs like a bug that can't turn over. He
does this so I'll rub his stomach. He literally does

this about twenty times a day. Usually I'll give him a good scratch, but if I'm busy, I have to ignore him. He just keeps hopefully lying like a bug. Now I sit cross-legged next to him. He has a couple of fatty tumors that I don't like, but his vet aspirated them and checked the fluid under the microscope and says they're nothing. But then I scratch behind his upper back leg, and it seems swollen. It's probably nothing, but I text my dad, even though he's in the next room. He texts back that I should make an appointment at the vet. When I turned ten, I told Dad I wanted to be in total charge of Sinbad, and he said fine, so it's always me who talks to the vet.

I call Dr. Andris, and it turns out that swelling in this part of the leg is considered important enough that they say they can get me in right away; they keep late hours three days a week. So I take some cash out of my at-home stash and put a leash on Sinbad, and Dad drives me to the vet. It takes about seven minutes, and when we arrive, there are several people in the small waiting room with cat carriers. Dr. Andris is the best vet ever, but to keep his prices low, he runs a basic operation. There's nothing much in the waiting room except old wooden chairs and throw-away magazines—a bunch of coupon booklets and about twenty copies of some paper called *Aquariums: Everything You Need to Know*. Sinbad is doing his half-whine, half-howl thing on account of all the cats.

I'm dripping sweat—it's hot tonight, but not *that* hot. I lean back and close my eyes, thinking about Sinbad's leg. It's not *super* swollen—it's probably nothing. When they call us in, I push Sinbad onto the scale: ninety-two pounds, so a little under his usual. I can hear all the dogs in the hospital portion in back, howling and barking. Dr. Andris comes in. He's this handsome guy who's great with animals and bad with people. He's so handsome he looks just like a photograph. And he seems like he's in total commu-nion with animals, but he doesn't make much eye contact with humans, like he's incredibly shy.

"So what is he here for?" Dr. Andris asks while looking at Sinbad.

"His back left leg seems swollen."

Dr. Andris nods. "How much does he weigh?"

"Ninety-two."

He writes that down, while I unleash Sinbad.

Then Dr. Andris lifts Sinbad onto the exam table. First he expertly moves his hands all over Sinbad, feeling for anything unusual. Then he checks Sinbad's teeth. "Teeth are looking good. You still brushing them?"

"Yes."

"Good."

He pets Sinbad a couple of times. "Beautiful dog." He leans his nose toward Sinbad and says in a high voice, "You're a beautiful dog." Then he sighs and turns to Sinbad's leg. He nods, frowns, stops frowning. "Popliteal lymph node. I guess we'll need to aspirate?" he says like he's asking me.

"Okay."

He taps his lips with two fingers. "How long has it been this way?"

"I just discovered it today."

He finally makes full eye contact. "Okay. Is that it?"

"Yes, thank you."

Dr. Andris sticks a small needle into Sinbad's lymph node, then withdraws the needle and leaves the room. He returns in ten minutes and says without looking at me, "Doesn't look like a fatty tumor, unfortunately. I guess we'll have to biopsy?"

I pause, then say, "Okay."

"Okay." He asks what he asked earlier: "Is that it?"

"Yes," I say, coming alive and leashing Sinbad.

Dr. Andris kind of shuffles out of the room, like he doesn't want to be noticed, which just makes him more noticeable.

I sit in the waiting room until they get Sinbad's chart, and then make an appointment to have the biopsy done. "So how much will it cost?" I ask. I even handle Sinbad's vet bills myself. This was my idea too, so I could feel like he was totally mine.

"Well," says the receptionist. "Let's see . . . four hundred. Did you want us to brush his teeth or clip his nails while he's under?"

"I already brush his teeth, but how much would it cost to do his nails?"

"Ten dollars."

I feel relieved about the price. I've always gotten a dollar a week for each year old I am, so I currently get eleven dollars a week for an allowance. I have about five hundred fifty saved, so I'm loaded. I look around, but Dad must have stepped outside.

When I get outside, he's looking up at the setting sun like he's trying to blind himself. He lays his arm around my shoulders. "It'll be fine," he says, but I can tell by the way he says it that he doesn't believe it. That's why he's trying to blind himself.

I don't answer, just look at the sidewalk for a second. Then when we get home, I remember how I stared at the wall when I was kid, and that's just what I feel like doing now. So I sit in front of a wall in my room and just stare at it for a long time.

When we drop Sinbad off at the vet's in the morning, he looks at me with surprise. Last year when I made AA, we went out of town twice for tournaments, so we've been apart before. But it's hard. I can hear him whining as I go out the door.

Dad drops me off at school with my bike—it's already third period. That's my music class. We sing show tunes, which I don't have a strong feeling about one way or another. Some of the kids love it, though— there're three girls and a boy who live for this class. Lunch, history, math, study hall. Then back on my bike for home—Dad has texted me that he's going to be late, but that he's contacted our two neighbors. When Aunt Mo started working during the week again, Dad and I went up and down the street knocking on every door in our neighborhood, getting to know everyone. We exchanged phone numbers with about twenty different neighbors, so I could call them if something happened. Dad also installed a security system. Canyon Country is safe, though, plus Sinbad loses his mind whenever a stranger comes to the door. Dad also gave me pepper spray to keep by my bed. I'm not supposed to tell anyone that, 'cause it's illegal for kids under sixteen to possess pepper spray in California. I also carry it with me when I walk Sinbad at night. The woman who lives next door is a stay-at-home mom, and on the other side the grandfather lives with the family, and he's home all day. At first, being alone, I would get scared and just hang out with the woman next door. But her three kids are under five, and I have to keep a close watch on Sinbad around them. This got pretty stressful.

I have several friends whose parents started to let them stay by themselves for short periods once they turned twelve, and other friends whose parents won't do that yet. When my grandparents were growing up, they said you could go to school by yourself when you turned six. Different world today.

Basically, Dad and I both do what we have to do. Dad's gotta work, and sometimes I gotta be alone. Except with Sinbad, I'm literally never alone . . . except today I am. As soon as I'm home, I check that all the doors are dead-bolted. I place the pepper spray near the computer mouse.

Then I go to my computer and read about lymph nodes and chemotherapy for dogs and find out that if Sinbad has cancer, it's going to cost thousands of dollars. I'm pretty sure we don't have thousands of dollars, so there's only one option: he just can't have cancer. One of our neighbors had a dog with mouth cancer who was given seven months to live unless he had five thousand dollars of treatment. The neighbor couldn't afford treatment, and his dog ended up living for five more years, until he was thirteen. So there's also that.

I've never actually added up all the stick time and skating lessons I take, but wouldn't it add up to thousands of dollars? I go on Excel and type in

all my training fees and team costs and airfare and
equipment . . . What else? Hotels for tournaments.
After I've got all the numbers in a column, I can't
figure out how to make Excel add them up. So I do
it the old-fashioned way instead. It comes out to
$15,300 a year!! I check my addition—same answer.
I stare at the numbers. My mind is black, total darkness. Time passes.

The house seems so empty without Sinbad that I
can hardly stand it. I try staring at the wall, but that's
not working today. I go for a walk, clutching my pepper spray. But I get only a short way up the burned-
out path before I feel lonely and turn back. So I work
with the medicine ball until I collapse to the ground.
Fatigue is good; it's one of my favorite things, that
exhausted haze that I get into sometimes when I
work out too much.

When Dad arrives home, he sets off the security
alarm, 'cause he didn't realize I had it on. It's even
louder than when your fire alarm accidentally goes
off! It kind of shakes us up.

At ten p.m., a vet tech calls and says the surgery
earlier went fine. "He's a champ," she says. "We could

actually release him now if you can get here right away before we close."

For a second I get excited, but Dad's already asleep, so I say, "We can't do it." I feel kind of embarrassed but add, "Can you tell him I love him?"

"Sure, of course."

Dogs are super amazing—like some of them know you're about to get home even before you get there. They're psychic. So I know that Sinbad knows I'm lying here thinking about him, and I know he's thinking about me. So basically, kind of, everything's okay.

The next day is early dismissal, and the last day of school. We visit our new homerooms at the junior high next door. Our new teacher talks about how each year is tougher as you get older—better but tougher. His name's Mr. Stoller. He's famous for being tough, and unfortunately, I'll also have him for history. Tough seems great for coaches, but I don't really like tough teachers, so I'm kind of disappointed. For teachers, I like inspiring. He says anyone who talks during his classes will be sent to the office.

Also that homeroom includes "character building." As he turns to the blackboard and starts writing, I look at the guy next to me, and we kind of roll our eyes. A book drops to the floor, probably deliberately. Mr. Stoller has written *I. Will. Make. You. Work. Hard. To. Achieve. Your. Potential.*

He has us go around the room and introduce ourselves, even though we all know each other. I get a little nervous—don't really like talking in front of people. When it's my turn, I say, "Conor MacRae. I play hockey. My dad's a cop. I have a Doberman named Sinbad." I think for a moment. "Sinbad's at the vet." Then I sit down.

When school's over, I don't get that free feeling I usually get on the last day of school. I just think about how I need to make it through a lesson with Ivan so we can go pick up Sinbad. A bunch of us are outside waiting for our parents when a guy starts yelling at another guy. They're older than me. Some of the kids get excited about the prospect of a fight. But my dad's a cop, so I know if any punches are thrown, I gotta break it up, especially 'cause one guy's a lot bigger and could basically destroy the other guy. I hover nearby, feeling the adrenaline flood through me. It's pure stress—I can hear a soft buzzing in my ears. There's a lot of yelling and then a little shoving, which some of the kids laugh at. The smaller kid starts crying. I guess this is my moment. I step up and the big guy goes, "Ohhhhhh," like he's excited to fight me.

I think of a fight I saw Dad break up once and do what he did. I hold up my palms to show I mean no harm. Then I rub my face like I remember Dad did. I say what he did: "I can't let you fight." When he said that, the man thought about it and backed down.

The big kid suddenly pushes me with both hands. I flounder backward but get my balance right away and surge forward, shoving him as hard as I can. When he falls to the ground, I stand with my fists in front of me, squeezed so tight it almost hurts. My fists are quivering—I guess I'm scared. The guy pushes himself up, but slowly, suspiciously. He's bigger than me, but not that much bigger, and I'm positive I'm stronger. He shows his palms, shrugs. "You're not the one I have a problem with," he says, then picks his books off the ground and walks toward the parking lot.

The little guy runs away without saying anything, and everyone moves off. I don't actually know any of these kids—most of them are older. As they leave, one of them says, "That's the hockey kid."

So I just stand there by myself, the adrenaline draining immediately so that I feel exhausted. I don't think I'm going to be able to do Ivan, but I know I have to, 'cause at this point we'll need to pay for the lesson whether I take it or not.

Dad drives up in a minute—he does an early shift most Thursdays so he can take me to skate with Ivan.

As I get in the car, he says, "Sorry I'm a little late—stopped at the bank to get four hundred out of your account." He gives me a funny look. "You look green. Everything okay with Sinbad?"

"Yeah. Now we gotta wait to hear back from the lab."

Dad nods. "All right. We just have to try to suspend our feelings until we hear, okay? Not time to panic yet. Actually, there's never a time to panic. Have I ever told you that? There's never an appropriate time to panic."

"Yeah. I mean, no, you never told me." I kind of

want him to know I broke up a fight, 'cause I think he'd be proud of me, but to tell the truth, I'm so exhausted I don't even want to talk.

We ride quietly to Garland. In the dungeons when I change, I just sit there for a minute in my underwear, completely out of energy. But I put on my gear, wearing a Grizzlies jersey that's getting a little small. Public skating starts at three, the same time as my lesson. Not many people show up for public skating on time, so Ivan uses the fairly empty ice to time me going at full speed around the rink. You have to be super alert when you do this, 'cause you don't want to hit somebody darting into your path.

Ivan is five-eight, good for figure skating but small for hockey. He played hockey, though, until he made the national figure-skating team for Bulgaria. He's thirty-six, which he likes to mention periodically like it's really old. And it is pretty old. But he's still got a reputation as one of the best skaters in California. One of the best skating instructors as well. At his peak he could skate around the rink in thirteen seconds. That's NHL-level speed. That's why he has a one-year waiting list for lessons.

When he shows up, he stuffs three pieces of gum into his mouth per usual before he says, "Why don't you take a couple of warm-up laps?" I use long, sweeping strides around the rink the way he likes and think I'm doing pretty good. He yells out, "You got lead in those legs?" Then he takes out his phone to time me. "Feeling like you got it today?" he asks.

"I don't think so," I say honestly. But I'm the master of focus, IMO, so I get in position and concentrate.

"Okay . . . go!"

I take exactly three hard-running steps before I change to a running-gliding hybrid. At the first corner I lose a fraction of a second 'cause one of my crossovers is too short, and then on the first straightaway, three of my strides aren't at full power. Otherwise I do okay. Ivan is nodding when I finish. He holds up the phone: 15.85! I should get in a fight more often!

"Super," he says. "I believe that's your record. Messed up a little on the first corner, and a couple of your strides lacked power. If you do it perfect, we could get it down to, uhhh, maybe fifteen point six. Okay, let's get started."

We spend the whole lesson with me doing intricate steps threading through some plastic cones. Every so often my eyes fall on my dad, waiting on a bench. When the lesson's over, Ivan and I skate over to him. "How did he do?" Dad asks.

"Fifteen, eight-five," Ivan says.

"Great!" Dad says. "He always misses that first crossover, though. That's a concentration issue. I'm also wondering if he's getting low enough when he skates."

Ivan walks off the rink and sits on the bench beside Dad, chewing his gum like a madman. "You know, I know what you're saying. It's like pulling teeth to get him to keep low. I wish I'd gotten ahold of him earlier. I believe he was nine and a half when we started lessons?"

"That sounds right," Dad says.

"I thought I got pretty low," I say.

"You need to get lower," Dad says worriedly.

Ivan's next lesson skates up, so he tells us bye and skates off. As soon as his next student pushes off, his dad is already yelling at him. "And work hard this week!"

There was only one time I remember Dad yelling at me over hockey. That was during the AAA
tryout, when I heard him shout "HUSTLE" from the
stands. When I didn't make that team, we both sat
in the car with our heads in our hands. I thought my
NHL hopes were over. Then Dad said, "Don't worry
about it—did you know David Perron played midget
B when he was sixteen?"

David Perron is a left wing in the NHL. I lifted
my face from my hands and said, "Really?"

"Yeah. He came out of nowhere and got drafted
in the first round when he was nineteen."

"Really?" That made me a little hopeful, but it
took a few weeks to really feel okay again.

I watch for a second as the kid with the yelling
dad glides around the rink. The father shakes his
head at my father. "He doesn't put his heart in it!"

Dad nods, and we walk off. I dress in a hurry, and
we head straight to the vet. The parking's all taken,
so Dad drops me in front—Dr. Andris has only three
parking spaces, and one of them is reserved for him.

Inside, as soon as I tell the receptionist who I'm

here for, I can hear howling. Sinbad! He hears me! "I'm here!" I call out, and my pup howls like he's dying of heartbreak. He's pulling hard on the leash as they bring him out, and wearing a cone around his neck. I fling my arms around him while Dad appears, and I pay the lady with my precious cash from my account. The cone looks pretty undignified for a Dobe. "Aw, you look like a wuss!" I tell him. His tongue hangs out happily. I check out his leg—it's shaven and stitched up. He pulls me out the door and immediately turns left, which ends up being the correct direction. Like I said, dogs are psychic.

CHAPTER 10

A WEEK LATER, all is wrong with the world. Sinbad has cancer. And it's going to cost almost seven thousand dollars to treat. That makes me feel frozen inside, like my blood's not moving for a minute there. I get the call from the vet while at my teammate Jae-won's house. He didn't make the AAAs either last year, and we both got so upset that our dads took us to a restaurant we all like. But me and Jae-won just ate really quietly and only wanted to get home.

I lie back on the floor and stare at the ceiling. Jae-won lives in an apartment in Koreatown, and the ceiling is stained. He and I were the two least rich kids on the team.

"'Sup?" he says.

"Sinbad's got big problems," I say. "He's got cancer."

"Aw, man, I'm sorry. He's such a great dog. Can't they help him?"

"Yeah, but it's going to cost seven thousand dollars!"

Jae-won's head flicks back a bit, like someone's pushed it. "Wow. Man. You got the money?"

"Nah, man, I got a hundred and fifty left in the bank."

"What about your dad?"

"I dunno. It'll be hard."

He lies back also. "Man. We're only eleven, and we're already in debt."

Jae-won owes his dad for the last pair of skates he got, which cost six hundred dollars. He had to pay for them 'cause his dad had just gotten him a different pair of six-hundred-dollar skates, and Jae-won decided he hated them after using them twice. It's tough when that happens. And you can't really resell top-end skates for much 'cause they're heat-molded 'specially for your feet. Still, they were able to sell them for two fifty.

We lie without talking. Like I said, sometimes staring at a blank space is a good thing. Then he says, "I'm sorry about Sinbad. Is he gonna live if your dad has the money?"

"Dunno. They say so, but I'll read up on it later."

Jae-won's great. He just lies there next to me, and I know he's not getting up unless I do. He's like the world's most sensitive hockey player. And he's got the most unbelievable hockey hands in history, though his skating's not that strong. But Dad thinks he's headed for the NHL. At worst, Dad says, he'll play Division I on a scholarship. I've seen him slip the puck through unbelievably small openings. In 1998 his dad played on a South Korean junior team that beat Thailand 92–0, which must be some kind of record. His dad is small, but Jae-won was the tallest kid on our team last season. There're no sure things, but I'm pretty sure that if he keeps growing, his future's golden. Hands like his are one in a zillion.

I sit up suddenly. "Do you think your mom could drive me home now?"

"Sure! Mom!" He rushes out of the room calling out, "Mooooom!"

I feel like I need to get home ASAP. I need to take care of my boy.

"She's ready!" Jae-won calls out.

Jae-won has five-year-old twin brothers, and we all go downstairs and pile into the car together. My friend sits in the passenger seat, and I sit in back, in the middle of the twins—they like the windows. That's the way we always do it when his mom drives us somewhere, 'cause even though Jae-won is a hero to the twins, they like to sit next to me, too.

This time his mother snaps a few sentences in Korean, and both twins turn to me at once and say, "Do you want the window?"

"Nah, that's all right," I say.

All four of them look at me like I'm going to have some kind of mental breakdown, but I don't. The twins start to bicker, and when they don't stop, I truthfully just want to knock their heads on the windows. Finally Jae-won turns around and shouts, "Shut up! He's thinking!"

"What is he thinking about?" one says, but then they don't say more.

When we reach my house, the entire family gets out to say good-bye to me, like I'm going away for a long time or something. Jae-won and I knock fists. "Lemme know if you need anything," he says.

"Yeah, thanks. Thanks, Mrs. Kang."

"Oh, yah, welcome, Conor. You call if need ride or anything."

"Thank you."

She puts a hand on each of my shoulders. "You call, right?"

"Yes, thank you."

When I go inside, Sinbad shoots into the air and hurls himself at me. "Sinbad!" I cry out, kneeling. He stays very still while I hug him, like he always does. I lean in, resting my head against his neck. I try to push him down so I can look at his stitches, but he thinks I'm playing and starts hopping around. "Sinbad, I'm serious! Down!" He lies down, then immediately hops up and slaps his front paws on the floor. He looks so happy, I decide to take him for a walk.

The house feels empty, so I go check Dad's room and see he's not home—I told him I'd be home at six, and it's only four thirty. Tomorrow's the AAA tryout—Jae-won and I decided not to do stick time like we do on some Thursday nights a couple of hours after I do Ivan. It just seemed like a good time to relax. And now I get to hang out with my pup.

I decide to take his cone off for a walk, then leash him up to go outside. We've been walking the streets instead of the hill 'cause so many of the leaves are burned and charred that it makes the hill kind of barren. There's a small park about twenty minutes away, so we walk there. Nobody's around, and I let Sinbad roam free. A squirrel appears; he tears off after it. He's super prey-driven, so chasing squirrels is his life's work.

The park's got a few swings and one of those big plastic playgrounds. Dad used to take me here sometimes when I was little. Now it seems so . . . young. Thinking about Sinbad makes me feel like I'm a hundred years old. He's running back, and I see something in his mouth. As he gets closer, I hear a bizarre screaming sound, which turns out to be coming from the squirrel in his mouth. "Aw, Sinbad! You gotta either kill it or drop it! Drop it! Drop!"

Surprisingly, he listens, the squirrel unsteadily loping off as I releash Sinbad. Watching how unsteady the squirrel is, I wonder if it would have been better to let Sinbad kill it. Now I feel guilty. But then the squirrel seems to have shaken it off, and he runs easily and quickly up a tree.

We head back home, Sinbad supremely satisfied with himself. I love seeing him so happy. I feel like I can't take my eyes off him. As we reach the house, Dad is just rolling his police motorcycle through the gate on the driveway. I feel super nervous about everything we have to talk about. I'm used to being a little nervous for big hockey games, but this feels different. This feels crappy. Sinbad and I pass through the gate. Dad is lovingly covering up his bike. When he's finished, he turns to look at me, and immediately I can see his concern. I didn't mean to show anything in my face, but I guess I am.

"Did you hear from the vet?" he asks right away.

"He's got cancer," I blurt out. "It's gonna cost

seven thousand dollars to treat him." I hold my breath and for some reason just keep holding it, like I do when I have the hiccups. Finally I gasp for air.

He just looks at me. Then he nods once and says, "If that's what it costs, that's what it costs."

I say louder than I meant, "I don't have to play hockey until Sinbad's better. Will that save enough money?" That makes me feel sick to say. I love hockey, but I love Sinbad better. I *really* love hockey, but I REALLY love Sinbad. It's all a sick feeling right now, though.

He thinks for a moment. "I'll have enough to pay for being on the team," he answers carefully. "But we're not going to have the money for you to take lessons for a while. . . . I'm sorry, Conor." He thinks for a minute. "But we'll do extra dryland! That'll help keep you strong. Russ discovered a workout video he's obsessed with. He's doing it every night and says he's hard as a rock. I'll order it for you. How would that be?" Russ is his former partner.

"Sure. I'll do it twice a day." I turn toward the wall, tap my fingers on it a few times. "Dad? I'm sorry I cost so much money." I see that makes him feel bad, so I close my eyes tight and wish I hadn't said it. When I open my eyes, he's just standing, staring. He looks stricken.

"Conor, you're my son. I don't care how much money you cost. All kids cost money, that's just part of having kids. You don't get new clothes. You don't get presents. You never went to private school. You never had a babysitter or a nanny. You haven't really cost that much, as far as kids go. Even in a small town in Iowa, I had kids on my hockey team whose parents spent a thousand dollars on them at Christmas. They had new bicycles. They had five pairs of shoes. They went on nice vacations. They went to camps. You're not like that."

I look down at the ground, just thinking. I mean, I know from school and my teams that a lot of kids get a lot more than me, and their parents don't have the slightest idea that they're giving their kids a lot. They just think what they're doing is normal. Dad's right. I've never been on a nice vacation. I have one pair of shoes. A nanny never took care of me or drove me anywhere. I don't resent kids who grow up with nannies or have five pairs of shoes, but I admit I resent that they think we spend too much on hockey. Dad was at some kind of school event once, and there were parents who told him it's insane how much we spend, and yet they spend forty thousand dollars a year on a nanny. Basically, they asked Dad how much he spends, he told them, and then they kind of attacked him for it, 'cause they know he's only a cop. Sometimes I think it's rich people who resent poor people, not the other way around. Not that we're poor. But we ain't rich, either.

"Well . . . I'm sorry anyway," I say. But then I see how hurt it makes my dad that I said that, like it makes him feel bad that he doesn't have more money. So I say, "I just mean thanks for everything. That's what I wanted to say."

He musses my hair. "We're going to get Sinbad better. I mean, look at him. Does that look like a dog who's ready to die?"

Sinbad's ripping apart an old blanket he picked up from the driveway. We give him blankets sometimes, 'cause he loves ripping them to shreds. Dr. Andris just said to be careful that he never swallows a long piece of it, since the cloth can get twisted up inside of him. He's growling like he's fighting a tiger. He most definitely does not look like a dog who's ready to die. He looks like a dog who's going to stick around for quite a few years. So that perks me up a bit.

As we head inside, Dad says he can take off work whenever I can get an appointment at the oncologist. I go to my room—Sinbad right behind me dragging the blanket—and call the number of the oncologist, even though it's five thirty.

"Vet Center," someone answers. "How can I help you?"

"Hi, I was referred by my vet, Dr. Andris. I guess my dog has cancer. He had a bad biopsy. So we need to see Dr. Tracey."

"Dr. Tracey is out of town right now. Would Dr. Pierre work?"

"Is he as good as Dr. Tracey?"

"She, yes, she's excellent. They're both excellent."

I hesitate, only 'cause Dr. Andris specifically mentioned Dr. Tracey. But I say, "Okay."

We make the appointment for Tuesday. Sinbad's lying on the floor with a big wad of blanket in his mouth. I sit next to him and search "cancer" on my phone. A few months ago, all the kids from my school started using DuckDuckGo to search the Internet, 'cause it has only a small number of employees in a small midwestern town, and its whole thing is protecting the privacy of users. So nobody uses Google anymore. Stuff like that happens at school all the time, where a few people will start doing something, and all of a sudden we're all doing it 'cause it's way cooler than what we were doing before.

I pause, wonder how much money it would save if we canceled my phone. Then I start to make a list of what else I could give up, but the fact is I've already given up just about everything to play hockey. There're the weekend fast-food restaurants, and my protein drinks. I could give up both of those. I don't know how much the protein drinks cost. Dad usually gives me twenty-five bucks for birthdays and fifty for Christmas, and everything I wear is a hand-me-down from the Garcia brothers down the street. My grandparents on my dad's side always give me thirty-five-dollar Ice Warehouse gift cards for Christmas, but on my mom's side we kind of lost touch over the years. Dad says they were really hurt that he didn't even wait two years to get remarried. To me, two years seems like forever, but what do I know? Maybe when you're old, two years is nothing. But it made Grandpa Takao and Grandma Toshi really sad when he got remarried so soon. They sold their house and traveled for practically five years straight. After that, they were broke—they'd run out of all the money they'd saved for their old age. Supposedly they live off Social Security now. I tried writing them three times, and then one day out of the blue they wrote me back. The whole letter was about a trip to Hong Kong they took. They stayed on a high floor at a fancy hotel in a place called Kowloon, and out their window they could see a harbor, and across the harbor were the sparkling buildings of Hong Kong. They said that Hong Kong and Kowloon were also famous for their crowded, impoverished tenements. But it's one of the safest cities in the world—they only liked to travel to safe places. I don't know why they wrote to me about Hong Kong, but they went on and on about it for two pages. That was a few years ago. Then last year for my birthday, they sent me a frame. It was a nice frame and everything, not that I know anything about frames, but I admit I thought it was kind of a strange present to send an eleven-year-old kid. But Dad said they loved putting framed pictures all over. He said they probably had two hundred framed pictures in their house, when they had a house.

Then I snap back to attention and turn to the phone and read about chemo. It looks like if you don't have a lot of money, you treat the dog with just one drug. But that's not as effective. For seven thousand, we're going to be able to get the full treatment. The drug doxorubicin is likely to be most effective when included in the mix, but it can be dangerous—heart toxicity and skin necrosis. I look up "necrosis," and here's what it means: *a form of cell injury that results in the premature death of cells in living tissue.* As many as 90 percent of dogs respond positively to chemo, but as many as 95 percent relapse. "As many" is a weird phrase, 'cause it can mean anything.

Suddenly I don't want to read any more about cancer. In fact, the thought of reading more about it makes me sick. I check my e-mail, and there are three—all from PETA. I gave them three dollars a couple of years ago, and now I get e-mails all the time from them. So I click through on one and read a really sad story about medical testing on dogs. This makes me sick too, but I scroll through the page to read about how in 2015 the United States became the last developed nation in the world to eliminate using chimpanzees in invasive research . . . which leads me to an amazing photograph of a bunch of chimps mourning the death of another chimp . . . and then I veer to photographs and stories of the ghettos in Hong Kong and Kowloon. I guess a lot of them have been torn down, but the poverty there was mind-blowing: totally dilapidated buildings where entire families lived in 150 square feet or less of sub-divided apartment space. People so poor that even if lightning struck and you happened to be born with the most hockey talent in history, you might never know it, and if you knew it, you might not even be able to buy the worst pair of used skates. *AWW*, I just suddenly feel like the whole world SUCKS! I mean, there are good things, but there's just so much that sucks. Except for my Sinbad, lying now behind me on the bed. I realize I forgot to put Sinbad's cone back on, so even though it makes me feel really guilty, I wake him up and put it back on while he gives me gloom eyes—he hates the cone!

I notice that it's somehow midnight. I suddenly feel flooded with relief that I managed to pass several hours without obsessing about either Sinbad or tomorrow's tryouts.

The last thing I think before getting in bed is that I'd like to save the world, like my dad, but I just don't know how.

CHAPTER 11

JAE-WON AND I send each other about fifty texts during the day, not always about hockey. Like, he texts me, *My cuz gave me some cool joggers. Should I wear them even tho it's hot?*

Dude, it's too hot for long pants, I text back, and he doesn't reply. I can't decide if I should walk Sinbad or not. I want to be totally fresh for tryouts tonight, but at the same time he loves his walks. I decide to take him on a short walk and then give him a bone while I stretch.

When Dad gets home from work, he asks, "Did you eat?"

"I forgot. What should I do? Is it too late to eat?"

"Why not just have a peanut butter sandwich?"

So I make myself a sandwich on whole wheat bread with this all-natural peanut butter and organic jelly we got at the store just for today. Dad read that NBA players almost all eat peanut-butter-and-jelly sandwiches before games, so that's why I eat so many of them.

When I'm finished, Dad puts out his fist, and I bump it. "You're going to do great," he says. "I can feel it."

"That's what you said last year before I didn't make AAA."

He thinks for a moment. "Yeah, I did say that. . . ."

As I pick up my hockey bag, I get that barfy feeling I get sometimes before big games. I let my bag drop back to the floor and kneel next to Sinbad. "I just gotta go do something important, and then I'm gonna come back and give you another walk, okay?" I swear he understands me!

Dad and I head to the car. I lie in the backseat. Just zone out and listen to hip-hop until Dad notices and says sharply, "Put on your seat belt." When we reach the rink, I see Madden walking across the parking lot with his parents. He played AAA last year, so he's a lock to make the team.

"Hey," he says.

"Hey."

I'm in the ninetieth percentile height-wise, and Madden's probably lower ten percent. But his skating is half ballerina, half most powerful man on earth. "Good luck," he says.

"You too," I say, even though the only way he won't make the team is . . . actually, there's no way he won't make the team.

There's a little nervous chatter in the dungeon, but the guys are pretty quiet. Jae-won's not around; it's not like him to be late. I call him and hear a phone ring in the room. He must already be in the rink. I head in, really aware of the stomping noise my skates are making, which I've never even noticed before.

Next to the ice, there's a snack table set up. That's not for us—someone says there's a figure-skating performance going on after tryouts. The rink is crowded with parents, both figure-skating parents and hockey parents. The air is filled with electricity. I can feel the anticipation of the hockey players, the figure skaters, and the parents. Dad's sitting in the stands.

I know Coach Dusan will be watching me carefully at the tryout, 'cause Dad has heard he's especially eager to find a second-year defenseman, which is what I am. A lot of last year's peewee AAA team are returning, so there're only a few true openings, though everybody has to go through the motions of trying out. There're several other guys who are also second-year defensemen, so I'll have some competition. And two of them are friends of mine. Pasha and Ethan. Actually, Ethan is my frenemy. We're supercompetitive with each other, but off the ice we're cool. He has a habit of checking me when he's trying to take a puck away from me. You're not allowed to check at the peewee level, so I don't usually check him back unless I'm mad. Checking is when you bang your body into another player, especially on the boards. It's where a lot of injuries happen in youth hockey. Anyway, I can see Ethan's here, and he looks focused. I allow myself a moment to do a long-distance mind-meld with Sinbad, and then I need to push him out of my mind and slide onto the ice.

We do drills for five minutes, and then Coach Dusan sets us loose to scrimmage. Half the players get red knit caps, signaling they're on the same team. We put the caps over our helmets. Pasha and Ethan are on the other team. For my first shift, it's like my legs are asleep. I let a guy whiz by me, and I bang my stick on the ice in frustration. Then I remember hearing that Coach Dusan hates it when guys act out their frustration.

So I go to a trick I have. I try to remember the time when my dad let me drink half a cup of coffee, just to see what it's like. I was so revved up I couldn't fall asleep until two in the morning. Now I try to channel that energy inside me. I focus on *expressing* that energy. *Focus.* Coaches love focus. I forget my fear that maybe I'm having a bad day. My next shift nobody gets by me, and every time I go to the boards with another player, I come up with the puck. I feel like my feet are flying, and I try to push off even harder. I bang a slap shot toward the net, and it just misses the opening. But it was a good, hard shot, and it was a good decision to take that shot.

Coach Dusan keeps me and the other defenseman on the ice for what seems like a long time, and I hope it's 'cause he's looking at me. Suddenly Jaewon's on the ice. That floods me with confidence—we've been playing together for years. He skates hard down the ice, and it's like I know just when he's going to turn his head. I flick a saucer pass to him, and he scores with a soft shot in exactly the right place, through a tiny crevice in the upper right. By the time Coach calls me off the ice, my mind is totally in the scrimmage. I sit on the bench feeling really good about that shift.

Coach Dusan goes to the scorer's table, and then Coach Andy, who was my coach on the peewee AAs, pulls me off the bench and says Coach Dusan wants to talk to me. I go over to the scorer's table, and Dusan says, "Do you want to be on this team?"

"Yeah!" I say. Sweat falls into my eyes, plus everything's feeling surreal, so I take off my helmet and wipe my eyes. "I mean yes!" I add.

"Are your parents here?"

"My dad."

"Go ask him if you can commit to the team now. If you can't, I'm going to take Pasha."

I feel a moment of guilt—I don't know Pasha well, since he's from another club, but he's one of my favorite people. But then excitement takes over. "I'll be right back!" I practically scream before running clumsily in my skates to the stands.

My heart is pounding. Dad has noticed me running, so he jogs over.

"Coach Dusan wants to know if I can commit to the team now! Otherwise he's taking Pasha!"

"What? Tell him yes!" Dad half shouts.

This time, I walk back like I'm completely cool. I knock on the scorer's door, and Coach Andy opens it. I tell Coach Dusan cool-like, "My dad says yes."

Coach Dusan nods and puts his fist out. "Just warning you I'm a perfectionist," he says as we bump fists. I head giddily back to the bench. I don't tell anyone I'm on the team now, 'cause I'm thinking, *Who knows what can happen between now and actually signing up?* Maybe Coach will change his mind!

Jae-won's out on the ice. His skating's not as good as last year's AAAs, so I hope he scores again just to show Coach Dusan what he can do. Instead he threads a hard pass between two players, a pass so awesome it's just as good as scoring. "YEAH, JAE-WON!" I scream. "YEAH!" He just made the team, I know it! He returns to the bench with a big smile on his face.

After that, the shifts go quickly. Nobody gets by me for the rest of the scrimmage. I'm trying to get out of the habit of dangling opposing players, 'cause I know that at the AAA level it's a lot harder to dangle your way out of a crowd. Dangling's the same as deking, which is using fancy stick-handling to get through a crowd. I try to flick a few choice passes, to show Coach that he hasn't made a mistake by sign-ing me.

The scrimmage lasts just thirty minutes. Then Coach Andy hands out envelopes to everyone who tried out. I take my envelope to my dad and watch over his shoulder as he opens it. There's the player name on top and three typed lines with blanks in front. The first line, which is checked, says,

Congratulations, you've been offered a spot on the Team.
The second line says, *Thank you for trying out for the*
Team, but we are unable to offer you a spot at this time.
The third line says, *Please see the coach.* I see Ethan
walking off, his shoulders drooping. I also see Pasha
just standing, his head slightly tilted, staring into
space. I feel bad that I took his spot, but at the same
time I'm a supercompetitive person, so I feel good,
too. But I wipe the smile off my face and tell Pasha,
"You played great, man. You deserved to make the
team." Which actually he did.

"Thanks, man. You made it?"

"Yeah."

"Congrats, I'm happy for you. You played better
than me," he says. Then he hits himself in the head
and says, "STUPID. STUPID."

"No, you weren't stupid," I say, shocked at how
hard he hit himself. "You—"

"I was STUPID!" He curls his hand into a fist and
knocks it hard against his forehead one more time.
Pasha's a great hockey player—he'll make AAA
somewhere else—but now he drops his chin toward
his chest and just stares at the floor.

His mother comes up and puts an arm around him, and they walk off together.

You can see who's happy and who's not. My dad's face is pure excitement. Other parents are saying "Congratulations" to him, and a couple of them congratulate me as well. He messes up my hair roughly, and I smile.

"I did it!" I say.

"You played amazing," he says. Then, just 'cause it's the way hockey parents are, he adds, "That first shift you were asleep, though."

I just laugh. "Did you like my slap shot?" I ask eagerly.

"Hardest shot you ever took!"

He messes my hair again, and I feel so proud! He's got a hundred-mile-an-hour shot, so if he says mine was hard, it must have been *hard*.

Someone lays a hand on my shoulder, and it's Jae-won. He looks teary-eyed. "What?!" I say. "Didn't you make it?"

"Yeah, I made it," he says, fighting back tears.

"Aw, cut it out, man, that's just embarrassing."

He smiles, then laughs. "I know."

Then I spot Rocko. He's listening to his dad, and his dad looks mad.

Rocko quickly approaches me and says, "You didn't play so great."

I ignore that and just walk away. Then everyone who made the team goes into a room, and the players get fitted for uniforms and socks. I see Lucas is there. He's from my AA team too. I like Lucas. He's all business. He doesn't mess around in the locker room, he doesn't throw your gear across the room or spray you with water. He doesn't take other players' sticks and bang them on the ground. He doesn't swear and trash-talk. He doesn't lock anyone in the bathroom. He just plays good hockey, gets dressed, and leaves. I don't know him well, but I'm a Lucas fanboy.

The parents pay, sign letters of intent, fill out a few papers, and if they're from other clubs, they show proof their sons are up-to-date on their tetanus shots. I had my tetanus shot last year, so they already have that on file. The players all sign a paper pledging to do their best and listen to the coaches. Aleksei texts me and asks how the tryout went. I text him back that I made the team. He asks me whether my dad signed the letter of intent. I say yes. He says that it's all because of his lessons, but he includes a smiley face. *You're the man,* I text back.

CHAPTER 12

IN THE CAR I start reliving the whole scrimmage. I remember every moment, not just every time I had the puck. Jae-won's magnificent pass. Lucas, Mr. Efficiency. Jesus Acosta, the fastest skater at the club's peewee level. Madden, who scored twice. The league requires that at least half a team needs to be kids who played with the club the previous season. I guess that's just to make sure that clubs develop their own players instead of constantly try to create all-star teams by recruiting guys from other clubs. I go through everybody who made the team. We have fifteen out of seventeen who played for the Grizzlies last season: twelve who were on the AAA team last year, and then Jae-won, Lucas, and me from the AAs. The other two guys are from the Racers.

"How many Racers did we have trying out?" I ask Dad. "It seems like it was a lot."

"I counted seven."

"How come?"

"I heard their peewee AAA coach got fired at the last minute, so their team is in disarray. They hired a new guy, but nobody likes him."

"Like *fired* fired?" Coaches are let go all the time, but I've never heard of one *fired*.

"Yeah, and he's one of the best peewee coaches in California. We watched his team play our AAAs once last year, remember? Those kids really understood the fundamentals. But he showed up falling-down drunk to a team function."

"Oh, wow . . ." I think that over, feel kind of sorry for the guy. "I would be okay with a coach making one mistake."

"Yeah, second chances. Absolutely, I agree."

Dad's pretty chill for a cop. I mean, I'm sure he can be tough on the streets, but he's chill, too.

He looks worried for some reason. "Is everything okay?" I ask.

"Yeah, are you kidding? Everything's great! I've never been so proud of you!"

Aunt Mo texts me. *Your dad says you made the team, congratulations!!!!! I knew you would!!!!!*

Thanks, I text back. *It was a lot of fun.*

She sends back a bunch of emojis and exclamation marks.

Dad's face seems sad, though, so while I glance at him curiously, I let him have his space.

When we get home, Sinbad's standing right at the door, his stubby tail wagging, totally oblivious to his cone. The cone is kind of like a goofy halo. I kneel down. "I made it!" I say. I feel a clench of worry inside my stomach as I remember that he may still be going through treatment when the team has its first out-of-town tournament. I give my head a quick couple of jerks, just to shake the thought out of my brain.

Dad goes right to his room, kind of determined, like he's got something to do. After I take out my gear to air it, I put plastic wrap around Sinbad's leg, take off his cone, then bring him into the shower with me. I know that's weird, but I do it sometimes. I soap myself from head to toe while he stands with his mouth open as water falls into it. After turning off the water, I get out and quickly grab a towel and dry off Sinbad really well before he shakes all over. Then I dry myself and decide to blow off brushing my teeth 'cause I'm suddenly exhausted.

In bed, I push Sinbad away so I don't get wet. He keeps scooting closer, and I keep pushing him away. We do that three times before I give up. Then I close my eyes and I'm gone.

Late that night something wakes me up. I'm suddenly 100 percent awake. Then I hear it: my dad crying. It's not loud, that's not what woke me up. And it doesn't sound like it's coming from his bedroom. I silently push myself up and walk carefully through the house. But he's not inside. He's on the front porch, on the top of the three steps. He doesn't see or hear me, but I see and hear him clearly. His face is in his hands, elbows on his knees, and he's crying hard. I can't decide if I should say something. I stand there in the throes of a terrible indecision. Finally I say, "Dad?"

His head jolts up and turns quickly toward me. His face is wet in the moonlight. "Sorry, Con, did I wake you up?" he asks.

"No, no problem, Dad. Um. Are you okay?"

"Yeah, yeah, I'm fine. Go on back to bed."

I hesitate. "But Dad . . ." I don't know what I want to say, but I know I want to say something, so I don't leave.

"I know," he says. "You want to know why I'm crying. I know." He wipes his face on his pajama top. He scoots over and pats the stoop next to him. I sit down. "Congratulations again. I'm proud of you, Conor. So proud."

"Thanks, Dad. That means a lot to me." And it does, too. It means everything to me. He looks really sad, though.

"But are you okay, Dad? Are you?"

"Yeah, yeah, I'm fine."

"But, Dad . . ." Then I just say, "I heard you crying the other day."

"You did?" He looks displeased, but not necessarily with me. Maybe with himself.

"Is it still the divorce?"

"It's different things. I got called to a bad accident today. Drunk driver." He shakes his head. "It made me think of your mother. . . . How proud she would have been of you today. And that got me thinking, just wishing I could have been driving the day your mother died. The reason she was alone was because I had a game out of town. I always felt like if I'd been driving, she wouldn't have died." My mom was killed by a drunk driver, in the middle of the afternoon.

"It's not your fault!"

"It just feels sometimes like it is. Even today." But then he half smiles through his sadness. "Seeing you play so hard in the tryout, you reminded me of me when I was your age. I never saw you play so hard. I'm glad you've had your hockey to distract you from . . . whatever. Real glad. I'm glad you have a passion, because I promise you having a life you're passionate about is the only thing that's worth a can of beans in this world." He wraps an arm around my shoulders and stares at the house across the street. It's a small house, like ours. It's painted a weird orange-yellow shade, but you can't tell in the night. Then he lifts his eyes to the sky. "There's going to be a blue moon this summer."

"What's a blue moon?"

"It's the second full moon in the same month." He nods, but kind of to himself, like he's forgotten I'm there. There's a long silence between us. He looks toward the door. "Where's Sinbad?"

"You know how he is. He likes his sleep." I'm pretty sure when I get back, he's going to be stretched across the whole bed.

"I need to get to sleep too. Come on."

He goes back into the house without making sure I'm following, and a few seconds later I hear his door close. I keep looking at the house across the street. I imagine dramas playing out in that house, kind of like they are here. And in every other house on the block. Even just the drama of daily life. Our little neighborhood, safe now from the fire, but full of the kind of drama Mr. Falco would be interested in, family drama. I think about the stuff I brought when we evacuated. I think I made good decisions. My hockey trophies represent a lot of battles. My computer. But mostly what I think about is what I didn't take, and I don't know why I didn't take it. The pictures in my bottom drawer, mostly of my mom, with the frame sitting on top of them. I don't know, man, I just feel like I can't look at those pictures. There's one that was taken in a photo booth, me and my mom when I was two years old. I wonder what the world would be like if she'd never died and Dad and I weren't here living the bachelor life. I wonder what would have happened if those pictures all got burned up. I don't know why, but there's a part of me that wishes they had been.

Three coyotes lope down the street, eyes glowing. There's a noise at the door, then deep growling. "Sinbad!" I say. He paws at the screen, ripping it.

"Aw, man! No! Bad boy!" Ordinarily, I would be the one to pay for that screen, but I'm not going to have any money for it. My heart just feels so low. I slip inside. "Come on, bad boy," I say softly so I won't wake Dad. He runs ahead of me, and when I get to the bed, he's lying on my pillow, acting like he's asleep. I think about how he's starting chemo next week, so instead of pushing him away, I lie down without a pillow. He paws me like he wants me to pet him. "I'm mad at you for taking my pillow, plus you broke the screen. I'm not going to pet you." But I'm already reaching for the top of his head as the words come out. He's acting exactly the same as he always does. He doesn't realize how hard the next few months might be. He doesn't even seem to realize he's got a hunk of white plastic around his neck.

The motion detector turns on outside. Who has a motion detector in Canyon Country, with all the animals? But Jenny wanted lights all over. And I haven't asked Dad to take it down 'cause, I don't know, maybe it'll remind him of her, or maybe he likes having little reminders of her around. I just don't know.

CHAPTER 13

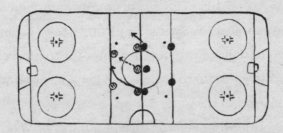

MONDAY THERE'S NOT much to do. Practice usually doesn't start until August. I'm so busy all the time that usually what I love about summer is having nothing to do for hours, just walking Sinbad and working out. But today feels kind of empty. Ordinarily I'd be playing in-house hockey this summer. Other guys like to take a few weeks off, but I'm not like that. I get super antsy when I haven't been skating. In-house leagues are four teams all based out of the same rink. A lot of in-house programs don't have very good players, 'cause there are no tryouts—the teams take anyone who wants to join. But there's one in-house program with a lot of travel players. Travel teams hold tryouts and go to different rinks to play as well as fly out of town for tournaments. Unfortunately, the in-house program I was planning to enroll in costs eight hundred dollars. Several guys I know are going to play there this summer, so I was looking forward to it. But it's okay.

After I eat a late breakfast, I sit out front with Sinbad, just so he can watch the neighborhood. Mr. Reynolds from down the street walks by. He's old, like in his eighties, but he takes a slow, slow walk twice a day.

"Hi, Mr. Reynolds!" I call out.

"Yes!" he answers. "Yes!" He walks a few steps and stops, then turns to look at me as if he's forgotten to say something, which he has. "Conor MacRae!" he shouts out. He immediately turns around again and heads off. He does that to everybody. He knows the name of everybody on the block, and when he sees them, he says their name instead of "hi." His hair is snow white, but he has a good amount of it, and he wears wide glasses, like, wider than his face.

After watching the world go by for an hour, we go inside and I do five sets of five pull-ups, thirty-three push-ups, and five hundred squats, which just about kills my legs. Then I clean the bathroom. I play video skateboarding and watch YouTube for five hours. Watching YouTube is one of my favorite things, but I'm just killing time until it's tomorrow, when we take Sinbad to the oncologist.

When Dad gets home, we go to a park and work out while Sinbad waits. Afterward Dad asks if I want to see a movie, but I don't, so we just sit in the park on our phones until it's almost dark. Sinbad lies close to me the whole time. At some point I start thinking of Mr. Reynolds, and then I think about old people, and then I think of my grandparents. I say, "Dad?"

"Yeah?"

"So after Grandma and Grandpa did all that stupid traveling, they just didn't want to know me anymore?" I don't know why I called it "stupid." I got nothing against people who travel.

"Conor, you need to understand—they were unbelievably close to your mother. She was the same way toward you, just unbelievably close." He pauses.

"After she died, they came over to our apartment, and they didn't leave for a week. I let them sleep on the bed, and I slept on the living room couch by myself. They slept with you in the middle. I don't think they even went out during the day."

"You never told me that!"

"Your grandmother especially. She just held you in her arms for hours. I had to make her set you down so you could walk around once in a while. Finally they went home because they couldn't remember if they'd left their heater on. They were afraid their house would burn down."

"Then did they come back?"

"Yeah, they would stay for days at a time. They only lived ten minutes away, but they didn't want to go home. I think they just felt like your mom was still around a little bit, in that apartment."

I think about my bottom desk drawer, and the pictures of my mom and me. There are some with us and her parents and her grandparents. There's even a picture of me with my mom's great-grandmother. I guess at one time, and maybe even today, the longest-lived people in America were

Asian American women in an area of New Jersey. That's where she lived.

"Remember that picture of my great-great-grandmother holding me? How old did she live to be?" I ask.

"I don't know. She was a hundred and one the last time I saw her."

"Was she nice?"

"To tell the truth, she mostly sat around watching TV and not talking to anyone. She did garden for two hours a day, I heard. There was one time we all went for a walk together. She got around the whole block. It was pretty amazing. But she never said a word."

The park is totally empty, but I don't feel like leaving yet. It feels nice to sit out here in the lukewarm night. Sinbad seems relaxed. So does Dad.

"When did Grandpa and Grandma stop coming over so much?"

"That first year, they were over all the time. Then when I started dating Jenny, they stopped coming over so much." He rubs his chin. "I know it really hurt them, and I thought about stopping with Jenny. But you seemed to like her, and she seemed to like you. So I thought it was a good idea. I liked her a lot too. She made me happy."

"Did you feel guilty?"

"Yeah, I felt real guilty. I thought about all of it a lot."

"Did you try to talk to them?"

"After I started dating Jenny, I went to their house to ask if they still wanted to take care of you when I was on road trips, and they said no. I went there another time to ask them how often they wanted me to bring you over, and they said once a week at first. Then they said they would call me when they wanted to see you, but they hardly ever called. I went to their house to talk a few more times, but they never said much, and sometimes we'd sit there for ten or fifteen minutes without saying a word. Your aunt already lived in Los Angeles, so when the next season ended, I decided to quit hockey and move to LA to get a new start. At that point, I hardly ever saw your grandparents anymore. But I went over there to tell them I was moving to Los Angeles."

"What did they say?"

"They cried. They were so close to your mom, I

can't even express how close they were." He rubs his face again. "And to be honest, Jenny didn't really like them. She was polite to them, but she wasn't feeling it. So I'm sure they intuited that."

"What's intuited?"

"They just felt it without anyone really saying anything."

"Like Sinbad just knows things?"

"Yeah, kind of."

"Wow, that all sucks."

"Yeah, it did. I mean, I was happy, you seemed happy, Jenny was happy. But they were sad."

"They came out to LA that one time."

"That was the only time."

I nod. It's gotten dark, the lights shining over the empty park. Southern California was in a drought for years, but the grass is pretty green now. But the lighting makes it all look unreal, or like a photograph. I look around; we seem to be the only ones left. It feels good to be here. I think about what my dad's just told me, and I guess I still kind of resent my grandparents for basically abandoning me. I understand they were hurt, but didn't Dad have the right to move on?

"We better get going. I want Sinbad to get a good rest tonight. I don't know if they'll start the chemo right away, but if they do, I want him ready."

That makes me hop up, which makes Sinbad jump up. We walk quietly across the park, Sinbad acting clingy like he does once in a while. I believe he knows what's coming. Even in the parking lot where we see a group of teenagers, he doesn't even seem interested in them. He just wants to cling.

"I had a Dobe once!" a guy calls out.

"They're great!" I say.

On the ride home, I think about how weird it is that time only moves forward. That means you don't really have a choice about a lot of stuff. Like if you wanted to stay a kid, you wouldn't be able to do that. And if you wanted to sit in a park with your dog and your dad for seven days, you really couldn't do that, either. You've got to move forward with your life. You've got to face stuff. I'm in the backseat with Sinbad, and he's still clingy. He *knows*.

CHAPTER 14

WE SIT AT the oncologist's. Everything in the office looks new and in good shape, the opposite of Dr. Andris's place. There's a chalkboard that says *WELCOME TO OUR PATIENTS!* Underneath are names of all the animals being treated today. It even says *WELCOME TO SINBAD! WE LOOK FOR-WARD TO MEETING YOU!* I flip through a scrap-book on an end table and see all the success stories—animals that went into remission for months and even a couple of years. Sinbad's going to set the record for that. Maybe five years! There are also handwritten notes from pet owners thanking the doctors.

I feel like spiderwebs are on my face. I've never felt this before and have to keep rubbing my hand across my skin to wipe away the feeling. Sinbad stands with his tail up, staring down a golden retriever. He's not dog-aggressive, but he's not dog-friendly, either.

A man leans out a door. "Sinbad!"

Sinbad looks at him with interest, then turns to me. We follow the man into an office, where he weighs Sinbad and takes his temperature. I'm surprised to see he weighs ninety, two pounds less than he weighed just last week.

Dr. Pierre comes in right away. She's a small black woman who looks like she weighs about as much as Sinbad.

"Hi, I'm Dr. Pierre." She shakes our hands, reads over the chart, then continues, "So a malignant lump on his left popliteal. How long ago did you notice the lump?"

"About a week ago."

"Good, I'm glad you got him in quickly. Do you think you could lift him onto the exam table?" She says that to Dad, but I do it with a little struggle. "Strong!" she says.

"I play ice hockey and work out."

"Oh, you do? Good for you. Uh, LA Kings, right?"

"Grizzlies . . ." There's an awkward pause. "Oh, you mean . . . yeah, the Kings play in LA."

"I thought so. Is Sinbad your dog?"

"Yeah, he sleeps on the bed with me."

"Aw, okay, well, we're going to take good care of him." She feels the back of his leg. "Right," she mumbles. "Wow, he's completely healed. You can go ahead and stop using the cone."

Dr. Pierre smiles slightly at me. "He's a good dog, isn't he?" I nod, and she continues. "So. There are some tests called staging tests that we do before we begin treatment to get an idea of the extent of the cancer. Different doctors will sometimes not do all of them. There are a set of the usual ones, which are chest X-rays, abdominal ultrasound, a full blood panel, a bone marrow aspirate, and a urinalysis. Many doctors like to do the bone aspirate, but it's expensive and invasive, and I try to avoid that. In the case of a Doberman, I also recommend an echo-cardiogram to make sure the dog won't go into heart failure during chemo." *Heart failure?* Wait, what? I can't ask. I need to concentrate. *Focus* as Dr. Pierre is still talking. "I'm going to tell you the sort of simplified version of things here, and then I'll also give you some papers for you to read."

I'm leaning forward as I listen. Then, glancing at Dad, I ask, "So that's all included in the seven thousand dollars?"

"Yes, it is."

I look at my dad questioningly, and he says, "Great, then do we get started now?"

"We do," she says. "We do. After the staging test results, I'll be giving him vincristine and doxorubicin intravenously. Then you'll give him prednisone and cyclophosphamide at home. We start out weekly, then move to every other week." Then she gives me a really sympathetic look. "Do you mind? I actually think things go more quickly without the owner. Do you think you could sit in the waiting room?"

She asks it kindly, but I know what the only answer she'll accept is. "That's fine," I say.

Dad and I return to the waiting room. I put on my earphones and chew gum as hard as I can. Then I close my eyes and listen to music, zoning out so big-time that I'm really surprised when someone in scrubs brings Sinbad out. We have a couple of hours to wait for results, so we find a cheap restaurant with outside tables and eat while Sinbad stands at attention, watching anyone who walks by. Sinbad loves to eat out, so even though I'm worried, it makes me feel good to watch him.

Then we return, and Dr. Pierre explains that the chemo will be given to Sinbad intravenously, and it'll probably take thirty minutes. I can't be there because the dog needs to lie still. Also, it's dangerous for me—the staff will be wearing impermeable gowns, N95 respirators, and special chemotherapy gloves.

So Dad and I return to the waiting room. The chairs are actually comfortable, nothing like the old, hard chairs at Dr. Andris's place. Earphones back on. Music cranked. Dad tells me not to listen to music loudly 'cause it'll hurt my hearing in the long run. But today is special, so I let the music blast away. I try to imagine sitting in the car, traveling up north to Vacaville, California, for a hockey tournament. One time we left at four in the morning and caravanned with some others families, going up the coast and stopping to play Frisbee on the beach. The parents sometimes complain about the travel, but then they end up having as much fun as the players. Truth is, hockey kids spend a lot of time with their parents, so most of the players come from super-close families.

I relive that whole trip in my head. Jae-won's little brothers were there. Mrs. Kang was trying to get them to wade, but they only wanted to be around the big boys—us. They were four then, and they kept running around in the middle of our Frisbee game, screaming and laughing and trying to make angels in the sand. I had a teammate named Jammer who was there, and when an ice cream truck came by, he ate seven bars, no joke. The great thing about hockey is you just have so many perfect days. When we got up to Vacaville, we won all four of our games. Jammer and Jae-won each scored a hat trick that weekend. Of course, you also have days that suck pretty bad, like when you lose a game and your coach has a mental breakdown about it.

Then really suddenly I think about Sinbad with an IV, not knowing what's going on, and I kind of feel like throwing up. He's lying there now, chemicals surging through his body, a stranger in a respirator and impermeable gown standing next to him. I groan a long, soft groan.

I like Amy Winehouse a lot when I feel sad after a loss, so I switch my music to that and actually feel better, 'cause her voice is so unreal that when you listen to it, you're not really where you are anymore; you're someplace else.

When the chemo is over, Dr. Pierre shows Dad how to give Sinbad a couple of more pills at home. I listen carefully, 'cause no matter what anyone says, I'm the one who's going to do it next time. We have to wait while Sinbad starts pawing at a wall. He does that sometimes if he thinks there's a mouse or something in there. Dogs can probably smell through the wall, so maybe that's what's going on. Dr. Pierre talks statistics: Average survival time is about one year, and 20 percent of dogs can live two years. Half will live longer than twelve months, and half less than twelve months. She has a patient who got cancer five and a half years ago, and he's still alive! That's Sinbad, I just know it.

Then we go home. Sinbad seems fine—great, even—so Dad and I are relieved. The only thing is, he might feel nauseous or tired in a few days. He probably won't. Hard to tell, though, since every dog is different. I take him for a short, slow walk right away. He pulls on the leash to go faster, but I heel him. Dr. Pierre used the phrase "quality of life" several times, as in, "With dogs we're not going to cure them, we just want to maintain as much quality of life as possible."

He pulls me toward the hills, but I don't want to take him up a hill 'cause he's supposed to take it easy. We walk past Mr. Reynolds's house. He's got a big sheet of blue plastic over some poles to make a shaded area with a lawn chair underneath. He also throws blue plastic over his car sometimes, and then it blows off and just lies there for days in his front yard. It all makes him look like he's homeless, but Dad says when you're in your eighties, you don't care what people think so much. Man, being eighty is so far away I can hardly imagine it! I can't even imagine getting through the next week, let alone another seventy years. I don't even want to be that old. I mean,

Sinbad will be long gone, and probably my dad, too. My hockey career will be way in the past. So what's the point?

We walk around the cul-de-sac. It's quiet and empty—Sinbad and me seem to be the only ones left in the world. Sinbad jumps up and places both his front paws on a tree, but I don't see any squirrels up there. He stares intently, totally in the moment per usual, then starts snarling. But he's just playing. I suddenly get that spiderweb feeling again and rub my face. Then I sit a long time with my face in my hands, like Dad does when he wants to get away without really getting away. Sinbad pushes his nose on my hands, and I feel a rush of love as I take hold of his head. "I got your back," I tell him. "Just like you always got mine. We're going to get through this chemo thing."

I like to think I'm pretty tough. One of the things you learn from hockey is that sometimes you're just wiped out, destroyed. You don't make a team you want, or you make an idiot move and cost your team the game. It's just like a tree getting burned down. Then you regenerate. That's what me and Sinbad are going to do, once a week at first and then every two weeks. Regenerate.

Finally I stand up. Down the block, Mr. Reynolds is in his yard, messing with his blue plastic. It's flying around in the wind like it's alive. He keeps trying to tame it. I hurry down to see if I can help, but he gives up and goes inside before I get there. His blue plastic lies in the middle of the yard, rippling in the wind. It's just crazy to think I'll be eighty someday. Crazy!

CHAPTER 15

SO DOG CHEMO usually doesn't make them lose their hair or anything like that, 'cause they're not given as strong a dose as humans get. When my dad picks up the prescription, he stops to buy latex gloves. So now I'm looking at two gloves sitting on the counter next to two meds on a paper towel. Dad watches as I stretch my arms and back and even my legs, like I'm getting ready for a game. Then I put on gloves. I get those spiderwebs on my face again, but I can't do anything about it just now. I chew on some gum, look at the pills. I'm a little surprised that they're vitamin-size. I was expecting something smaller.

Dr. Pierre doesn't want me to wrap the meds in pill pockets or food. I squeeze the top of Sinbad's snout and pull open the bottom while holding the first pill. Then I stick the pill as deep down his throat as I can, blow on his nose, and he swallows! He lopes a few feet away, sits, and looks at me. I hang out cross-legged on the floor like nothing's going on, just sitting here chewing my gum and studying the ceiling.

After a minute I say, "Sinbad!" but he doesn't budge.

I get up, but he runs off. Dad and I have to chase him down in the living room, but I don't want to touch him with my hands. Dad picks him up and carries him into the kitchen. Sinbad's not happy, but he takes the second pill. Okay! Dad holds open a plastic bag, and I drop the gloves in.

"All right!" I say. We high-five.

Sinbad chews a bone for about an hour, but then he stops almost mid-chew and lies there with the bone in his mouth. I pull it out and set it aside, and he closes his eyes and lies very still. He doesn't seem to be breathing, so I panic. "Sinbad!" He opens his eyes. "Sorry, I'm sorry. Just rest." He closes his eyes.

I wonder whether I should have given him some water after the pills. What if he gets thirsty but feels too tired to drink? I think about petting him while he sleeps, but maybe he just wants to be left alone. Sometimes when he goes to sleep, he goes out hard, so I'm not exactly worried. I check e-mail on my phone—got two e-vites for birthday parties. One's from my new teammate Ryan Morgan, and the other is from a kid at school. The friend from school is having his party at Magic Mountain, which means I'm not going. The last time I was there I got a sore neck from a roller coaster and had to lie in bed with headaches and dizziness for two days. The only thing I'm willing to get hurt at is hockey. Other than that, I'm a wuss. Never getting on a roller coaster again. Period.

I answer both e-vites and sit on the floor next to Sinbad, watching a movie about a tsunami on my phone. Even on such a small screen, it's pretty lit—*super* realistic. Think I'll avoid the beach for a couple of years, maybe forever. So, no roller coasters, no beach. I'm down to 1 percent battery. I plug it in and lay a pillow on the floor next to Sinbad. In the dark, chewing some gum. Sinbad's been totally still for hours, not even shifting his body. I stop chewing and listen to him breathing deeply. I try to breathe with exactly the same rhythm as him, over and over, then over and over some more, until we're totally in sync: just me and him, floating through space together.

CHAPTER 16

EVEN THOUGH THE pills aren't supposed to affect him that much, Sinbad mostly sleeps for an entire day, but then by the morning of the second day he's so eager to go for a walk that he jumps all over me, yelping and barking. He's acting like his regular self!

Outside, he pulls so hard I have to hold him with two hands. "Sinbad, heel!" He starts yelping, and I see it's a squirrel, the bane of his existence. I let him pull me to a tree, where he jumps up, whining and pawing at the bark. The squirrel is hiding in the leaves. Sinbad sits with his head raised. I look around, see Mr. Reynolds moving slowly toward us.

Sinbad lets out a half whine, half howl. He just sits, panting, while I wait.

"Conor MacRae!"

I turn. "Hi, Mr. Reynolds."

"You know, you could do me a favor."

"Sure thing."

"You know anything about washing cars?"

"Yeah, I wash our cars, except my dad won't let me wash his police motorcycle 'cause it's his love child."

"I'll pay you—" He's reaching into a pocket.

"You don't need to pay me," I quickly reply.

"Yes, yes, I do. I'm a man of my word."

I don't know what that means, since he hasn't said anything that would be breaking his word if he didn't pay me.

"I'm not too old to wash my car, but I just pulled a muscle in my back. Darn muscle! Darn back!" He takes a crinkly one-dollar bill out of his pocket. "I don't have much . . . Social Security."

"You don't have to pay me."

"Don't insult me!" he says sharply, so I take the bill and thank him.

"Sinbad!" I yank on the leash, and we walk—slowly—with Mr. Reynolds.

"I owned many dogs in my life," Mr. Reynolds says. "I owned a chimpanzee once!"

"Is that legal?"

"Unfortunately, it was. I didn't give him the life he should have lived, out in the wild. So I always felt bad about that. There are still people left who own chimps in the country, but there's nobody selling them anymore. So this is a good thing." Then he places his arm around my shoulder like my dad does sometimes. "I've had a good life, Conor MacRae. You're going to be the same way, I can tell you that. I've seen you walking around."

I'm a little surprised at all this, 'cause literally the only thing he ever says to me is "Conor MacRae!" Somehow he even knows my aunt's name, 'cause he was strolling by once when she was there, and he said, "Maureen MacRae!" as he passed.

When we reach his house, I tie Sinbad to one of the poles holding up the blue tarp. Hopefully, he won't pull on it and knock the whole thing down! Mr. Reynolds struggles to drag the hose out, but when

I offer to help, he snaps again, "Don't insult me!"
Then he goes and gets a bucket, then he goes and gets
soap and wax, and then he goes and gets rags. Fifteen
minutes basically pass. Not complaining, just saying.
I text Dad: *I'm washing Mr. Reynolds's car. He paid me
$1.* Dad texts back: *That'll go far.*

Mr. Reynolds disappears while I work. He's got a
big, old car. He hardly drives faster than my dad and
I jog, to be honest. Once we saw him in a nearby shopping area, and another driver yelled out at him, "Get
off the road!" That made me mad, so I yelled back,
"He's *old!*" but I don't know if the other guy heard me,
since he was already speeding off.

Mr. Reynolds has got me using dishwashing
soap, which I'm pretty sure is bad for the wax, so I
go home with Sinbad and grab some car-wash detergent. Sinbad seems tired, so I have a moment of
indecision—he hates it when I leave, but I don't want
to stress him out by making him walk even a little
bit more. So I leave him behind, then hear him howling in displeasure, then run back to get him. When
we return, Mr. Reynolds is standing there with his
hands on his hips.

"Thought you abandoned me."

I hold up the detergent. "Got car-wash soap."

He nods. "Fancy." Then he sits in the lawn chair under the tarp while I tie Sinbad back up.

I actually really like washing and waxing cars. It's so relaxing. It takes me about an hour 'cause I don't like to do a lot of things, but I do like to get it right when I do something. At one point, there's a big crash, and I see that Sinbad has pulled down the tarp and poles. My jaw drops— What if he killed Mr. Reynolds? I rush over, the blue tarp moving around as Mr. Reynolds tries to get free. When I pull it off, he continues to flail his arms around. He says, "Those poles have never collapsed before. I got them in there good."

"I think Sinbad did it. Are you okay?"

And he just laughs suddenly, which makes me smile. He nods. "Reminds me of something my chimp would do."

"I'll put the poles back in when I'm done."

"No, no, that's my job."

I finish waxing, and the car looks brand-new. I love that feeling of seeing a shiny car I've just cleaned and waxed. I take a picture of it on my phone, then turn around proudly. Mr. Reynolds is kneeling down, messing with a pole and grunting. I walk over and say, "I'll do it," but I know what he's going to say before he says it.

"Don't insult me!" Then he says, "*Aw*," and grabs at his back. I kneel down, and he says, "Don't insult me!"

I reach into my pocket and say, "Here's your money back. For knocking the poles over."

He says, "That's fair," and takes back the dollar. He gets up with a grunt, mumbling, "I'll get those poles up later."

"Bye," I say as he walks off. "Let me know if you need your car washed again."

He says, "Conor MacRae!"

That all gets me thinking, so the next day I knock on doors up and down my street, asking anybody who's home if I can wash and wax their cars for twelve dollars. Ten of them say yes. I do three a day, letting Sinbad hang around with me, and by the end of the week I'm in the money again. Except for the pepper spray, Dad's one of those cops who's a stickler for the law, and he says as he understands California child labor laws, I'm not allowed to have a *regular* car-wash route without getting a work permit from the superintendent of schools. He thinks I'm allowed to wash people's cars in an *irregular* and *intermittent* manner. All the laws in the world sometimes drive Dad crazy. He read an article once that said just about everybody in America is committing felonies all the time without even realizing it 'cause there are so many laws. He mostly just keeps up on traffic laws. So after I wash each person's car, I don't try to set up appointments to wash their cars *regularly*. I do give them my phone number and ask them to call me if they need their car washed again. I try to do a perfect job on every car so they call me soon. If I manage to wash a hundred or even fifty cars over the summer, that might help out Dad quite a bit.

And that's the way it goes for the next few weeks. I wash cars, except for I don't do anything a few days after Sinbad's treatments, 'cause he gets super tired, and then a couple of days after that he acts like a puppy again. We spend every minute together. When it's my birthday in July, we go with Dad to work out at the park. No party, and three presents, including a *Star Wars* sweatshirt from Aunt Mo. I wouldn't be caught dead wearing a *Star Wars* anything—I mean, I'm twelve now!—but I'll wear it next time I see her. Cards from my grandparents and my ex-stepmom. She signs her card *Mom*. She's sent me two notes since she moved out, and she signed one *Jenny* and one *Mom*. I don't know how I feel about her right now. I guess I've never known, ever since the day she said she wanted a real kid.

I offer my money to Dad, but he won't take it, says I can use it for hockey. It's not enough for me to play in-house. I decide to wait until I accumulate more before starting lessons again, just in case something comes up and Dad needs money after all. So there's a lull in my hockey world. Dad does drive me to public skating a few times to keep me from getting rusty. I glide around the rink feeling like a superhero next to all the newbies. I have an incredible hunger to be around the rink, so Dad and I and a couple of times Jae-won watch some in-house games.

Several of the best bantams in Southern California are playing in-house at this rink right now. They probably all discussed it and decided to get some serious off-season competition against one another. There's a set of twins who used to play at the Grizzlies—they're probably six feet, a hundred and ninety. They're so good—especially one of them— that at one point Jae-won actually lays his head against my shoulder, and when I glance at him, he's all starry-eyed with his mouth hanging open, like he's in love. He lifts his head, and we look at each other, and I know exactly what we're both thinking: hopefully, that'll be us after we go through puberty. Puberty is always going through the heads of a lot of peewees. It's the future, man. And it's a mystery.

CHAPTER 17

WHEN IT'S TIME for Ryan's party, I wear my usual T-shirt and athletic shorts. A lot of my shirts have holes at the collar 'cause I have a bad habit of chewing on my shirts when I'm at the computer. So of the shirts without holes, I choose a light blue one that's kind of dressy for a T-shirt. Aunt Mo got it for me, and Dad said it cost thirty-five dollars—*on sale*. Ryan lives all the way in Los Angeles. I have a feeling he's rich, 'cause he told everyone that he has a private hockey coach he skates with five times a week for an hour. There're quite a few rich kids in hockey, and a few are seriously loaded. That's probably

'cause of how much money hockey costs. But the
ice is the great leveler. Like, Jesus's family doesn't
have much money, but he's the fastest skater in peewee by far. I'm a fast skater, but he's a god. Some
people think he's the best kid skater in California.
Madden's probably more agile, but he's not as fast.
And Jae-won led our team in scoring last year. He
came in first in scoring in Southern California peewee AA. His hands are touched by God, man. Honestly, sometimes it makes me want to kill him from
jealousy and bow down to his awesomeness at the
same time. I hope he works out his skating problems, 'cause if he does, he's going all the way. Me, I
skate better than Jae-won, and I have better hands
than Jesus. I have better ice vision than either, like
I just have a sense of what's going on all over the ice,
where everybody is, and where they're going. But
I need to bring my skating up to the level of Jesus,
and my hands up to the level of Jae-won. Basically,
if you're in youth hockey, you got lots of stuff to work
on in terms of your game.

Anyway, in our old Volvo, we ramble up to what
turns out to be Ryan's freakin' *mansion*, and Dad

waits while I walk up to the front door holding a birthday card with ten bucks inside. I'm thinking I should have brought fifteen, but . . . priorities: I don't know Ryan real well. He played for a different AAA club during the regular season, but he played for the Grizzlies during the spring session. I didn't make the spring AAA team, though . . . that was another sad thing I forgot to tell you about. Spring's not as important as regular season; still, it was a disappointment.

A smiling woman answers the door, holds her hand out, and says, "Hi, I'm Ryan's mother. And you're . . . ?"

"Conor MacRae."

"From the team or school?"

"The team."

"Go, team!" she says, kind of passionately. "Do you think it's going to be a good season?"

"I hope so."

"Yay! We hope so too. That's why we came over to the Grizzlies. Go on in, sweetie."

I glance back and nod at my dad, then follow Ryan's mom. There's a huge double staircase in the living room, like something out of a movie. The living room is about the size of our whole house. A really small dog with long hair is stuck to Mrs. Morgan's leg. The dog is shaking like crazy and growls softly at me.

Mrs. Morgan picks him up. "She hates some people!" She rubs her nose on the dog's. "Don't you, cutie?" She looks at me. "Did you bring your swim trunks? We thought we'd start out with swimming."

She leads me through the house. There are a few pillars on the border of the living room and dining room, plus a couple of pillars by the staircase to upstairs. Mrs. Morgan opens the door to a bathroom the size of my bedroom, and I change in there, stuffing my clothes into my backpack. When I get out, Ryan's mom is gone, so I wander into the backyard. The yard is huge, but not super huge—we're right in the city, so maybe there's not that much space. The pool takes up a third of the yard, and it's shaped like some kind of three-limbed jelly-monster. I don't see anyone I know yet, but what the heck? I drop my backpack, run across the concrete, and jump into the water.

Then I spot Ryan and say, "Hey, Ryan. Happy birthday."

"Hi, Conor. Thanks. You play D, right?"

"Yeah. I played forward in squirts, but the coach switched me over last year."

He nods. "What's Coach Dusan like?" he asks.

"I don't know him real well, but everybody says he treats you like you're already professional. He might not even know we're still kids. I guess that's good." I pause, wipe water from my eyes, then add, "But it might just mean he's really tough. His squirt team won CAHA two years in a row, and he also won a state championship with a bantam team in Michigan in 2006. They came in second in nationals. He's never had a team miss the play-offs." CAHA is the California Amateur Hockey Association, so winning that means you've won state.

"I've never made the play-offs before."

I start to say, "Really?" but Ryan spots someone else, his face lighting up before he swims off. I take a few laps, then float on a plastic raft until I spot Jae-won. I wave, and he jumps into the water, then climbs on another raft. We lie in the sun together, not talking much at first. Then he paddles closer to me and says in a low voice, "This is the biggest house I've ever been in."

"Me too."

"Want to explore?"

"Sure."

We spill off our rafts and clamber up the side of the pool. There's a bunch of fluffy towels folded up on chairs, so we grab a couple. First we look around the backyard. It's my dream backyard. Most of it is mowed, but it still has a wild feel, with trees and bushes arranged in a forest-like way. I know I said it's not that big, but I just meant compared to how huge the house is.

"When we're in the NHL, we'll have a house like this," Jae-won says.

Most guys don't talk out loud about being in the NHL someday, even though we all secretly hope we will be. But Jae-won is like that, very honest about stuff. He wants to be in the NHL, so why shouldn't he say so?

The grass is soft on my feet as we head back to the house. We go inside, our towels thrown over our shoulders. The floors are marble. Jae-won's dad lays marble, so that's how I know what it is. The company he works for gave us marble counters at a discount, 'cause Jenny wanted them. I guess it looks good. Fancy-like.

We stumble into a room with a big screen on one end and really comfortable-looking leather chairs in front of the screen. We look at each other and laugh. "I watch movies on my computer," I say, then remember that Jae-won doesn't even have his own computer. If he wants to watch a movie, he uses the TV in his parents' room.

There're twelve chairs in the dining room, eight chairs in the movie room, six chairs at a table next to the kitchen, three chairs at a counter in the kitchen, two couches in a room with a pool table, two couches in the living room, and two couches in a room with a big painting over a fireplace. "They got lots of chairs," I say.

We count three bathrooms on the ground floor, then go upstairs. I kind of look around guiltily, like maybe we shouldn't be exploring. But Jae-won's face is all lit up, like he's six years old. We open one door, and there's a guy who looks like he's about sixteen lounging in front of an Xbox, playing Call of Duty. He frowns at us. "What do you want?"

"Just exploring," Jae-won says totally honestly. That makes me laugh, and then we both start giggling like little kids and close the door. We don't open any more closed doors, just peer into the rooms that are already open. There are seven bedrooms, all of them big and one of them humongous. We count three more bathrooms, but Jae-won says there are probably more attached to the bedrooms.

When we get downstairs, everybody's singing "Happy Birthday" on the patio, so we hurry out and join in. Most people eat cake, but Jae-won and I don't 'cause we've made an agreement to start avoiding sugar, even though the season hasn't started yet. Last year the team got nutritional guidelines, and most of the players followed them during the season. Some of the other guys from the team are here now, so we stand around eating these round sandwiches that I've seen at Costco. My dad says there's almost nobody who doesn't shop at Costco. It's a national religion.

A kid named Naveen says, "Hey, did you hear

we're playing pond hockey in Minnesota next season?"

"Really?" I say. That's kind of cool, I think. Then I think of something less cool. "What if I fall in?"

"You can't fall in. They make sure the pond's frozen all the way through."

"Is that before or after the tournament in Chicago?" Lucas asks.

"After."

"I can't wait to go to Chicago," I say. "My dad says it's one of the biggest hockey tournaments in the world. He went there when he played hockey as a kid."

Then we spend the next hour standing around stuffing our faces and talking about hockey. We don't go swimming again on account of the pool's so crowded, so we play Ping-Pong at a table that's been set up in the sun until we get so sweaty we can hardly hold the paddles. After about an hour of that, Mrs. Morgan comes by and tells me that my dad's here.

"See you, man," I say to the guys.

"You gonna be at stick time Monday?" Roberto asks.

"Nah," I say.

"Why not? You used to always be there on Mondays."

"Yeah . . . I'm focusing on dryland right now, so not skating much."

"Oh, okay. See you, man."

"Yeah, see you. Later, Jae-won."

"Yeah."

I go outside, but before I can get the door closed, another dog runs out. It's a puffy little white cloud-thing that I have to chase for about five minutes as it barks hysterically before it finally decides to run back toward the front door. I flip the door open, and it rushes in, stopping once to bark at me.

In the car, Dad says, "A dog like that bit Russ once on a domestic dispute call. We made fun of him about it all year."

"Why did you make fun of him?"

"I dunno. The look on his face." He chuckles. "You just have to laugh at stuff sometimes, you know? Memories . . ."

And he smiles kind of sadly, like he's remembering good times—good times that are gone. I sort of

understand, 'cause I love good times, although they
never seem quite gone to me. Could be 'cause I'm just
a kid. Could be this memories stuff is related to Dad
crying. Could be a lot of things. But I can't think of a
thing to say.

So I just go, "Good times!"

And he smiles. And he's back to the present.

CHAPTER 18

ON THE DRIVE home, I think about taking Sinbad for a walk, but it's over ninety degrees. Dad and I each have air conditioners in our room, though we don't use them unless it's over ninety-five. Then I think, since it's gonna be practically as hot inside as it is out, maybe I should take him for a walk after all if he seems up for it.

The second I open the door when we get home, Sinbad flings himself at me so hard he pushes me back. "Hi, boy!" I say, bracing myself for the next hit. When it comes, it's just as hard as the first one. Dad says, "You got a letter. No stamp." He waves an envelope at me. I take the letter and tear it open.

Dear Conor,

Got another job for you. Stop by when you have a chance.

Mr. Edwin Reynolds

So I leash Sinbad and we head out. At Mr. Reynolds's house, I knock and wait a long time, on account of how slow Mr. Reynolds is. When he opens the door, he says, "Conor MacRae! Don't you ever go anywhere without your dog?"

"Not really. Well, I play ice hockey, so I don't take him to games or practice. Otherwise I'm with him all the time. He has cancer!" I blurt out.

"Oh!" He reaches down and pets Sinbad, who kind of ignores him—he's only friendly to selected people.

The house looks small, and it's kind of empty, like no decoration or anything. There's a big pile of the blue plastic in a corner in the living room. I think about how Mr. Reynolds might be the only person in the whole big world with a pile of blue tarp in a corner of his living room. "Did you want me to help you?" I ask.

But he's studying Sinbad. "Cancer, you say? Is he going to die?"

"No, he's going to live for five years, but the chemo costs a lot of money." I don't know why I say that, but I guess I do believe it's true.

"Good! Good! Sit down, let me get you scissors."

So I guess he wants me to cut something?

There's a couch, but it's full of notebooks or albums or something, so I sit on a recliner, even though I have a feeling it's Mr. Reynolds's chair.

When Mr. Reynolds returns, he offers me the scissors, then brings over two albums. "I'm transferring all the pictures in this album into this new album I bought. It's hard for me to cut perfectly because of my arthritis. I can cut, but not perfect. I want to give the new album to my grandniece for her birthday. She's turning five."

"Sure, no problem." I sit on the floor, so he can have his chair. But he stands over me while I open up the old album. It's all pictures of a chimp.

"That's Mack," Mr. Reynolds says proudly. "He

was like our son when he was a baby! My wife and I loved that chimp like he was our flesh and blood. Then he got too wild to handle, and we didn't know what to do with him. We had to give him away to a lab, and we know they did medical research on him." His eyes go far away, then come back. "I'll never forgive myself for giving him away, but I thought he might hurt my wife while I was out of the house one day. Dropping him off at the lab was the worst day of our lives. . . ." He presses his lips together and frowns, then after a big breath adds, "Fortunately, the lab eventually gave him to a wildlife sanctuary, so the end of his life was good."

The pictures are glued onto the pages, so I carefully cut around them and place them into the pockets of the new album.

"That's Mack when he was still a baby," Mr. Reynolds says. "Cutest baby I ever saw, human or chimp or anything."

There are pictures of Mack on the bus, at the beach, lying on a human bed in a bedroom. Mr. Reynolds says, "He looks like he's having fun, but in truth he didn't really like the beach much. That's the only time we ever took him."

Then he goes to the corner, picks up a huge sheet of blue plastic, and pulls it out of the room toward the back. I work steadily, Sinbad pressed up next to me. The chimp is supercute, with a really emotional face. In the final picture, he's quite big. He must have been really strong by then. He looks as happy as Sinbad at his happiest. I think of him being experimented on, and I have to shut the album so I can't see his face anymore. Dad texts me: *What's going on?* And I realize it's been two and a half hours. *Almost done,* I text him back. I place both albums on the crowded coffee table. The table is covered with stuff that all looks old: mugs that aren't shaped like mugs are today, coasters that say LAS VEGAS 1963, dusty Christmas ornaments with angels on them. I wipe the dust off with my shirt, then say, "Come on, Sinbad, let's tell him we're done."

We step into the hallway, and I call out, "Mr. Reynolds?"

He calls something back, and I wait as he comes out of a room and moves slowly toward me, calling out, "Conor MacRae! All done?"

"Yep."

He reaches into his pocket, draws out a dollar, and hands it to me. I figure I should take it so as not to insult him. "Thank you," I say.

"No—thank *you*! Before you go, I was thinking I wanted to tell you something. Just because of your dog having cancer, I thought you might be interested in this. One night when Mack was living in the sanctuary, I woke up at night and I was wide awake. I wasn't dreaming. And I saw some electricity, right there in the room, in the shape of Mack. It was sparkling. It sounds crazy, and I know people already think I'm crazy. But that was Mack. I know it was. He just came by to tell me he was okay, and that he forgave me, and then he died and went to heaven. The sanctuary called me the next day to tell me that he had died."

I stand there looking at him. I mean, I don't want to think of me ever waking up in the middle of the night and seeing Sinbad as a bunch of electricity! So I try to get the image out of my head. Also, I feel like I know Mack by now, and for some reason what Mr. Reynolds just told me really messes with my mind.

I say, "I guess I better get going. Call me if you need anything. It's no problem."

"Thank you, thank you, you're a good boy. My grandniece will be very happy with her picture album. She loves animals."

We say bye, and Sinbad and I step outside into the setting sun. I text Dad that we're going to walk a bit, and then we go for a long stroll through the neighborhood. At first Sinbad has fun, but he seems to get tired when we're several blocks away. I even think about calling my dad to pick us up, even though not long ago several blocks would be nothing to Sinbad. Instead we sit on the curb for a few minutes while Sinbad rests his head in my lap. He's panting hard, so finally I do call Dad, and he drives over to get us. When we get home, he says, "Why don't you go ahead and turn on your air conditioner?"

"Thanks, Dad." I switch it on, and Sinbad has enough energy to hop onto the bed to rest. He doesn't even come out when I go into the kitchen for food. Dad has made our go-to dinner of boiled chicken with potatoes and vegetables, so I take a big bowl and carry it into my bedroom to eat at my desk. In the middle of eating, I open up a drawer and take five of my precious dollars and place them in an envelope to send to PETA. Like I mentioned, they don't do invasive experiments on chimps anymore in the United States. But I can't get Mack out of my mind, so I write out the envelope, stamp it, and print *This is for Mack* on the outside. They won't know what that means, but who cares? Then I go to the front porch and clothespin the envelope to the mailbox. I hesitate, think about how I could get a dog bone with that five dollars. That's the thing about money, man. There are a million good things to spend it on. I just stand there for a few minutes. But you can't use up your whole life standing around. You gotta make choices. So I go inside and try to forget about it.

CHAPTER 19

DAD AND I start working out six days a week, jogging with Sinbad when he's up to it, or doing muscle work at the park. Neighbors call me to wash their cars, and I wander farther into new neighborhoods to find customers. It's all great, but at the same time I feel like I'm going to lose my mind if I don't skate soon. I feel caged!

Dad can tell, so one night he decides to take me to do stick time at Ice House, since it only costs thirty dollars for the both of us. We load up our gear—we have identical bags—and climb into the car. We both own high-end gear, 'cause we're *extremely* picky.

Like we can spend hours at a hockey shop when we only need to grab a few minor things like mouth guards, socks, tape, etc. You gotta always get the right socks so you look lit on the ice. Plus, what happens is we also get involved in looking at the stuff we *don't* need. Dad wears nine-hundred-dollar skates, and mine cost five hundred 'cause they're not senior size yet. Yeah, it's crazy, the prices. But expensive skates are stiffer than cheaper skates and hold up better to all the work you put in when you play tier hockey. Also, there can be a four- or five-ounce difference in weight between a high-end and low-end skate. An extra five ounces would feel like lead on the feet of a top skater.

My skates are getting small, and my toes are start-ing to hurt. But I don't mention it; there's no money for new skates. I also need a new stick—mine has lost its pop—but no way I'm mentioning that either, 'cause high-end sticks cost two hundred or more. Sticks are super hard to choose, 'cause they all have a different curve and different angle and different flex and different weight, among other things. But don't even get me started on sticks, 'cause they drive me insane. Someday I'm going to find the perfect stick. Hasn't happened yet.

A lot of guys happen to turn up at the rink, so we all get together for an informal half-ice scrimmage. Man, it feels good! Everybody oohs and aahs at my dad's skating, and people gather in the stands to watch us. I'm not on Dad's team, 'cause I'm super-competitive and I like to try to beat his butt. A couple of times he hits a slap shot from way out that rockets into the net, causing applause and cheers even from the opposing players. After he establishes dominance, he lets everybody else play their game—he swoops in, grabs the puck, and immediately passes to the other skaters so they can score and puck-handle.

At one point I check Dad, even though nobody ever checks each other in scrimmages like this. I know checking isn't allowed until you're thirteen, but I do it anyway to surprise him. He *is* surprised and momentarily loses the puck, but he immediately takes two powerful strides and catches up with me. I try to flip the puck to someone else, but Dad bats it out of the air. No mercy! When it touches the ice, he hits a slap shot that unfortunately caroms into one of the guys, who doubles over in pain. We all rush over, but after a couple of minutes of leaning over, the guy's all good. Last year I had the hardest shot on the team, but I'm probably forty miles an hour behind my dad. His shot is scary hard, and his skating is scary good even as an old guy . . . old*er* guy.

When the scrimmage ends, we all gulp down water together, and the other skaters ask Dad about his background. When they hear he played three weeks in the NHL, you can see they're halfway between wanting to bow down and playing it totally cool. I feel so proud of him, but I also know making the bigs for just three weeks isn't all good. Dad once said that the hardest year of his life was after those three weeks, when he got sent back down and he realized that was it: his NHL dream had ended. But those three weeks, being out there on the ice, even as a fourth liner in garbage time, was so much fun he felt really *filled up* for those few games he played in. I guess it's pretty amazing sitting on the bench surrounded by fifteen thousand people. He'd started playing hockey at seven and made the NHL at twenty-four, so fifteen years after he started. And he said those fifteen years of hard work were worth it for those three weeks. At the same time, it was sad, 'cause when he got to the NHL, he went from being the best player on his team to the worst, and he realized for the first time that he just wasn't good enough.

Now, watching the guys gathered around Dad as he talks about what champion trash talkers some of those NHL players are, I think about Jae-won and Jesus Acosta and me, going after the same dream my dad chased. Is the NHL really a possibility when I don't have one truly amazing skill like Jae-won and Jesus? At the same time, Dad has told me many times that it is possible, so I'm going for it.

Dad is talking about the time a so-so NHL player hit him so hard he went flying five feet. "I thought I was strong, but man, I was shocked how strong this dude was. It's a whole different level."

My dad can still bench-press four hundred, but he said during his heyday he could do four fifty, which makes him a beast. I don't do weights yet 'cause Dad thinks I'm too young.

Stick time is over, so a few guys knock gloves with Dad, and we go change in the locker room. Coming out of the showers is a totally naked man, which I've actually never seen before. He's hairy! Whoa, next time I'm changing in one of the locker rooms without a shower! I turn my head away and say softly to Dad, "I think I need therapy now." He chuckles.

On the car ride home, I stick my head out the open window like I'm Sinbad. The warm air hits my face, and for just a minute I get this sense like I know exactly how my dog feels when his head is out the window. Just taking in the smells, appreciating the breeze. It's not thinking, it's *experiencing*. Maybe it's the same way as when I'm on the ice. I mean, I'm thinking out there, but things are moving so fast it's not normal thinking.

"We've got to get you lower when you skate," Dad is saying as I bring my head in. "That'll be one of the things we focus on in AAA. When you reach bantam, you're gonna need to be low when you check and when someone checks you. You want to be in a position of power at all times. Bantam is unforgiving at the elite level. By second-year bantam, you'll be playing against kids who are six feet three, two hundred pounds."

Fear of bantam—*checking!*—flashes through my whole body, and I close my eyes to shake it off. When I open my eyes, I spot a man hitting a woman on the sidewalk. "Dad!" I say, but he's already swooping to the side of the road, shouting, "Stay in the car!" to me as he rushes out. My heart pounds, and I hear what sounds like a waterfall in my head. The man is on top, pummeling—*pummeling*—the woman. Dad pulls off the man, who swirls around and starts to rush Dad. Dad gut-punches him, and when he folds over I realize I should be calling 911, so I do. The woman lies unmoving on the sidewalk. Then the man, who seemed to be in pain, abruptly rams into my father, and I feel sick to my stomach. I stumble out of the car and run forward. "Dad!"

Dad turns his head, giving the guy a chance to hit him in the ear. They tumble to the ground, wrestling. A woman wraps her arms around me. "Stand back, hon," she says.

Dad has the guy on his stomach, with his left arm twisted behind his back. "Police officer!"

The man is screaming, "You're breaking my arm!"

"Then hold still!"

"YOU'RE BREAKING MY ARM!"

Then the guy seems to relax his body, and Dad loosens his grip. Dad makes the guy lie on the ground facedown until the cops and ambulance arrive. I notice that just about every single person who has gathered around is filming on their phones.

"That arm twist was definitely harder than necessary," I hear one man saying as he comes in closer with his phone.

Another man says, "The cop sucker punched him."

But thankfully someone else says, "Aw, come on, man, you saw he had to do it, the guy rushed him."

"Go sit with the lady until the ambulance comes," Dad says to me. "Did you call 911?"

"Yeah, in the car." He has told me a million times that if I ever see anything awful going down, call 911 before doing anything else, and be a good witness. He says when I'm older, I can think about helping.

I approach the woman on the sidewalk and kneel beside her. "Ma'am, are you okay?" I ask. I reach out, draw my arm back, and reach out again to touch her shoulder. She's Asian, maybe Thai, and small. Her nose is punched off-center, and there's blood dribbling down her face. "An ambulance is coming," I add, trying my hardest to make eye contact. But the second she closes her eyes, I turn away so I don't have to see the blood.

"It was my fault," she said. "Don't let them arrest him."

I can't think of a single thing to say to that. I mean, there were a lot of times when Jenny got mad at me when I thought it was all my fault, and I remember how awful it felt to think that. A couple of EMTs pile out of an ambulance, and police arrive at almost the same moment, so I step back into the crowd. A couple of police officers talk to my father as well as to everyone who's watching. They keep talking well after the ambulance takes away the woman. A use of force requires half a day of paperwork, so I wonder if the police are gonna want my father at the station. But finally they let him go.

When we get back in the Volvo, he says sternly, "I told you to stay in the car. You coulda got me killed."

"I thought I might have to help you."

He looks at me squinty-eyed, like he's not sure if I'm mouthing off, but then he starts the car.

"So are you gonna be in trouble? You didn't break his arm, did you?" I ask.

"I don't think so." He glances at me. "Why, did it seem like his arm got broken? If so, then, yeah, I may get in trouble."

"Everybody was filming."

"Yeah, sometimes they film you even when you pull them over for speeding. They just hold up their phones the whole time you're talking. . . . I hope his arm's not broken."

"I don't think it was. I don't know why I said that."

"Okay."

"Are you kind of shook up?"

"I may have a beer," he answers.

Since he has a beer many nights, that doesn't seem like much.

"Is that it?" I ask. "One beer?"

"That's it."

We pull onto the freeway. I feel like I'm still processing, so I ask, "How come that doesn't shake you up?"

He shrugs. "It's not that unusual."

"Soooo, like how many times have you been in a fight like that?"

He reaches into the ashtray and pulls out a piece of gum, which he hands to me to open. After he's chewed on it for a minute, he says, "Uh, I can't really remember. Too many to count."

"That guy looked strong."

"He was. But that's one of the reasons I left patrol for motors. It's fun when you're in your twenties and you think you're saving the world. Then when the world doesn't get saved, it's not so fun anymore. Some guys never stop feeling like they're saving the world. But I did."

"You can still get hurt during traffic stops."

He chews vigorously. "The only guys who've ever attacked me during traffic stops have been drunk, except one. It's easier to handle a drunk man."

"What about the one person who wasn't drunk?"

"Ex-con."

I wait for more, but it doesn't come.

"With a gun?" I finally ask.

He blinks a few times, like he's seeing the whole thing in his head. "Yeah, he had a gun. When I got to the car, he opened the door real fast, slamming it into me. He had a gun, but he couldn't get a shot off because he hadn't spotted Russ. I was surprised to see Russ there, because he'd been pulling over a different car. He got a shot off, which surprised the guy so I could grab the gun."

"Well, why was Russ there if he was pulling over somebody else? Don't you ride with your partner?"

"Sometimes you ride together, but often you're in radio but not visual contact. Anyway, Russ came because he had a feeling."

My eyes go wide. "So you were saved by Russ's *feeling*?"

"Yup."

"Whatever happened to Russ?"

"He got shot in the arm in another incident and quit to start a contracting company. He was a good cop—real good—but he'd had enough. After Russ shot that guy, he thought a long time about being a cop. He wasn't sure he wanted to keep doing it. Then when he got shot, he decided he'd had enough."

I stare out the window, keep processing. I think about those times when you just somehow know what's going to happen on the ice before it happens. That's the best feeling in all of hockey. Maybe that's what Russ felt? He just knew? One of the crazy things you learn when you get deeply into hockey is that there's just stuff in the world that can't be explained. You get into the flow, and it's like some kind of Einstein time-bending thing . . . not that I know anything about Einstein. The more I think about it, the more I believe that must be what saved my dad's life. Russ entered the flow. And saved a life.

CHAPTER 20

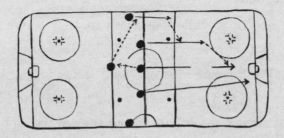

THE FIRST TEAM practice isn't until mid-August, but in July, Coach sends everyone a dryland workout schedule to start. Dad and I just keep doing our own thing instead—it's harder. We're also sent food forms to write down what we eat all day so that Coach can determine if we're getting proper nutrition. I'm eating pretty good this summer—haven't had fast food once. Sometimes Dad makes super-rare grass-fed meat and brown rice. To be honest, he doesn't make me eat cooked vegetables with every single meal, 'cause he doesn't like them either. Oh, and wild salmon once a week. It's expensive, but he thinks it makes you live forever or something. But our main dinner thing is boiled chicken with onions and potatoes and maybe a vegetable.

Once in a while Jae-won's mother drives him over, or Dad drives me over to his house. One day Mrs. Kang drops him off, then takes his brothers to the nearest rink. I don't know how Mr. and Mrs. Kang are going to afford it, but they're trying to get the twins into hockey.

Jae-won and I play Minecraft for a few hours. He builds a four-level house that's pretty brilliant, while I build a house that's pretty lame. We both go mining, and I get more stuff 'cause I'm stuck on mining. The kids who are really good at Minecraft are more into building. But I love getting diamonds and gold, and just basically hoarding it all instead of using any of it.

We fix a couple of turkey sandwiches and sit at the dining room table. "Do you ever just wish you were eighteen already?" Jae-won asks. "So you'd already know how good you're going to be?"

"Dad says there were actually some guys who suddenly got better even after eighteen," I say.

Jae-won pauses. "Are you gonna play in another country if you don't make the NHL?"

I think this over. One guy at a rink I skate at didn't make the NHL and went to play in Finland. The Scandinavians have some of the best clubs—the kids there can spend all their time on homemade rinks in their backyards. I don't know much about Scandinavia, though. "I haven't thought that far ahead. I'm kind of focused on getting better today."

"Yeah, I know what you mean." He pauses again. "My dad is worried about my skating not being good enough yet. He wants my mom to get a second job so we can afford more lessons. A part-time job. She already has a full-time job."

Working an extra job when you have two little kids would probably mean a total lack of sleep for Mrs. Kang. The Kangs live in the same building with a couple of their relatives, so they have a babysitter nearby. But I know how obsessed Mrs. Kang is with her kids, and I'm sure she'd rather be at home with them more. One thing I notice when you have no money is that you have to make some winner-take-all choices—one thing loses, and another wins. Sinbad needing cancer treatment versus me needing more ice time. Mrs. Kang wanting to be with her kids more, versus Jae-won needing to work on his skating. "I wish Ryan would give us some of his money," I say.

"I know, right?"

We laugh, but Jae-won starts rubbing his head and groans. "Conor, if my mom gets another job, I feel like I got so much pressure on me."

"That's 'cause you're so good," I tell him. "If you were bad, your dad wouldn't want your mom to get another job."

Jae-won seems to think about this. "So how did you get to be such a good skater?"

"I'm not like Jesus," I counter. "He started when he was two, I started when I was six and a half. Also, my dad has been having me do squats and stretches since I was six. I think that helped a lot. He also made me play soccer, even though I hated it. But he says all the researchers say if you want to be an elite athlete, you have to play more than one sport."

Jae-won hits his head. "I wish I'd started that young! I didn't start skating until I was almost nine. Do you think it's too late for me?"

I gape at him. "Seriously? I didn't know that. Seriously, you've only been skating for what, three and a half years? You're awesome! I wouldn't worry, man," I tell him. "My dad says hockey players usually do have to start young. He says that sports like hockey, gymnastics, and figure skating, you gotta start young. But you started in plenty of time. There was some amazing figure skater Ivan mentioned once. I forget his name, but he didn't start skating until he was twelve. I honestly think you're gonna be fine, you're gonna be great. My dad says so, in fact."

"Really?"

"Yeah."

"Cool."

We chew on our sandwiches. Coach Dusan likes carbs for athletes, so I've been trying to eat more bread. But since I don't use mayo, it tastes pretty dry.

So then I ask Jae-won, "Do you ever feel guilty, like about all the money hockey costs?"

That makes him start rubbing his head again. "Yeah, I think about it all the time. But I have to do it. It's hard for some of the kids at school to understand. Even some of the jocks don't get it, because they're just casual jocks. It's not, like, their whole life. All I ever want to do is play."

"Plus, don't you think your dad would die if you quit? I think my dad might literally just die," I add.

"My dad would kill himself. I don't have any doubt about that. But I ain't gonna quit." He presses his hands on his forehead. "But it's so much pressure, man. If my mom gets another job, it's just so much pressure."

My dad has something to say about that too, so I tell Jae-won, "My dad always says that elite athletes don't get caught up in the pressure or guilt or nothing like that. The pressure just makes them focus harder. He says if you feel too much guilt or pressure, you have to compartmentalize it."

Jae-won looks at me eagerly, like he wants advice in the worst way. "What does that mean?"

I don't answer, 'cause I realize I'm not 100 percent sure what that means. But Dad has said it a few times. So I rack my brain, and I come up with, "I think it means you put it in a separate box in your head, and then you just think about your goals and don't let that other box bother you. The best athletes don't get all mental about stuff."

But I can see by the look on his face that none of his worries are in a separate box. They're all messed up with the rest of his brain. That's Jae-won for you. The world's most tormented youth hockey player, for sure, and all 'cause he was born with magic hands.

CHAPTER 21

SINBAD IS NOW being treated every other week. Strictly speaking, he's in remission. I know that sounds like it should be exciting, but all it really means is that the doctor can no longer feel a lump on his leg. So the lump is gone and ... that doesn't really change much. The treatments continue. Then one of his doses doesn't go as well as the others, and he stays sick for two days, though he gets a little better each day. He's too out of it to jump onto the bed, so I take out my sleeping bag and stay on the floor next to him both nights. I call Dr. Pierre, and she says I should bring him in, but at the same time if I do bring him, there's nothing she can do except put him on an IV and have him watched in the hospital. Since I can't sleep at the hospital, that doesn't seem like a good idea to me. Plus, I'm pretty much a 1,000 percent sure we couldn't afford that. But this is the first time I really feel like he could die. And I know that if he dies, it needs to be with me lying next to him. That's the way he would want it. I'm positive about that.

On the second night, I go through my usual presleep regimen of filling Sinbad's mouth with water from a syringe Dad got me from a mail-order pet-supply store. Sinbad gulps eagerly, so I give him a few drinks.

Back in my room I think about how Lucas and his family are all Christians, so I text him and ask him to pray for Sinbad. We're all on TeamSnap, an app for sports teams, so I've got everybody's e-mail addresses and phone numbers. This is what Lucas texts me back: *I'll pray for him every night. I have three dogs that sleep with me. #Godisgood.* I text back, *Thanks!*

I don't feel sad. I feel really, really, really focused on making Sinbad better. I pet him for a long time, but then I get the feeling this starts to bother him.

Dad's dad—Grandpa Adley—mailed me a magazine about alternative health care and nutrition. He complains a lot about how doctors have become pill dispensers, and he thought I might get some ideas on how to treat Sinbad during his chemo. There's actually a story about dogs, and how you should chop up greens for their food every day. Sinbad is kind of obsessed with lettuce, so he probably gets enough greens. He'll even eat watercress. Watercress is one of Grandpa's things, so Dad buys it once every couple of weeks.

Then right before I fall asleep, my phone dings and Lucas texts: *I've been praying for a long time. Is he doing better?* Me: *He's been sleeping. Thanks for praying!* Him: *You pray too. God will hear you whether you believe in him or not. Night.* Me: *Night, thanks again!*

That little exchange makes me an even bigger fanboy of Lucas. He wasn't really close to anyone on the team last year, but he was one of the guys who always hovered around any man who went down on the ice, even if it was someone from the opposite team. Most guys skate away from an opposing player who goes down—that's the way some coaches like it.

But Lucas seems like he just *has* to be there, in case he can do something, whether it's pray, run to get the kid's parents, whatever. That's more important to him than what the coach wants.

I get on my knees in front of Sinbad and look upward. Is that right? I try holding my palms faceup. *Please, God, I'm not going to lie—since you know everything, you probably know I don't believe in you. That makes no sense, but you know what I mean.* I pause; God is going to think I'm nuts. So I start again. *Please, God, take care of my friend Sinbad. He had a hard life before he came home with us. He has scars on his skin. If you could let him be okay, I'll* . . . I don't want to lie or say something that I know I won't do. I think about what God might like. *I'll make sure I only get rescue dogs my whole life, even though I used to have a dream of buying an expensive Doberman if I make the NHL.* Then that feels like I'm trying to bribe him. But I can't think what else to say except: *Thank you. I'll rescue many dogs.*

I remember all those dogs in the various shelters we went to. For some reason, there have always been two that I've never forgotten. One was a white dog that looked like she might have been half shepherd. I tried to talk her into coming forward, but she just lay at the back of the cage. She seemed very, very depressed, and her sign said she was sick. It just made me sad how depressed she was, and since the sign said *sick*, I figured nobody would take her home. She was probably dead within days of when I saw her, from euthanasia. Then the other dog I can't forget was small and tan, and when I paused at her cage, she jumped up and down hysterically, and I knew exactly what she was trying to tell me: *Take me home! Don't let me die!*

Grandpa Adley says that Dad should never have taken me to those places; he should have just bought me a dog at the store or a breeder. "You upset him! And you don't know where those pound dogs have been. They're dangerous!" That's the way Grandpa is. He's supercool about some stuff, like alternative health and nutrition, but he's kind of in the Stone Age about other stuff, like animals. He practically thinks PETA is a terrorist organization. He came close to having cardiac failure when I told him that I sent PETA a few bucks. He's got a big heart when it comes to humans, though, so I really like driving out to Iowa to visit him every Christmas vacation. We bring Sinbad, and Grandpa and Grandma treat him pretty well. He also puts together an ice rink in his backyard just for the two weeks I'm there. He says it costs a few hundred dollars, which is why he can't afford to give me any actual presents, except the Ice Warehouse gift card I mentioned earlier. But I think it costs more than a few hundred. Nobody will tell me. It's crazy to think there are kids out there in foster care, and me and everybody on my teams always have parents and grandparents who do stuff like make backyard rinks for you and drive a billion miles a year taking you to practices and games.

Sinbad suddenly retches.

"You okay, big guy?" I ask.

He stands up, gives himself a big shake, scratches at the carpet, and then instead of lying down where he's been scratching, he hops onto the bed. He feels better! Just like that, I zoom from thinking he might die to believing everything's going back to normal. Just like that, I'm in a totally different mood than I've been in. Just like that! I touch my nose on his, but he seems to be asleep already—he can fall asleep in literally one second.

The bed feels so comfortable it's like I don't even want to sleep, I just want to lie there feeling incredibly comfortable. I never really thought about how great sheets are. They feel so soft! Sinbad keeps shifting over until I'm on the edge of the bed and have to get up and move to the other side of him.

As soon as I wake up in the morning, I'm going to send Lucas a text thanking him for praying. I admit I think of reneging and buying an expensive Doberman when I grow up, but then I say, *Just kidding, if you're listening!*

CHAPTER 22

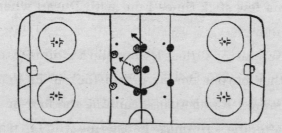

FRIDAYS, THEY'VE BEEN holding peewee four-on-four scrimmages over at Ice House. It's twenty-five dollars, and Dad decides I should do it. It's just once a week, and I'm desperate to get some ice time.

It turns out to be a fast-moving score-a-thon that teaches me a lot about how much I like having the puck. When you're D, you don't handle the puck that much. In four-on-four, when I get the puck, I move with more speed than I knew I possessed, and instead of trying to dangle my way out of log-jams, I use a few neat saucer passes that leave the opposition with their ankles broken. A saucer pass is a pass that you flick into the air, over your opponent's stick. I learned the power of the saucer pass from a few stick times I did with Dusan when we had money.

Now all my various lessons and scrimmages come together into one glorious dream: the four-on-four.

Samvel Karapetian is running the four-on-four, and after the scrimmage he asks me who I'm playing for next season. I tell him, and he says, "You should have tried out for the Jets. We're going to beat you." But he says it kiddingly.

"Nah," I say. "Ain't gonna happen." It won't, either. Four of the players Coach Dusan turned down are going to be playing for the Jets' peewee AAA, so theoretically we should be better. These are the Jets guys who didn't make the Grizzlies:

Jimmy Alexander. Jimmy has a lot of talent, but after he hurt his ankle and later his shoulder in the same season, he hasn't been the same. His ankle and shoulder don't still hurt, he just doesn't love the game so much anymore. I played AA with him in the spring.

Ethan Brown, my frenemy. Ethan puts in a lot of ice time and is a solid player, but for some reason he fell asleep out there during the tryout. I mean, we all disappear and go in and out of our best selves, but his case of this kind of disappearing is worse than usual. He also constantly sprays people in the face with water bottles in the locker room, which gets old. And he grabs other people's gear and throws it outside in the parking lot. He's tall and strong, but a stiff skater.

Pasha Zharov. Like I said, Pash is one of my favorite people. He's such a cool kid and such an awesome hockey player. I can't speak for why Coach Dusan didn't take him. I wish he'd made our team.

Shawn Johansen. Nobody has any idea how Shawn made a AAA team. He can't skate, can't stick-handle, can't defend, and can't pass. And he doesn't listen to the coach 'cause his mind wanders so much. My team played against his once

last season, and he hardly got any playing
time. His greatest skills are trash talking
and dropping F-bombs. He can shoot okay,
so maybe that's why he made the team. He
was super excited about making the AAAs,
though, and claims that his team will have
its own plane.

In the car after the four-on-four, I'm feeling super
psyched. Dad says, "You were looking good out there
for someone who hasn't been playing much."

"That's the most fun I ever had playing!" I say.
"They should start a league for four-on-four. I bet
crowds would love it."

"Maybe so," Dad says, "but hockey's a pretty perfect game as it is."

I can't disagree with that. "Yeah, I guess you're
right. A regular game is *deeper*." The four-on-four is
incredibly fun, like a milk shake, but a regular game
is like steak. Then I say that out loud to Dad, and he
just laughs, like he's really happy.

"A steak, huh?" And he laughs some more.

That's when I realize that he doesn't laugh as

much as he used to. So I continue. "Four-on-four is like . . ." But then I can't think of anything.

Dad says, "Four-on-four is like a bouquet of flowers, and a regular game is like a tree."

"Yeah!" I say.

I feel good, and I can see he feels good. Four-on-four, man! It makes the world right!

But then that night Dad gets an e-mail that pretty much ruins our day. It's a ninety-page playbook from Coach Dusan. He says he expects us to know it backward and forward and will be testing us on it.

The playbook is full of information and contains almost fifty plays, which are made up of both diagrams and text. I actually think I can remember fifty plays if I learn them on the ice, but I'm pretty sure I can't memorize plays just from reading about them in a book. Like if one of my coaches demonstrates a drill on the ice, I catch on right away, and I can transfer the drill into reality during the next game. That is, it takes me a while to instinctively use the drill or play, but I don't have any problems remembering what I've learned on the ice. However, I have a memory problem when it comes to the written word. I have to work twice as hard as the other kids at school to be able to remember things. I flunked seven tests last year that I studied hours for. I still forget my multiplication tables sometimes, even after my dad coached me on them three times a week for two years. If I work hard and long and study a lot, sometimes I just suddenly remember everything I'm supposed to. When that happens, I'm flooded with relief—until I have to memorize the next thing. I've never had to memorize ninety pages. I can't even memorize one. Now Dad prints out the playbook and solemnly hands it to me. I take it and don't move. "You okay?" he asks.

"If I gotta memorize this, then I gotta memorize it," I answer. Coach says in his e-mail that he wants all this understood by the end of September when we get out of the preseason. And Dad and I both know that he isn't known for patience. I go into my room, close the door. I feel like a broken man, for sure. I want to play AAA like I want to live. Sinbad can sense I'm upset and presses against my legs.

"Can you believe this?" I ask him. "Why didn't anyone ever tell me about playbooks? I thought they were more of a football thing."

He doesn't move, just lies across me looking at the side of the bed. He does that sometimes, just lies or sits somewhere staring. Got no idea what he could be thinking about.

Dad knocks at the door, and I call out, "Yeah."

He opens the door. "Do you want me to help you somehow?"

"I don't know how," I say. "I just have to start reading. I will in a minute."

"Okay. Okay, well, give me a yell if you want to talk."

"Thanks, Dad."

He closes the door and I'm back alone, thinking. Everybody at the Grizzlies organization has a super lot of respect for Coach. He's got a reputation for being one of the best coaches at developing talent in Southern California. Dad and I have been planning to get me on one of his teams for years. That's the only reason we stuck with the Grizzlies when we have a club closer to our home.

Coach Dusan loves the kids he picks for his teams—he had a player get cancer one year, and I heard he was so upset about it he could barely function after he heard. To help out the parents, he drove the kid's little brother to school every morning whenever the player was having chemo. But I understand sports at this level. Your coach will leave you behind in a split second if you can't cut it. Coach is a famous screamer. He'll call a player out and scream at him during a game or practice. I've heard some of the things he hates are if a player is out of shape, if he doesn't lay it all out there on the ice, if he loses concentration, and if he has to be told something more than twice. It's that last category I'm worried about—in Grizzlies tier hockey you have a theory class once a week, and I'm pretty sure he's going to need to tell me some stuff quite a few times. Tier hockey is AA and AAA, but last year my coach was kind of a slacker when it came to theory class.

I figure this can all be tough, it can be lonely, and your only reward is playing in a game. But playing in a game is worth any amount of toughness and loneliness and yelling.

One thing I never question—never—is if hockey is worth all the work. I just love the lifestyle. I love everything about it: the rinks, the cold air, the camaraderie, the speed, the parents screaming in the stands, and yes, the uniforms. The uniforms are so fire. We're all kind of weird about what we look like. Like last season, a guy showed up with a new, expensive helmet, and a bunch of people started roasting him 'cause the helmet made him look like a mushroom. So then even though his parents had paid more than two hundred dollars for that helmet, he refused to ever wear it again. And I don't blame him a bit.

CHAPTER 23

SO I GO sit at my desk, staring at the first page. It's just a picture of a hockey player. On the next page, the playbook starts out with rules for both players and their parents. I start reading, and I understand it all. Understanding isn't my issue. It's remembering what I understand. But at least it's a little easier to remember stuff if I understand it. The rules take up several pages. It's things like you're not allowed to bring your phone into the locker room, a rule I'm sure exactly nobody will follow. And no texting or e-mailing with your teammates, and no social media with them. That's a new rule, just to keep kids under control and not embarrass the club—players can send each other some crazy stuff on their phones, and the club wouldn't like that stuff getting out. Once last season, two guys got mad at each other 'cause of misunderstood comments that were made on Instagram, and they kind of lost their minds and sent each other some insanely angry DMs. It's possible, though, that we'll follow some of these electronic rules with Coach Dusan, 'cause we're all in awe of him. What else? There's a rule against swearing. A lot of coaches start dropping F-bombs on the players in peewee, but the players themselves aren't allowed to swear, which is another rule nobody follows. And your parents aren't allowed to talk to the coach until twenty-four hours after a game has ended. This is a firm rule that everybody will follow if they want their kid to stay on the team. This puts the brakes on parents angry about something the coach has done—like benching your kid—during the game. They can talk to the coach after they've calmed down. Coaches feel extremely strongly about this rule. Reading all this, I feel relieved. I know this stuff!

I'm surprised when I look at the clock and see that it's nine thirty, my bedtime. But I can't stop myself, so I turn to the back of the playbook and start reading through one of the plays. I groan softly. First of all, I have no idea what any of it means. There're lines this way and that, and circles with F1, F2, and F3 inside them. I know what these are—they stand for which forwards are in the play with the puck, with F1 being the closest to the puck, F2 next, and F3 farther away. But I can't figure out all the lines. Some of the lines are solid, and some are dotted. Maybe the text and the solid lines describe the main play, and the dotted lines show an alternate play in case the main one is broken up? How am I going to memorize something when I can't even understand it? I think about how my father hit a wall when he reached the NHL, and wonder if this playbook is my wall. Then I don't even look at the page, just gaze at the window shade ... it's dusty, gotta clean that.

Dad knocks and opens the door. "Time for bed, Con."

"Dad," I say, "I don't understand the playbook."

"Really?" he says, interested. "Why don't you give

it to me? I'll look it over before I go to bed. What part don't you understand?"

"The plays in the last half. They don't make any sense to me."

Dad takes the playbook, and I get ready for bed. I did so much reading tonight that I forgot I was planning on taking Sinbad for a short walk. He's sleeping anyway.

Before I get ready to go to sleep, I search for, *Do athletes have to read a playbook?* And I come up with an article about NFL players saying that learning a playbook is a three-year process. It also says you should spend an hour a day on your playbook. That makes me feel super relieved. I'm happy to put in an hour a day, and three years seems like a century away—I'll be through with bantam by then! But I remember that Coach Dusan said in his e-mail how he expects everyone to know the playbook by the end of September. So I spend another hour online trying to figure out diagrams of hockey plays, and totally failing.

That is, I thought it was an hour, but somehow two hours have gone by, and it's eleven thirty. I do my before-bed routine in the bathroom but skip flossing, and when I come out, I can see Dad's light is on, and I know he's reading the playbook. I stop at his door, which is closed, and say, "Good night, Dad! Thanks for reading the playbook."

"No problem. Get some sleep."

I get in bed. The idiot motion detector has been activated again for some reason, and the light shines into my room. Someday I'm getting a ladder and disconnecting that thing if I can figure out how.

Sinbad lies with his eyes open. "Hey, Sinbad," I say. "What if there's a robber who comes in here in the middle of the night? Are you gonna get up and protect me?"

His eyes flick from my right to the left—a lot of dogs' eyes do that when they look at humans, 'cause the right side of your face shows more emotion, and they want to understand what you're feeling. Anyway, that's why scientists think they do that. I put my arms around him and say, "I love you, Sinbad." He stands up on the mattress and leans his long nose on me, licking my cheek. That's unusual—he hardly ever licks. Probably he read something in my face that made him feel he should lick me. He nestles back into the bed and closes his eyes.

It's warm, so I turn on the ceiling fan and push the blanket down to the foot of the bed. I'm so worried about the playbook I can hardly stop from screaming. I can be a great AAA player, I just know it. But no question, the playbook is a big, big hurdle for me. One year I flunked social studies 'cause I couldn't remember enough, even though I studied hard. The teacher thought I wasn't trying. On the other hand, I usually remember most of the stuff I read on WikiLeaks. So what does that say about my memory? I turn on the light and get on the floor and stretch my back. Sinbad jumps off the bed to bug me like he always does when I stretch.

The door opens up, and Dad stands in the doorway.

"Everything okay in here?" he asks. "How come you left the bathroom light on?"

I look at him. "I forgot," I say. "Sorry."

Dad nods. "It's midnight. Are you worried about the playbook? Because we're going to conquer that. I've seen a lot of playbooks, and they all seem impossible at first. This is your first one, so you're just not used to them yet. We've got time." He taps his fingers on the doorjamb. "An athlete's relationship to the playbook is complicated. They're abstract, so you need on-ice practice. What you're really looking to do is not memorize them, but own them. That just means they become second nature for you. I don't have the slightest doubt that you can do that. In fact, it's one of the things that you're good at. Okay?"

Frustration kind of explodes inside, surprising me—it's like my gut just broke open. I almost need to spit on the floor. "It doesn't make any sense! Do I really need to learn it if I play good?"

"Actually, you do. You have to understand your coach's system. And you're going to. I was looking it over, and it's not that bad. I've seen worse."

He's got work tomorrow, so I say, "Thanks, Dad. I'm fine. I really am. I was just having a moment with Sinbad." Having a moment with Sinbad? What was that supposed to mean?

Dad nods again. "He's going to be fine. We caught it early." He taps his fingers again on the doorjamb.

He closes the door, which he started doing earlier

this year. I guess it's 'cause I'm older now. Previously he always left it open a crack. And you know what? Dad seemed so sure that I'm going to learn the playbook that I realize I do feel better now. So I get up and go knock on his door.

"Yeah?"

I peek in. "Thanks, Dad. I feel better now."

"No problem. You're going to do great."

I get in bed, turn on my phone to check for texts and e-mails like I usually do before bed. There's an e-mail from Jae-won and one from my aunt. Jae-won and I have a tradition of e-mailing each other. Most of the guys don't use e-mail, but we got started 'cause sometimes we just had stuff to say that was too complicated to text about.

> Hey, Conor. Did you get the playbook? Do you feel as crappy at me? I started it but wanted to give up as soon as I got to the plays. Made me want to quit hockey, seriously. Then tonight my mom and dad had a big fight about how much money hockey costs. Anyway, are you still on Xbox Live? I haven't seen you. Let's play COD.

Actually, my Xbox Live subscription ran out. To tell the truth, I was sick of Call of Duty—it takes up too much space in your head. I decided I like games where I can be more of a vegetable. For a few months there I was more interested in COD than in hockey. Then I lost interest. Plus, my dad makes me pay for Xbox Live with my own money, and even before Sinbad got sick, I realized it doesn't mean enough to me that I'll pay the sixty bucks. That makes me think of a birthday party I went to at a paintball field, and how I was obsessed with paintballing for a few months. But that got old. I don't know why other obsessions get old but hockey never does. There's something about hockey that I just can't get out of my system. It's like hockey is just *me*, and COD and paintballing are outside of me, even though they're both really fun.

I type in an e-mail to Jae-won.

Hey, J-W. Yeah, I know what you mean. The playbook is tough. How are we gonna get through this?? My dad says he's gonna help me. You can come study with us if you want.

My stepmom and dad fought sometimes about
me playing hockey. Sucks. Don't ever give up
hockey, man, you got the softest hands in SoCal.
I'm not on Xbox Live anymore. See ya. —C

I really relate to the whole parents-fighting thing.
Even when I was playing on a B team, our lives
revolved around my hockey schedule. Hockey is
really involving that way, I don't know why. At team
parties when I hear the parents talking, it's hockey,
hockey, hockey. The first year there were some dis-
agreements between my parents about me playing
hockey, but they weren't yelling at each other. The
second year, when I was still on a B team but skating more and more, there was some yelling. The
third year, when I made an A team, there was a lot
of yelling. Then last year, when I was on the AAs,
I skated or worked out twenty hours a week, plus
travel time to and from the rink or park, plus dress-
ing and undressing, plus shopping at hockey stores
for gear, plus team parties. So I can see how my stepmom was upset, especially since she didn't consider
me her "real" kid. At the same time, I wanted to skate

so bad—SO BAD—that I was glad my dad stood his ground. I would lie in bed listening to them yell, and think about how it was all my fault, and I just didn't see a way out. Quit hockey? Not an option. But the truth is, hockey is a curse if both your parents aren't on board. After the fights, sometimes Dad would stick his head in my door and say, "Compartmentalize, Conor, compartmentalize." Thinking about it now, I can see how there was no way they could have stayed together if I kept playing hockey. So even though she's the one who wanted the divorce, I guess he kind of did too, 'cause he refused to give up on my hockey like she wanted.

I check Aunt Mo's e-mail.

Hi, hon. I got a surprising call today. Your mom's parents want to visit with you in Los Angeles this Thanksgiving. I said I would check with you and your dad first, but mostly with you. What do you think? Love, Me

Well. That's a shocker! Anger suddenly rises up in me. Immediately. I kind of feel about them the way I feel about Jenny, like they're just two people who rejected me. Maybe they're even worse than her, 'cause they blew me off and I'm their actual grandson. That's just not right. But I push it hard out of my mind 'cause it'll just make me angry.

Then I lay my hand on Sinbad's side, feel him breathing easily. The touch wakes him up, and he paws at me before starting to breathe evenly again. He was doing great during the day—we even went for a couple of walks. I put my other hand on his side as well and try to merge like we did once before, breathing in sync. But for whatever reason, it doesn't work, and I feel disappointed.

My mind automatically goes back to my grandparents, and anger toward them wells up again. I don't want to see them. They cut me loose to travel around the world. I don't know them. I don't need them. I'm fine right here, in my little house with my little family—my dog and my dad and my hockey gear. What else do I need?

CHAPTER 24

WHEN SINBAD IS sick or getting IV treatments, it makes me question whether this whole chemo thing is fair to him. I mean, he doesn't know why he has to go through all this. Is it just for me? But he's so happy sometimes. Isn't it worth it to be sick when the result is you end up being really happy? Supposedly, most dogs don't get sick when they get chemo, so maybe their owners don't have so many doubts. I wish that was me.

About a week after his previous chemo, I take him for a long walk, up and down our usual hill, and then up another hill. He hears a noise and whines, so I unleash him and he runs off. When he disappears from view, I sit down and wait, and it dawns on me—there are already plants regrowing everywhere! Some of the weeds are several inches high. Green's my favorite color, so it's cool to sit in the middle of all that new growth. It's only eighty out, which is pretty good for summer in Canyon Country. I check my phone but know there's no signal up here, so I just reread the e-mail I finally sent Aunt Mo this morning. I told her that I don't want to see my mom's parents. It wasn't a hard decision. There were times early on after Dad married Jenny when I really wanted to see them. I'd just be there in my room with nothing to do 'cause Jenny wanted to have some "parent time" alone with Dad. Even when we all went somewhere together, I felt like Dad was more with her than with me. I'd even asked Dad about Grandma Toshi and Grandpa Takao. He said they were going through issues and couldn't see anyone at the moment 'cause they were still upset about my mother's death.

I roll my head and neck in a slow circle, then close my eyes and let the breeze hit my face. Sinbad doesn't show up for twenty minutes. He's done that before, but with him being on chemo, I start to feel pretty worried. "Sinbad!" I call out, but he doesn't come.

Then I hear a commotion, and it's him, bounding through the brush with a rabbit in his mouth and a wild look in his eyes. He shakes his head back and forth, the rabbit's body whipping around. He looks like a complete madman. I know some people might think this is mean of me, but I feel so proud of him! In fact, I think it's my proudest moment as a dog owner. Even when he caught that squirrel, he didn't look *this* wild.

"What a good boy!" I exclaim. "You're the best good boy in the world!" I rub his head. He might be the best dog the world has ever seen! Then I wonder what to do with the rabbit, since wild rabbits can have worms. "Drop it!" I command. He shakes it vigorously. I wonder if it's too late, whether he's already got the worms. Then I grab his upper and lower mouth, pull apart, and shout, "NO! NO!" He wants to fight me for it, and his jaws don't budge.

"Sit!" I say, and surprisingly he does. But he

doesn't open his mouth. I try to pry his jaws open again while saying "NO!" This actually goes on for several minutes. Finally I can see there's no way he's letting go. "Oh, all right, let's head home." I'll have to offer him some dog food or something to get him to drop the rabbit.

And he literally carries that bloody carcass for forty minutes. Back on the street, we pass Mr. Reynolds's house, and he's out there with his blue plastic, pulling it over his car. He looks happy and involved, like he always does with his plastic. He spots me, though, and calls out, "Conor MacRae! What's that your dog's got?"

"A rabbit," I reply. "He won't let go."

"Oh, that's nice," he says.

At home Sinbad doesn't give up the rabbit for dry dog food. He doesn't give it up for wet dog food or lettuce, either. There's a drumstick from yesterday's soup, and when I wave it in front of Sinbad, he drops the rabbit immediately. I throw the rabbit in the sink temporarily, wash my hands, and tear the meat off the chicken bone.

Dad comes home just then and for some reason

heads right to the sink. All he says is, "Oh, that's pretty," then goes to the fridge, takes out a carton of milk, and heads to his room.

"Sorry, rabbit," I say. I bag it three times and bring it to the outside garbage can, Sinbad following me eagerly. He does his best sit in the driveway. "Not giving it to you. No!"

I know this probably won't help with worms in his mouth, if he even has worms in his mouth, but I take him in and brush his teeth early—I usually brush them at night—and give him a bath for good measure. Meanwhile, I'll have to watch for worms in his poop. But it feels great to have these "problems." Life is good! It's a weird thing, like one day everything in the world seems to suck, and another day everything seems to be working out. Aunt Mo says that's just 'cause I'm a kid, and kids are "dramatic." I don't know about that. I mean, sometimes we're just responding to the grown-ups, right?

I go stand in Dad's doorway. "Aunt Mo says Grandpa Takao and Grandma Toshi want to come visit me on Thanksgiving."

He sets down his milk carton. "Yeah, I heard. So what do you think?"

"I told her no. . . . How come they asked her instead of you?"

"Actually, they keep in touch with her more than they do me. . . . Okay. All right. Are you sure? Sometimes I think . . . I mean, your mom didn't have any siblings, and I have one, but she doesn't have kids yet. It might be a good thing to have more relatives in your life."

"Nah."

"Want to talk about it?"

"Nah." I pause. "Sinbad caught a rabbit."

"I noticed."

"It was pretty cool. He was super excited. I never saw him so excited."

"I'm glad he's doing well."

I get a feeling then that Dad's had a bad day, so I wander off.

In my room, Sinbad's ripping apart a blanket . . . my blanket. "Aw, Sinbad!" I say. "Seriously?"

He's so busy ripping that he doesn't notice me. I know I should scold him so he never does this again, but since he's been sick, I can't make myself do it. But I do take the blanket from him and throw it back on my bed. I've only been using it 'cause I let the air conditioner run all night a couple of times. I'm pretty sure it's just a cheap blanket; still, we can't afford to be destroying stuff right now. It's torn, and there are a couple of holes, but it's still usable. I look at Sinbad suspiciously. The rabbit, the blanket—it's like he knows he can get away with anything right now. I pat the bed, and he jumps up. I sit next to him while I work on the playbook. Jae-won and his family are on their annual trip to Redding, where Mrs. Kang's parents live, so we haven't studied the playbook together yet. Dad, of course, has basically memorized the whole thing. Then we've been going over old video of my games while he tries to point out plays that are similar to the ones Coach Dusan has diagrammed. On my own, I just keep reading it over and over.

Next thing I know, I'm waking up, and it's three in the morning. I can't sleep, so I go to my desk, thinking I may read the playbook more. There's an envelope on my desk—Dad must have put it there after I fell asleep. It's from Mr. Reynolds.

Dear Conor,

Here's something I thought you might like. It's a real fingernail clipping from Mack!! He hated getting his fingernails clipped, but we used to do it once a month. I would keep him calm, and my wife would do the cutting. Then afterward we would give him a special treat like carrots and apples. He was a funny chimp. He wouldn't eat a whole apple and then a whole carrot, no, he liked to eat some apple, then some carrot, and so on until he was finished. It was something special we thought you might like.

Yours very truly,
Edwin Reynolds

I notice he accidentally said "we" thought you might like—referring to his wife? I examine the nail. It's so different from Sinbad's narrow black ones. It's shaped like mine, but it's dark with a pink spot on it. It's unbendable, like Sinbad's, though maybe not quite as steel-like. It's dead . . . but alive. I stare at it in my open palm. Maybe I'm still half-asleep, 'cause I get this weird feeling, like I can kind of sense Mack. I wouldn't say it's a scary feeling exactly, but it feels weird, for sure. Then the feeling's gone, and I think I might be insane. Life'll do that to you sometimes.

CHAPTER 25

THE NEXT MORNING Jae-won sends me a link to a story his parents had just read. It's about a cop who shoots an unarmed man, and it turns out the cop is in the middle of a brutal divorce. That really gets to me, and I wonder if I should call someone at the police department so I can tell them my dad is maybe not 100 percent just now. Then I realize that the thing to do is talk to my dad about it, and see if I can talk him into taking some time off. I think he needs it—after I got back in bed last night, I heard his alarm go off, and then I heard him crying in the hallway. It sounded like he was just standing there, doing nothing but crying. Then after a couple of minutes, he got in the shower. So yeah, I'm going to talk to him.

I have one customer that day, several blocks away, so I take care of that and place the money in my drawer. I've got more than four hundred dollars! It makes me feel good seeing that money in there. I feel like I'm helping to protect my family: my dad and Sinbad and me and even my aunt—you never know when someone might need four hundred dollars!

When Dad gets home later, he takes me to four-on-four. I think about trying to talk to him in the car, then wuss out and decide to do it on the way home instead.

When we get to the rink, I'm surprised to see Owen Karnataka there. He's the guy I mentioned who went to play hockey in Finland last season. He's kind of a legend, cause his 16U AAA midget team won the national championship seven years ago. My dad never won nationals. There are three levels of midget: 15U, 16U, and 18U. Owen's team won when they were almost all fifteen-year-olds, which is beyond beast. His dad is from Southern India but immigrated here before Owen was born. I've seen his dad around the rink—he's the Roaster in Chief, but then again he's not. Like Owen was playing a game in one of the rinks, and my dad and I stopped to watch for a period. And Mr. Karnataka was yelling out stuff like, "That was not good! Not good! I know you don't have so much talent, but please don't embarrass me!" But then after roasting Owen for about ten solid minutes, he suddenly turned to my dad and said, "I honestly think he is one of the best hockey players in America. Really the best."

Owen, in a sleeveless T-shirt, strides through the freezing rink carrying a hockey bag. He must be twenty-two or -three now, and he basically looks like he's at the peak of his peak, buff like I can only hope to be someday. He nods at me when he walks by—he was a coach on an in-house team I played on once. "Owen!" I call out as he passes.

He turns around. "Hey . . . Conor, right?"

"Yeah, thanks for remembering. What's Finland like?"

"It's cold, man. But I love it. It's an adventure. It's as much fun as I had in bantam and midget."

"Cool. What's the hockey like?"

"It's high level. We had a guy on our team make the NHL. He managed to stick with his NHL team the whole season, and hopefully he'll stick next season as well."

"Wow!"

"How about you?" Owen asks.

"I made peewee AAA for the next season."

"Great, man, congratulations! I knew you had it in you, seriously. You had the best all-around game I've seen in a young kid. But are you getting any lower?" He looks at my dad and nods. "Is he getting any lower?"

"He's doing better, but we've still got work to do on that."

"He'll get it." He winks at me. "Maybe you'll end up in Finland one day. Bring a warm coat." Then he gives a quick wave and walks off.

I go change in a locker room, psyched. I love talking to these older guys, just about where they go with their careers. There are a lot of options. I mean, I know I'm not the kind of kid who's going to grow up and get a PhD. I'm the kind of kid who could go to college and *still* not get a good job. Like, what I don't understand is, everybody says if you go to college, you'll get a better job. But what if *everyone* went to college? If there are only a certain number of good jobs, then the same percentage of people are still going to end up with a good job, and a lot of people with college degrees are *not* going to get good jobs. It all depends on how many good jobs there are, not on how many people go to college. Right? I've been trying to figure this out. Basically, I just gotta understand what all the options are. Why can't we have jobs for all kinds of people, including people like me? How does that work? Sometimes, thinking about it, I just don't want to grow up at all.

But then I go out there, get on the ice, and I'm pushing off on my skates, and it feels even greater than it did last time. There's so much open ice in four-on-four—it's just constant flying up and down while skating your fastest, passing, and scoring. I score five goals, and we win 21–17. Makes me wonder if I'd like to switch to playing forward someday. I love playing defense, but I know Dad wonders if I have the killer instinct you need for it. I have a killer instinct, but maybe it's not the D type of killer instinct. I mean, in bantam some guys have the attitude like they wanna check five players a game just to make their day worthwhile. Plus, playing defense is a lot of pressure, 'cause if someone scores it can be all your fault, and then you have to feel like crap for the rest of the day if it was an important game. On the other hand, playing forward is constant movement, constant puck-handling. You feel pressure, but it's a different kind of pressure.

But maybe that's just four-on-four. Dad believes in letting the coach put you where he feels is best for the team. He says, "In hockey the best players integrate fully with the team," whatever that means. Or, "The coach is in the best position to see the team as a whole." I'll do anything my coach asks, especially 'cause I'm not really sure what I'm best at. On my team last year, the six defensive players were the six fastest skaters on the team and blew the offensive guys out of the water when it comes to skating backward. I was actually the worst backward skater of the six of us. The offensive guys last year had better hands and were more agile. We had one center who couldn't skate that great and didn't score that much, but he had this superpower of being able to win every single face-off. There was a guy who stuck in the NHL for years just 'cause he had that same superpower. This is the kind of stuff you have to spend half your time thinking about if you play hockey. Like should I work harder on my backward skating, or should I work more on my hands and hope to make the move to offense at some point? Basically, I try to work on everything.

But today, once I'm out of the locker room, I switch back to thinking about my dad, 'cause it's so important. I don't see him around, so I go to the car, but he's not there. Some guy starts walking across the lot, waving his arms wildly and spinning and talking to himself. He's between me and the rink door, so I just stand there. When he starts moving toward me, I drop my bag but hold on to my stick. Then he spits out "HOCKEY!" and moves on.

A young girl has spotted him and suddenly screams "Mommy!" and runs across the lot toward a woman. I look around, and the guy is already across the lot and almost out the gate. I sit on the ground next to my bag, look up Finland on my phone. Ice hockey is the biggest sport there, and they have one of the best hockey teams in the world. They're the most stable of all 178 countries, according to some organization. Not sure what "stable" means, though.

I look around at the parking lot, surrounded by its huge, black, metal security gate. Dad's walking toward the car, so I get up and heave my bag off the ground.

"How'd you get past me?" he asks. "I didn't see you."

"I didn't see you, so I just came out."

We get inside the car, and he immediately flicks on the radio and turns it up loud. So I'm not sure if he feels like talking.

I start by asking, "Did you ever think of playing in Finland?"

He turns down the radio right away. "Well, I started out pretty cocky. I was sure I was going to make the NHL, so, no, I didn't think of leaving the country. That might have been fun, though, to see the world. My parents spent so much on my hockey, we didn't really have the money to travel. And I guess we didn't really want to travel either. I just wanted to play hockey, and my parents just wanted to watch me play hockey. I feel sorry for my sister, though. She kind of got dragged along all the time."

"Have you ever been out of the country?"

"Once. I never told you? Your mom and I went to Japan for our honeymoon. It was your grandparents' wedding present to us."

"Do they play hockey there?"

"Yeah, but they're honestly not that into it. I think there was a promising kid whose family apparently decided to move him to Canada. Not sure what became of him."

"I kinda worry that there aren't that many players with Japanese blood who ever made it in the NHL. Do you think I'm going to fail?"

"There are some making their way up the ranks now. At least two will probably be first-round draft picks. One is very small, but his skating is off the charts for a teenager. And you have to look at the greatest guy who did have Japanese blood—have you heard of Paul Kariya? Really high-skill player. If it weren't for all those concussions, who knows what his stat line would look like. I actually played his team once, but we were never on the ice at the same time."

Like a lot of the guys on my team, I don't watch many professional hockey games. Those guys are so far beyond us that Jae-won and I just don't like to watch them. I'd much rather see a good bantam game than go see the Kings or something. I did see a YouTube video of Kariya, but I only watched that one video of him, where he got creamed by a blind-side elbow. Seeing that illegal hit on him, then seeing him lying on the ice afterward, I couldn't watch more. I guess you just gotta grow up tough in this life . . . whether you play hockey or not, probably.

I look at Dad, frowning at some guy weaving way fast on the freeway. Dad's kind of the ultimate in tough, or so I've always thought. So this crying busi-ness is definitely a problem. I gotta ask him.

So I say, "Dad, did you hear that story about the cop who shot that unarmed seventeen-year-old guy up near Redding? The one with the toy gun?"

"It was a pellet gun, not a toy gun. The news

called it a toy gun, but its real name is a pellet gun. It's very realistic-looking."

"So you heard about it. . . ."

"Yeah."

"Yeah, but Dad, that officer, the one who shot the kid—he was going through a bad divorce. He wasn't his best self out there. You know, like how you always tell me to be my best self out there on the ice."

He doesn't answer for a moment, and I think he might be offended that I don't think he can do his job. Then he says, "I've actually thought about this, Conor, but I think I'm okay out there in the streets."

"But Dad, maybe that guy thought *he* was okay out there. I mean, what if you're not the best judge of that, you know?"

He glances at me and says, "And who would be the best judge?"

"Well, me. I mean, I know I'm only a kid, but I know you, right?"

"You know me as a dad, not as a cop. All good cops learn to separate their personal lives from their jobs. Compartmentalize. If you can't do that, it's the wrong job for you. But I tell you what, I'll think about what you've said." He makes a face like he ate something sour. "Hand me a gum wrapper, Con." I hand him an old gum wrapper that's sitting in the cup holder. He spits his gum into the wrapper. "I think I'm finally sick of cinnamon gum."

He just seems really tired and old right now, so I let it go. I suddenly get that feeling I mentioned before, like when I can sense the bad stuff from his job, the bad things he's seen, welling up in him and kind of making a cloud around him. And it makes me feel bad when I feel this way, but I really need to get away from this cloud. So I look out the window. I asked him once why he didn't get a bodyguard job, or maybe work some kind of private security. He said he had a friend who got a job doing security for a rich guy who was good friends with a politician. Some of the politicians this friend met, he liked, and some he thought were pure evil, even though they seemed nice when you saw them on TV. That was something Dad didn't want to deal with. And he doesn't want to do security for some rich person. That really doesn't motivate him. He wants to be a cop. So sometimes he's just going to have this cloud.

I think about that window Dad has talked about, where you have 1.5 seconds to make your decision to shoot. Wrong decision, you die. "Right" decision, someone else may die. That there is what you would call a tragic decision, either way. But you gotta make the decision to live. I would. And that's why I would never want to be a cop.

Jenny wanted Dad to quit being a cop as well, but maybe for different reasons. She started to get pretty ambitious about the kind of life she thought we should be living. She wanted him to go to college, and he had no interest. I would say all together, if you added up the good days we had together, out of all the years they were married, we had maybe three months or so of times that were really nice.

I remember the one road trip we took with Jenny when I was six, right before I started skating. We stopped on an empty highway, just the three of us, and took pictures of the horizon, the empty blacktop stretching into nowhere. Jenny said, "Wow, sometimes nowhere is the best place to be." She suddenly picked me up and kissed my face and said, "I love you SO MUCH." That was the first, last, and only time she ever told me she loved me. But I kind of don't mind, 'cause that's honest of her.

And . . . so, yeah, to me, Hockey = Divorce. "Why do you have to push him so hard?" Jenny screamed during one argument.

"I'm not pushing him!" Dad yelled back. "He wants to do it. Ask him!"

"He doesn't know what he wants! He's ten years old!"

"He wants to play hockey! I repeat: ask him!"

And I did want it, even when I was ten. I wanted it more than anything, more than I wanted my parents to stop fighting. I would lie there hoping my dad would win the argument, and I could keep playing.

CHAPTER 26

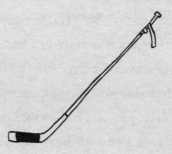

WHEN I HIT five hundred dollars, Dad suggests I start taking lessons again. "We've got the Sinbad thing under control. Now let's get you ready for the season."

So Sunday at five a.m., there I am at the rink to skate with Shu. He looks surprised when I slide onto the ice. "What happen you? I thought you quit hockey!"

"Nah, just took a break."

"Break okay. Kid need break." Then he swings his stopwatch at me so that it clanks on my helmet cage. I flinch. "You skate fast today or I make you go home."

He times us one by one, around the ice. I'm a full second over my usual time.

He shakes his head sadly, doesn't even bother to pinch me. "Lazy today. No NHL for lazy kid."

"I think I'm rusty. I'm having a bad day."

"Nick never have bad day."

Nick is nineteen and plays major junior hockey like a lot of NHL players did at one time. He's one of the best players I've ever personally known, after my father and Owen. Nobody who skates with Shu at five in the morning can touch Nick, and there are some darn good players who skate with Shu at five in the morning.

When Nick tapes the shaft of his stick, he leaves a little piece of tape hanging, so for a few weeks I did that too. Aleksei thought it looked unprofessional and sometimes pulled it off and yelled at me, "Why you do that?! I don't like!" But I kept doing it again, 'cause I wanted to be like Nick. Then I decided the tape hanging there distracted me, so I stopped taping that way. You gotta try different stuff to find your style.

During the scrimmage portion of Shu's workout,

I fall down and go headfirst into the boards. You're supposed to get right up from a fall when you're at peewee level. If you don't, you have to sit out two shifts. I don't know if that's national, but it's the way the Grizzlies do it. But my bell's rung, and I lie there for a minute. Shu ignores me. If Aleksei were here, he would poke me with his stick and say, "Get up! This is hockey!" Then skate away.

A couple of players lean over me and ask if I'm okay. I don't know why, but I just have trouble getting up after a fall. When I'm hurting or dazed, it feels so good to lie there on the ice. Like, I don't even struggle to get up like the tough kids do. I just can't push through a hurting. So after maybe a minute and a half, I pull myself up. I don't look over at my dad, 'cause I'm kind of embarrassed, since I'm basically fine.

After I get up, Shu looks at me and just shakes his head like I'm a whiner or something. Speaking of whining, my skate blades are dull. We didn't get them sharpened 'cause the guy who usually does it was out sick when we came by Friday, and I won't let anyone else sharpen them. So I'm skidding a bit out there. Nobody who doesn't know hockey would notice, but my dad probably sees that I'm not skating as well as I usually do. Even a tiny nick on the blades can throw me off my game 'cause I'm so picky.

Then Shu has me and two guys from my new team named Aidan and Aidan go up against Nick by himself. I don't know why, but sometimes it seems like half the guys in hockey are named Aidan. Even as good as Nick is, I don't see how he can get the puck from the three of us. We're all good passers. But somehow on Aidan 1's first pass, Nick lunges and just tips the puck, then speeds over to it, and it's game over. He scores with a flick of his wrists. Shu whips his stopwatch on Aidan 1's helmet, making a clang. "Go again," Shu says.

So we go again, and this time I'm the loser. I execute what I think is going to be a perfect saucer pass to Aidan 2, but Nick whips his stick through the air and hits my pass, then flashes over to the puck. He hits a blazing slap shot into the net. How can this guy not be in the NHL?

"How can you not be in the NHL?" I ask him.

He just smiles, but I wonder, seriously, how is

this guy not in the NHL? You must have to be a freaking superman to be in the NHL. I mean, if Nick can't make it, who can? Or maybe Nick will make it someday? The major junior level is way up there in the hockey hierarchy. Not as high up there as my dad got, but pretty darn high.

Then Shu has two AAA midgets go up against Nick, and he still beats them, though it's a struggle.

We're on the ice for three hours, alternating drills and scrimmages. I can hardly see with all the sweat pouring down my face. All in all, a great workout. Then we finish up with a few dryland exercises outside.

Later, in the car, I ask, "So, Dad, will Nick make the NHL?"

"He's a great talent. NHL? I don't know."

"But he's so good."

"He's awesome. But, you know, with Nick I feel like he can't see the whole ice at once. When things get too intense, he starts focusing on one area of the ice at a time. Tunnel vision. Playing against peewees and bantams you can't tell, but when he plays against top talent, you can really see it. I watched him scrimmage with some guys from Sweden once, and he didn't really have their vision and hockey sense. Great skills, though. Unreal reflexes."

I think that over. "So when you don't make it, do you feel bitter?" I ask. "Mr. Falco says bitterness is the great enemy of life."

"Nah, I never felt bitter. I asked myself whether there was anything more that I could have done. I moved out of the house at sixteen to play junior hockey. What more could I have done? It was lonely out there, living in a strange family's house like you do in juniors. Man, it was lonely! But when you're out there playing at a high level, it's worth it. The games make everything worth it."

"So if you're not bitter, how do you feel exactly?"

"I got my shot. That feels good."

A feeling wells up in me, explodes in me actually: *I want my shot.* And yet, would I really want to move out at sixteen? That sounds scary, plus Dad says it's lonely. And it's only four years away. If I have a choice, and I'm good enough for juniors, I'll wait until I'm eighteen to move out. But, realistically, that's a hundred years away at the moment. Hockey-wise, the coming season is all I need to be focusing on.

"So, Conor, switching subjects here, I've been thinking about what you said. I talked to the sergeant at work. I'm going to be taking a couple of weeks off."

"Are we going somewhere?"

"No, it's not a vacation exactly. I've just been thinking . . . you have to be alert in my job, extremely vigilant at every moment. And maybe I'm not able to do that right now. I'm distracted. I need to focus more, and there's also the problem of I'm just not feeling it right now. Do you know what I mean?"

"Uh, sort of?"

"Sometimes when an officer has a lot going on in his life, the department likes them to take some time off. When I say I'm not feeling it, I'm kind of thinking of some of the things you gotta do out there, get yelled at, get insulted, maybe get shot at. Some days I don't know why I'm out there." He pauses. "I have something else to tell you."

Uh-oh, that sounds big. "What?"

"I know you've already said no, but your mom's parents really want to see you, and they say they're going to see you."

I stare at his profile. He can feel me staring and glances my way. "What do you mean, they're *going* to?" I ask.

"They're coming out for Thanksgiving. They said they're flying out here, and they're going to be in a hotel, just waiting, for you to call them." I don't say anything, so he adds, "Anyway, just keep thinking about it. It's a long time away."

I wait for a feeling to come, 'cause I literally don't know what I feel. Then I think, *That makes me feel really tired.* I don't actually like having complicated stuff in my life. Jae-won and I talk about that sometimes. We just wish everything could go smoothly. Then I feel sad. I look at the back of the front seat. I'm not really into forgiving people, even if they're related to me. Like there was a guy who punched Jae-won during a game last year, and I punched the guy about five times before someone pulled me off. Got suspended for a game. But I wasn't sorry at all, and if I see that same player again, I'm gonna hate him. That's not right, but it's the way I feel. Forgiveness sucks is the way I feel at this moment.

CHAPTER 27

THAT WEEKEND, JAE-WON stays over Saturday night. We discuss the playbook for about an hour with Dad. Dad has found old clips of youth hockey games from YouTube and Vimeo, and he goes over the clips with us, explaining how the players are executing drills that are the same as or similar to drills that Coach Dusan has drawn up. Watching film really helps a lot to see what the diagrams mean. It sounds corny, but it's like the clouds just opened up and the sun shines through. I truly get it!

Afterward, we eat three peanut butter sandwiches apiece, then drive to the park with Sinbad to work out in the cool night air. Sinbad had a treatment Monday, but he got over it quickly, sort of. I've started to realize that in reality he seems off compared to a year ago. There's something about him that just isn't the same. I try to tell myself that it's my imagination, but I know it's not.

Still, he jogs along with us, then lies and watches as we do the stairs. Afterward, Jae-won's wiped out, plus he likes to hang with my dad, so I walk Sinbad alone. Since it's night, I stay in sight of Dad, 'cause if I were a perv, I'd hang out in dark parks.

Sinbad pulls hard on the leash. Sometimes I let him pull, since it seems to make him happy. I used to use a prong collar—those are supposed to be better for dogs' necks than choke chains. But when I found out he had cancer, I got him a halter to hurt him less. But he likes to pull more in the halter. "Heel!" I say, yanking on the halter. He heels well in the prong collar but ignores me now. "Sinbad, heel!" I say louder, and we get into a pulling match. Here I used to think I had a little control over him, but now I see it was just the collar!

When we return to Dad and Jae-won, they're

talking about Dad going to nationals as a bantam AAA and losing in the final.

"Was it fun anyway?" Jae-won asks.

"Yeah, it was amazing. We all cried after we lost, though. Then we started talking about how we were going to make it back next year, and we cheered up. We didn't make it back. Three of our best players aged out of bantam, and the team wasn't as good the next year. But the final was amazing, one of the most fun games I ever played in. We lost in overtime—it was incredibly intense."

"Cool," Jae-won says.

They don't have a national championship for peewees, so that's all in the future. Nationals can probably be a shock, 'cause you're one of the best teams from your area, and you probably think you're pretty hot, but then you meet up with a bunch of kids who are the best team in *their* areas. Some of those teams from Minnesota are supposed to be scary good. I actually know a kid whose parents moved the family to Minnesota specifically to advance his hockey career. He was super talented for sure, so his parents just decided to completely go for it.

It's weird. Sometimes it seems like there are a lot of godly players out there, and then sometimes it seems like there are hardly any. But the bottom line is, there are enough so that it's practically impossible to make the NHL.

"Do the coaches yell at each level?" Jae-won asks Dad.

"Yeah, you gotta get used to that. Actually, not all of them yell, but most of them believe in maintaining appropriate fear, which usually means yelling."

"I wrote a paper in school about the F-bombs the coach dropped on us last year, and my teacher said she was going to report him to the authorities, whoever they are," Jae-won says.

Dad laughs. "The F-bomb authorities?"

It's nice, it's really cool, to be sitting around in the middle of summer with my dog and two guys—Dad and Jae-won—who totally understand where I'm coming from, and I totally understand where they're coming from. We all get not having money, we get sports and working out, we get respecting each other. And we're superclean. There are some kids at the junior high who smoke pot, who've gotten drunk, who've stolen prescription drugs from their parents. That's a whole other world from mine. I watch it like I would watch a documentary on my computer or something. It's interesting, but it's completely separate. It might as well be a whole different planet.

CHAPTER 28

DAD SPENDS HIS two weeks off working in the yard, planting stuff, which is a first. At one point I ask him if he's enjoying his time off, and he says, "I gotta tell you, gardening is not my thing. The sergeant at work suggested it." He laughs. "So that's a waste of two weeks off." Still, he seems pretty relaxed, and I haven't heard him crying in a while.

"So did you, I don't know, think about anything while you were gardening?"

"Actually, I did," he says, but doesn't say more.

I can tell his favorite thing to do is take me to lessons or work out with me and Jae-won. He gardens and then watches TV, holds a couple of poker games. But he does seem a little bored, I'm not sure with what exactly—the gardening, yes, but something else as well. I try to think back, and it seems to me he wasn't always bored. On the other hand, all that boredom looks like it was good for him, 'cause he's laughing more than he used to. I can hear him laughing and talking loudly during his poker games. So I think the two weeks off were good for him, and maybe everything's okay now.

And then finally—suddenly—it's here, mid-August, *triple-freaking-A*. The season begins!! All the way in the car as Dad drives to the rink, I sit up straight and stare ahead, taking big breaths. It's unbelievable that it's here. It's gonna be just me, Jae-won, and Lucas from AA. Are we gonna be the worst players on the team? I wonder if the other guys will be nice to us, or if they'll think they're better than us.

I don't see either Jae-won or Lucas as I walk across the parking lot with my heavy bag and stick. That sucks. But in the locker room, they're sitting together in the far corner, so I join them and start getting changed.

"Hey," Jae-won says.

"Hey."

"How's your dog?" Lucas asks.

"He's good. He had that one real bad stretch, but he's doing better. Thanks for praying for him. It actually helped—he got better. I'm praying now sometimes too. So seriously, thanks, man."

"Cool that it helped. It was no problem, I pray every night anyway."

"Cool."

"You pray every night?" a kid named Avery asks loudly.

The locker room goes silent. I wince a bit, like maybe Avery's going to make fun of Lucas.

"Yeah," Lucas says kind of cautiously.

But Avery just nods. "Cool."

The AAAs from last year are sitting next to each other, joking about how some of them have gained a few pounds over the summer. Three of them have a push-up contest while the others count and laugh. They're super relaxed, while I feel tense and worried, like maybe I'm not going to skate well next to the AAAs.

"Do you go to church on Sundays?" I ask Lucas. "I mean, I guess not. You were always at the games."

"My parents don't actually belong to a church. We're independent Christians. We read the Bible together every night."

"Cool," I say, then pause to think about how many times one of us has said "cool" just since I got here. Lucas bows his head and closes his eyes for a moment, like he always does before practice. He does it for just a brief moment, so you could almost miss it. Lucas hardly talked to anyone last season. But now I feel bonded to him since he prayed for Sinbad and it worked.

One of Jae-won's laces breaks, and he panics a bit, 'cause he doesn't want to be late. He's still changing his laces as we all leave. "Don't worry, you still have a few minutes," I tell him.

He nods, but I can see he's stressed. We march through the hallway and into the rink. The Zamboni's already finished, and Coach Dusan stands with his clipboard, talking to a couple of parents. One of the assistant coaches throws a bucket of pucks onto the ice, and I chase one down. Jesus skates around the ice, and I stop what I'm doing to watch. I saw how skinny he was in the locker room with his shirt and pants off. It's unbelievable how that skinny body can skate so fast. All of last year's AAAs race around with Jesus. Wow, some of them are awesome skaters!

Coach Dusan slides onto the ice, puts his fingers into his mouth, and lets out a piercing whistle. We rush to him. He looks at Andrew, who arrived last. "Ten push-ups, Andrew," he says, and Andrew falls to the ice. He only manages seven.

"Seriously?" Coach says. He shakes his head.

Jae-won is running across the floor and slinks onto the ice while the coach is looking at his clipboard, drawing on it. He doesn't look up but says, "You're late."

"I'm sorry, my lace broke, Coach Dusan!" Jae-won cries out, like we're in the marines.

Coach Dusan rubs his forehead and closes his eyes. He seems to think a moment before saying, "I wanted to talk to you all about something important. I know some of your parents put a lot of pressure on you about your hockey. Not all of your parents, but some of them. I don't want anyone on this team who doesn't love the great game of hockey. I want you to work your butts off, yes, but I want you to do it because you love the game. I understand that you're not always going to love practice, you're not always going to love working out, you're not going to like it when I get on you to work beyond what you think you're capable of, but you have to love the game of hockey. I love this game. But if I had to go through all the work I went through and I didn't even love the game, my life would basically be ruined. If you don't love the game, talk to someone. If your parents won't listen, talk to me. I'm all about the human potential as it relates to hockey, but reaching that potential is the opposite of what will happen if you put in the hours to do something you don't even love. I had a player like that once, and some bad things happened just because his parents couldn't hear that he didn't want to play. So talk to me. Pull me aside and talk to me. Any questions?"

Whoa, that's the last thing I expected to hear. We all stand there quietly. Coach is pretty intimidating, so I can't imagine that anyone will have any questions. Then Jae-won raises his hand, and Coach Dusan nods at him.

"I love hockey," Jae-won says. "Especially the actual games. I lie in bed and think about hockey until I fall asleep. But I feel a lot of pressure, too. Is that okay?"

"Good question!" Coach Dusan exclaims. "Pressure, unfortunately, is part of elite sports. So you're going to feel pressure. Some of that pressure will be coming from me. But only you know if the pressure is too much for you. If you think you're reaching a point where it's too much, I encourage you to come and talk to me. But I want to be honest with you, you *will* feel pressure, and that's normal. If you love playing the games, then I think you're all right. I had that kid who didn't love the games. . . . Does that help, JW?"

"Yes," he says, nodding.

Then Coach suddenly looks right at me and says, "Conor, did you read the playbook?"

I freeze. What?? Why me? "Yes," I say, scared for no reason, since I understand most of the book now. Then I say "Yes!" louder.

"What do I want you to do in practice today, and every day?"

Relief floods over me. "Practice with intention!" I answer.

"Good! Practice with intention, everybody. Twice around the ice, full speed."

A boy named Nikita suddenly yells out, "Grizzlies on three, one-two-three!"

"GRIZZLIES!" we all shout.

"One-two-three!"

"GRIZZLIES!"

We take off around the rink, our skates digging in. The ice feels slow today, maybe 'cause it was a hundred degrees outside this afternoon. I feel like I'm dragging, but I try to concentrate on speed until I stop with a spray of snow.

"Twenty push-ups!" Coach Dusan calls out, and we all fall to the ice.

Practice is a lot harder than I expected. I haven't played defense in two months and feel like I've lost all my instincts. Then when we work on our saucer passes, it turns out that mine aren't smooth enough, so it's harder for the other player to get them. I always thought I made great saucer passes. To tell the truth, I thought I was a master. And everybody's always told me I have a hard slap shot. I do, but it turns out I miss the net too much, Coach Dusan says. But the hardest part is that we're supposed to have memorized about fifteen plays that were written up in the playbook. I've read all the plays, and watched film with Dad, but wouldn't you know it, Coach has us practice a drill that Dad couldn't find film for. I feel like I'm in way over my head, but then I see that a lot of guys don't understand either. It's also hard 'cause Coach'll draw twenty lines all over his board, and the lines start to get mixed up in my head.

The playbook says to ask questions, so at one point I skate up to Coach Dusan and ask, "So during the forecheck drill when F1 skates to the strong side, where should I be?"

"Just for the purposes of this drill, stand on the weak side but slightly toward the strong side," he says. "During a game, you need to be creative and make your decisions on the fly based on the situation." I start to walk off, and he says, "Conor."

"Yes?"

"If you have an opening, don't be shy about taking

a slap shot. Your slap shot is one of the reasons I picked you for this team."

"Okay."

So during the next drill I take a shot from a couple feet inside the blue line, and I'm surprised when it explodes toward the net and just misses, hitting the goalpost. "There ya go, Conor!" yells Coach Dusan, and suddenly it seems like a perfect day.

In the locker room later, I feel good, relaxed. Everybody's showing each other their biceps—Brian's are biggest. He's one of the kids from another club. I've never talked to him, but I think everybody has talked *about* him, 'cause he's already hit puberty, so he's five feet seven and practically sounds like a grown man.

"How tall are you, Conor?" Brian asks.

"Five-four," I say.

"You're fourth tallest on the team. Andrew is shortest."

"Yeah, but I've got the best hands," Andrew says.

"Jae-won has the best hands!" I answer.

"No, he doesn't—he's AA!"

"Jae-won does have good hands," Brian says. "I saw him play last year."

Then Andrew wants to arm wrestle Jae-won, which has nothing to do with how good your hands are, but they do it anyway, and Jae-won wins. So everybody's laughing and starts insulting Andrew, but he's good with it and laughs as well.

I pack up and say, "See ya," to Lucas and Jae-won. Outside, it's dark—we've got an eight thirty start time. That might be hard during the school year, when I probably won't get home until ten thirty. But the club has a full slate of young teams—they're called squirts and mites—and they get priority for the earlier slots.

In the car, I ask, "How did I do?"

Dad starts the car and backs up, saying, "You looked a little lost out there at first, but you came on strong later. But what happened to your saucer pass?"

I feel kind of disappointed, but I also know that Dad's always honest when I ask him how I did. "I couldn't get it to stop shaking in the air."

"All right, well, let's go to Aleksei this week."

I can't wait to go to Aleksei again, but I immediately worry about the money. Then I switch worries back to how I looked at practice.

"Cool . . . Anything else? How did I look compared to everyone else?"

"Most of them looked rusty. It's always that way
at the beginning."

"But do you think I'm as good as them?"

"What? Yeah! Absolutely!"

That's all I wanted to hear, so I zone out for the
ride home.

At home Sinbad jumps around and whines at the
door. "It's too late. I'll walk you three times tomorrow,
okay?" I go right to my room, throw off my clothes,
change my boxers, and climb into bed. I have literally
fifty or sixty pairs of underwear, 'cause when I don't
feel like taking a shower, I just change my boxers
instead. That would probably sound disgusting if I
was a girl, but I'm not. When Jenny used to want me
to take a shower after a late practice, and I just wanted
to sleep, Dad would say, "He's a boy, Jen, he's a boy."

Sinbad hops onto the bed. He's had good energy
lately. Still, I get out of bed, kneel next to the mattress,
and say softly, "Thank you for taking such good care
of Sinbad. I still plan on rescuing lots of dogs someday." Then I get back in bed. While I was kneeling,

Sinbad slid over to my pillow. Since he's feeling well, I push him out of the way. He doesn't help—I have to push really hard.

My phone dings: Jae-won. *Dude, practice was lit. Let's try to make first line.*

I text back *Yeah!* He doesn't answer, but now he's got me thinking. Except for my first season, I always tried out first for a better team than I made. So every year, I was one of the best players on the team that I did make. I think about how Dad made the NHL and was the worst player on the team. I hope that doesn't happen to me this year. I gotta admit, I'm a little surprised how fast the AAAs skate. I've seen them play before, so I knew they were fast, but when you're out there with them, you can really see how you're at a whole new level. That makes me feel tired. Like I've been working for years, and now I gotta work even harder just to keep up. And then I've got a sick dog. . . . Life is tiring, man. I feel sorry for myself for a second. But Sinbad lets out a snort, and my whiny moment passes. I smile. *Sinbad's gonna make it! I'm a AAA! I'm gonna work like hell and make first line!* I press my face in Sinbad's neck. Life doesn't get any better. It just doesn't.

CHAPTER 29

THE TEAM HAS three ice practices a week, an hour of theory, and three hours of dryland, plus everyone has various lessons and dryland that they do on their own. I work as hard as I can, but some practices I come home feeling like I'm barely keeping up. It seems like everybody else is better than me. I might be the actual weakest player on the team. Simple truth is I need to be getting on the ice more. Dad says Coach told him I'm doing great, but I don't feel that's true. I don't want to be third line or even stuck on the bench, so I add an extra hundred squats a day, like that'll change my fate.

Jae-won comes over a couple of times and Dad discusses film with us, and then one day the three of us go jogging with Sinbad, except he quits early and just watches us, panting in the sun. Later, while Jae-won and I wait for his mom to come pick him up, we sit on the front stoop talking about Rocko. Jae-won has heard he quit hockey and then had some kind of breakdown.

"Just like Coach Dusan was talking about with that player he had . . . What *is* a breakdown exactly?" I ask.

"Not sure. I guess you have to go to a shrink."

"I had to go twice, once family therapy with my dad and stepmom. And another time I had to go 'cause I was sitting with my chair tilted, and the teacher thought I was going to fall and hurt myself. I did it three times even though the teacher told me to stop. The vice principal made me stay in her office during recess and lunch, and then when I kept doing that with my chair, she made me go to a therapist one time to help me think about my life."

"Wow, she sounds like a freak," Jae-won says.

"She was evil, like, I really think she was some kind of secret Satanist or something."

"Scary. What was the shrink like?"

"Sucked. He just asks you these questions in a really calm voice. He kept saying, 'How do you feel about that?'"

"Did it help you stop tilting your chair?"

"Nah, man."

"I had to go to a therapist three times, because I wasn't conceptualizing what I was doing before I did it, or something like that. The vice principal said I was supposed to conceptualize, take three big breaths, then walk away. Instead, I guess I threw bread at another boy during lunch because he was bothering my friend. Then another time all of us got in a fight because the other boy tripped my friend on the stairs. But his parents gave a ton of money to the school, so they believed everything he ever said. It was a charter school, and they were always begging the parents for money."

"So did the therapist help?"

"Nah, my parents just put me in a different school. We're using my cousin's address for my home address, and I'm going to a school in their area."

"I didn't know that. Glad you got away!"

"I like this school a lot better. The principal's, like, totally sane. I went from Cs and Ds to straight Bs. I even got an A once."

Sinbad's sitting next to us, Jae-won petting him. "You really don't need a shrink if you have a dog," I say.

"I wish we could have one in our apartment. Someday when we get a house, I'm gonna get a German shepherd or a Doberman." Sinbad seems to understand and places a paw on Jae-won's knee.

"He's psychic," I explain. My mind goes back to Rocko. "Hope he's okay." I take out my phone and text him. I have his number 'cause we had exactly one playdate earlier this year. *Hey, Rock, it's Conor. 'Sup, I heard you quit hockey.*

He texts back immediately. *I freakin' hate hockey.*

Glad you quit then. You okay?

I am now. Thanks for asking. But my therapist says I'm not supposed to be in contact with hockey players anymore.

How come?

She says they're a bad influence. Too competitive. Bye forever.

Bye, good luck!

Jae-won is looking over my shoulder.

"Do you think he'll be okay?" Jae-won asks.

"I don't know."

Mrs. Kang pulls up, and the twins jump out of the car and run full speed at us. Sinbad looks alarmed, so I hold his leash and say, "It's okay, boy."

The twins fall all over Sinbad, petting and nuzzling him. He lets out a low rumble—he hates it when anyone besides me puts their head near his head. It's just a thing of his. "Cut it out!" Jae-won says.

"He's getting annoyed, be careful," I say, and the kids fall back.

Mrs. Kang walks up and says, "How is dog?"

"He's doing better, thank you."

"Good, good, you take good care, I know you make good father someday." She laughs like she's really happy she said that, and I smile.

Then Jae-won's brothers each take one of his hands and pull him away. "Sit in back with us!" one of them says. Even though he yells at them sometimes, he's their hero. They know he's got magic hands. He's a legend in his own home.

I get up and walk Sinbad around the neighborhood. We haven't been to the hills lately, 'cause one
day I took him up a hill and down the other side, like
I used to do a lot. But he got tired on the bottom, and
we still had to climb up again to get home. I'm waiting for him to get back to a 100 percent, but it hasn't
happened yet. The last couple of weeks, he's probably
at 85 or 90 percent compared to a year ago. Dr. Pierre
says that may be the best we can hope for him. She
said it super nice-like, but it made me sad. At the
same time, when I take him off leash and hear his
paws go *ka-thump ka-thump* on the sidewalk, it makes
me so happy I can hardly stand it. It's such a fantastic
sound!

Phone dings—Rocko again. *Good luck with your
hockey, you're really amazing at it. Bye, don't text me
back.*

That was nice of him. I text him back anyway.
Be happy, man. He doesn't answer, so I guess I won't
be hearing from him ever again. That happens in
sports. Old guys drop out, new ones join the club. I've
known Jae-won for three years, though, so I think
we're friends for life. But then I think about how my

mother died, my grandparents abandoned me, Jenny left, I barely talk to kids I was friends with just two years ago, Rocko and I used to be good friends, etc. Dad keeps in touch with people he knew from elementary school, but he's not good friends with them. He does stay in close touch with some of the guys from his first juniors team when he was sixteen. He also keeps in touch with a bunch of the cops he knew early in his career. Once, not many months after we got Sinbad, we drove up to Oregon with him for the funeral of Dad's very first partner. He'd moved up to Portland and gotten killed there during a domestic disturbance call. After the funeral, we took Sinbad to the Oregon coast, and I let him off leash. He ran around bothering everybody and wouldn't come when I called. But when he finally let me catch him, he started licking and licking my face, and after that and for the first time, he was really mine.

Dad had sat with Jenny in the sand, talking to the widow. I didn't want to sit with them, just 'cause, I don't know, that was one of the first times I realized that sometimes I didn't want to be around it, the sad part of a cop's life. I remember how Sinbad's scars

were almost faded, and his fur looked smooth and
jet-black and shiny in the sun. He kept licking, even
though today he's not a big licker. It was like he was
suddenly overwhelmed that he actually loved me. I
wish we could go back to that day, but we can't. It was
a sad day, yet a happy day for me and Sinbad. Dad
was still really into Jenny then, kind of doing whatever she said she wanted him to do. That day it felt
like me and Sinbad against the world. But it felt good.

CHAPTER 30

MY BUSINESS SEEMS to have slowed down. Basically, everybody's car is clean. There are people who like to keep their car constantly clean, but apparently not many in my neighborhood. But I have six hundred dollars, and one evening as Dad's having a poker game, Aunt Mo picks me up for Aleksei. Aunt Mo actually wants us to ask her for help more, but Dad doesn't like to bother her too much. Plus, he wants to watch me skate.

"Work hard!" Dad calls as I leave, even though I always work hard. People who don't understand sports might think that's annoying, but for an athlete, it's no big deal to hear stuff like that. I do work harder sometimes, don't know why that is.

And some games I play great, and some games I don't. I guess it's true of any athlete, but some are more consistent than others. I notice that a lot of the kids my age can be inconsistent. It drives all the parents crazy, especially the fathers . . . though there are a couple of mothers who are absolutely insane.

Every so often when you're on the ice during a game, suddenly you can hear one of the parents yelling at the top of their lungs at the refs—you can actually get suspended for that. And of course, they're all cheering during the game, but sometimes they cheer especially loud. And then there's Nikita's mom—Nikita and I played squirt A together. One game, there was a quiet moment in the rink, and then suddenly we all heard, "NIKITA, YOUR MOTHER LOVES YOU!!!" That made the whole team smile. You gotta love those Russian moms.

"So what are you doing today with Sasha?" Aunt Mo asks when I get in the car.

"Aleksei," I say. "I'm doing power skating and then stick time." She puts her hair behind her ears, and I realize half her hair's been cut off. To me, it doesn't look better or worse, but I say, "Nice haircut."

"Thank you!" she says. "I just felt like I needed a change."

She actually says that pretty often, so I only say, "Cool."

"Isn't it all stick time? What's the difference between stick time and power skating again?"

"Stick time, or coaches' time, is an hour-long workout with sticks, and it's not regular practice." "Stick time" also means when the rink lets a bunch of random players practice casually, but why confuse her?

We're waiting in the car 'cause Mr. Reynolds has stopped his car right in front of our driveway for some reason. Aunt Mo watches him in the rearview mirror. I turn around and watch as well. He's got a big sheet of his blue plastic that he's messing with. I swear that stuff is like his pet dog. Then he pushes it all into the backseat and starts driving slowly down the street. "He's really into his blue plastic," I say. "He's obsessed with it."

She laughs. "Some people like movies, and I guess some people like blue plastic."

We back out and start driving slowly behind Mr. Reynolds. He brakes every three seconds, literally. "I wonder if he should be driving," Aunt Mo says.

"He only goes to the store a few blocks away. He drives *really* slow on side streets, but he takes it up to twenty miles an hour on the bigger streets."

When we're free of Mr. Reynolds, my aunt steps on it. For a low-key person, she drives a little fast. You wouldn't expect it from her. She's a great driver, though. She and her old boyfriend used to do some kind of race-car driving. I don't know much about it, but supposedly you get to drive fast around a track, and some people think it's a lot of fun.

We drive quietly for a few minutes, and then she asks, "So did you have any more thoughts about your grandparents?"

"No," I say honestly. "I mean, I've had some thoughts, but I don't know what to do."

"Do you want to tell me what your thoughts were?"

"I don't really know. I don't mean I was having

specific thoughts. I was just more kind of having it in the back of my head."

"Okay." She screeches around a corner. "That's fair." She talks about why some *Star Wars* movies are better than other *Star Wars* movies. Then she sighs. "But it's kind of sad. Lately, I don't like the movies as much as I used to. I don't know if they're not as good, or if I'm just changing."

That's about as shocking as my dad not feeling the same about work anymore. It seems like things must change all the time when you get to be a grown-up. I don't know why, but I would have thought your personality basically stayed the same when you got older. My aunt is quiet for the rest of the way, just concentrating on her driving, since it's one of her favorite things to do.

When we reach Ice House, she asks, "Now what's power skating again?"

"It's to get your thighs strong so that you can skate faster. You do all these boring, really hard exercises up and down the ice until your legs burn so much you can hardly stand up."

Aleksei is arriving as we walk up to the rink. He

doesn't say hi, just says, "Next two week I take off. My girlfriend will be here from Russia. She says I have to take off lessons. Who am I to argue?" He looks at Aunt Mo like she's here all the time.

He's one of my favorite coaches, and I used to get nervous when he took time off. My puck-handling gets rusty when I don't skate with him for a while.

"It's always nice to get away from hockey sometimes," Aunt Mo says.

"You talk to me?" Aleksei says. "I never get away from hockey. It is my destiny."

"I mean, just to take a break," she explains.

He points to his head. "In here, I never take break. This drive my girlfriend crazy. Natalia." Then he looks annoyed. "Conor! Go change, late again!"

When I'm changed, Aleksei is his usual yelling self. As soon as we get onto the ice, he barks out, "Work hard! You need to work hard!!" He beats his stick on the ice. "Conor, did you hear me?! I AM GOING TO HAVE HEART ATTACK!!"

We start out with me going up and down the ice twice on my left leg only, and then I go up and down the ice twice with my right leg only. I don't see what skating on one leg has to do with hockey, but I have to admit that since I've been taking power skating, my skating has gotten faster and stronger. Then I go up and down the ice kneeling on alternate legs. On and on. At one point I exclaim, "Aren't we done yet?" As soon as I ask that, I look at the clock and see there are ten minutes left. Aleksei shakes his head at me like he pities me.

He says, "If I teach you the way they teach in Russia, I will get arrested for torture."

Every year a Russian team flies over to play against our best Grizzlies bantam team, and every year the Russians win. The Russian players are flat-out amazing. They're beautiful to behold, that's the only way to put it. They're creative, like they just do things that you totally don't expect but that make so much sense after they do it. I'm a total Russian fanboy.

"Do they do power skating in Russia?" I ask.

"Five time a week for hour!" Aleksei exclaims. "You done resting?"

"Yeah, I'm ready." I never know if he's telling the truth to me about how they train in Russia, but

judging from the kids who play against us every
year, they're obviously training hard. I didn't mention it earlier 'cause these days you kind of forget
about Aleksei's past, but before immigrating here,
he played for the Red Army team that was one of
the best hockey teams the world has ever seen. So he
understands training like nobody else.

Next he has me skate up and down the ice while
keeping my feet close together. I do some ladders,
which are every hockey player's least favorite drill.
You skate up and down the ice, going a shorter and
shorter distance each time. Your legs start to feel
more and more sluggish, like you're pushing through
mud. After that I pull Aleksei up and down the ice as
he hangs on behind me. We do this six times.

When it's over, I collapse to the ice like I always
do. I lie there a few seconds feeling gratitude that it's
over. Then I get up and go wait at the other rink to
start stick time with Aleksei. My frenemy, Ethan,
is already there waiting. Ethan pretends he can see
right through me, like I don't even exist. I say hey to
him, but he doesn't acknowledge me. He's probably
still salty 'cause he didn't make the Grizzlies.

The Zamboni finishes up, and we glide onto the ice. Ethan is a very good hockey player, but he's not like the best guys. 'Cause of his size, though, he'll probably do okay in bantam. That's when everything changes. Size matters from then on. It's not the most important thing, but it's more important than in peewee.

Sometimes when I pray for Sinbad, I've taken to also praying that I grow to be six feet minimum. Dad's six-two, so there's a chance I'll be big. But my mom was only five-two. Dad says she was the most flexible person he ever met. She was practically a contortionist. That's probably why I can do yoga, but I never do it 'cause it's so boring. Being flexible is just something Mom gave me without knowing that she was giving it to me. Sometimes when I think about that, it seems pretty cool.

There are seven of us here for stick time. Aleksei sets up the cones, tires, and danglers into a maze and shows us how he wants us to skate through them with the puck. It's kind of complicated, and unfortunately, I'm first in line. So I give it a try, and I hear "CONOR! TEN PUSH-UPS!" I do the push-ups, thereby missing the next person so that I still don't know how to do the drill correctly. I get up, and the next two guys get it wrong and have to do push-ups. Finally one of the bantams does it right, and now I get it.

We do drills for forty-five minutes before Aleksei starts the scrimmaging. In the very first scrimmage, Ethan checks me hard, banging me against the boards when I steal the puck from him. I rest on the ground, my bell thoroughly rung. Aleksei roars, "Ethan, go sit on bench!" Then he pokes me with his stick, and I know what he's going to say before he says it. "Conor, get up! It's hockey!" I get up and see that my aunt has opened the door and stepped onto the ice. She's one of those relatives who are kind of really great and really embarrassing at the same time—not that I have so many relatives.

"I'm fine!" I call out, and she steps off the ice again.

Later, in the car, she says, "That boy really hit you hard. Is that allowed?"

"It's not allowed for peewees like us," I say.

"I remember him from once before. He wasn't always that mean."

"He is now."

"His mother should have a talk with him. Was that her sitting near me?"

"Yeah. She'll never have a talk with him. She thinks he walks on water."

She pauses, then smiles and ruffles my hair. "Well, we all think that of our boys."

Like I said, really great and really embarrassing at the same time. But mostly great.

We do the drive-thru at In-N-Out, where I get protein burgers—they're just the meat and lettuce, since I decided to stop eating white bread for the season. When Aunt Mo drops me off, she says, "Did you know I never knew my mother's parents? They were in a feud with my mom."

"About what?"

"They didn't think her husband was good enough for her."

"Grandpa? He's great!"

"I think so too. Later they wanted to make up, and my mother said no. Sometimes I think she should have said yes, but maybe there were other factors. But I'm just thinking that you might want to see your mother's parents on Thanksgiving. I don't know them extremely well, but your mother was a really lovely, sweet person, and they raised her."

"Maybe they're not as nice as her."

"Maybe they're not, and maybe they are. It must have been devastating for them when your mother died. Why not try to see them this once? I wish I could have known my grandparents." She tugs on my ear. "Okay?"

I squirm. "But I like just chilling on Thanksgiving."

"Okay, I don't want to push you."

I sit still, staring down at my hands in my lap. And, I don't know, I feel like digging in my heels. So I say, "Thanks for the ride, Aunt Mo. You're the greatest."

She pulls me over and holds me to her, then nuzzles her nose in my hair and says, "Oooooh, you're such a little cutie." Great. And embarrassing.

Sinbad does his usual crazy dance when I get home. After lunging into me a few times, he settles down and sniffs at the bag of In-N-Out. Dad's having his poker game in the living room. I think about eating on the couch, 'cause I like listening to cops talk, but somehow now that Sinbad's sick, I'd rather spend all my home time alone with him. So I go into my room to sit on the floor and eat. First I close my eyes for a second and give my head a quick shake. I know it's hockey, but whenever I get clocked, I always need to mentally reset. I truly hate getting laid out, back on the ice, trying to breathe.

Sometimes in a game I'll be playing great, and then I suddenly think about getting hurt, and I start to play worse, not aggressively enough. Most of the players aren't like that, but some of us secretly are. I mean, we all act like it's a secret, but we know some players get a little intimidated out there sometimes. I never used to be like that, so I hope this is just temporary.

Sinbad's nosing at the bag, so I hand him a piece of lettuce. His teeth come down hard on my fingers. "Ow!" But I give him more, with a piece of meat this time. When we're done, I write down what I've eaten for dinner, for Coach Dusan's food report. So far today I've had four bowls of whole milk with no-added-sugar cereal, two bowls of whole-milk yogurt with bananas, seven glasses of water, three apples with a ton of sugar-free peanut butter, plus dinner. More than three thousand calories.

Dad and his poker buddies are talking super loud, laughing about a mouth beef one of them got. A mouth beef is when a member of the public complains that you were rude to them. Mouth beefs go into your permanent record, even if you're exonerated, so too many of them can influence promotions.

I hop onto my bed over and over thirty times, then do thirty push-ups. Then that's it. It isn't as much as Coach Dusan wants, but Dad, Sinbad, and I jogged in the morning and physically I've had it for the day. Note the word "physically." Mentally, I've got work to do. I open up the dreaded playbook and randomly see page 57, near where the diagrams of plays start. I look at the squiggly lines and straight lines, at the red arrows and blue arrows, at the purple circles and the red circles and the triangles. "'For example, if the L forward has the puck, the forward on that side shall be in the (red dotted) shooting lane of the L defense while making sure a pass can't go through the box to the high slot forward.'" Does that make sense? Then I laugh out loud and close the book. 'Cause it doesn't make sense, and it's not gonna make sense, I realize, without Dad finding film that relates to it. Realizing that liberates me for the rest of the night. "We're free!" I say to Sinbad. "Going for a walk," I call to Dad, and Sinbad and I go out into the warm Canyon Country air, just like we have a thousand times before. Maybe more like two thousand. Not sure—you do the math, it's not my thing.

CHAPTER 31

THE TEAM HAS two assistant coaches. Coach Kyle is ten feet tall and makes a lot of jokes and encourages everyone to work hard, but he never yells. He'll just be like, "Come on, Conor, you can do better than that!" He cracks jokes to you after you get yelled at by Coach Dusan, to balance things out. Coach Brendan is the most serious person I've ever met. If you mess up, he leans forward and looks at you super intensely as he explains what you should have done. So like the actual mistake might have taken less than three seconds, but he'll spend five minutes explaining it. Everybody else will be on to a new drill, but he'll still be explaining to you. But he's cool, I like him.

When we mess up on a drill once, Coach Dusan corrects us like we're his own sons, but by maybe the third time we mess up on the same drill, his face turns red and he yells really loudly. "WHY ARE YOU STANDING FIVE FEET AWAY WHEN I SAID THREE FEET?!" Sometimes me and the other guys discuss whether he's really mad, or if he's just trying to scare us. We haven't figured that one out. One time I didn't understand something he said about a drill, so I skated up, super scared-like, and asked him about it. He told me really nicely what I was supposed to do, and when I got back in line with the other players, they all surrounded me and asked what he'd said, 'cause they didn't understand the drill either but were afraid to ask. We hate getting yelled at, but at the same time it would be a fate worse than death not to be on this team. Like I said, we're all in awe of him. He's one of those people who go full-out on everything they do. Even when he's just standing there doing nothing, he's doing it really intensely. He's literally the only person I know who I never see standing around looking at his phone.

Early on, the Grizzlies hold testing. Slap-shot velocity, snap-shot velocity, pull-ups, high jump, long jump, forward skating speed, backward skating speed, endurance, and push-ups. I'm pretty shocked when I come in second in forward skating speed and first in slap-shot and snap-shot velocity. When my dad gets the e-mail about it, I literally pound my chest and yell, "Yoooooouuuuwwww!" Dad just chews his gum and says, "It's what I figured." The test scores give me some swagger, and I don't feel like I'm one of the worst ones on the team anymore. I ignore the fact that I came in ninth in push-ups and eleventh in endurance. All that shows is what beasts we've got on this team.

Until school starts up again, life is pretty much perfect. Yeah, some days I got my doubts about my standing on the team, but I get to spend all the time I want on hockey, exercise, and Sinbad. Then school starts after Labor Day, and I can tell Sinbad really misses me every day. He just seems more depressed. I take Mr. Falco's writing class again—we have a couple of special programs and teachers that kids in sixth through eighth can take once a week if they want. I just kind of drift through the rest of school all day, and then perk up for his class. He picks up right where he left off, riffing on family this and family that. He's full of energy, striding back and forth in front of the room. He apologizes, 'cause he never sent us our stories over the summer. Says he had a family emergency. But he hands me my story first thing.

It says, *You need to write more about cops killing people unjustifiably.* That's all it says. I take the paper, immediately crumple it up, and put it in my backpack. He said it was supposed to be a *family* story, not a *political* story. I feel anger rising up in me, but I just walk out. He calls after me, but I don't turn around. I sit on the curb outside until the bell rings to end school.

Some kids gather, a couple of them drinking sodas as they wait for their parents. Coach Dusan practically thinks soda should be illegal. Dad only allows me to drink it on three holidays: Christmas, Thanksgiving, and the Fourth of July. I always pour it over ice and savor it like I have since I was seven years old and had my first can one Christmas.

When our old Volvo pulls up, I hop in. As soon as I see my dad, I feel like I have to protect him from the world, even though he's twice as big and strong as me.

"How was your first day at school?" he asks.

"You know" is all I say.

"Yeah. But try hard anyway, okay?"

"I did."

"Great!"

I think about how he's seemed better since he took off those two weeks. I ask, "So how was your day?"

"Aw, man!" he exclaims. He pulls slowly into traffic. "Paperwork. A woman refused to give me her driver's license, so it took four hours to deal with her."

"How did you find out who she was?"

"We finally had to arrest her. We gave her an hour, and then we arrested her."

"Your partner was there?"

"I called him over. When things start to go sideways, you'd like someone else there for a witness, backup, whatever you need."

"So you had to put her in handcuffs?"

"Yeah, but then after we cuffed her, she spit at me. We put her in the car kicking and screaming, and then she suddenly got perfectly calm and said she would give me her license."

"So then you took her license and wrote her the ticket?"

"No way, you spit at me, I'm arresting you." Someone runs a stop sign and almost hits another car, but my father's face stays perfectly blank. Usually he comments on stuff like that. Now he just rubs at his nose and looks after the car that ran the sign. And something about the way he's so blank when he's usually so emotional makes me realize that he's not so okay after all, that maybe all that crying has just morphed into something else. So I still gotta protect him. I gotta take care of him. I don't know how, but I gotta.

CHAPTER 32

ON SATURDAYS WE have three hours of practice: an hour of ice, an hour of dryland, and an hour of theory. Before theory one day, Coach gives us a speech about the kind of effort he expects. Any perceived lack of effort will result in benching during games. At every level, he says, there will always be someone to replace you if you don't give full effort.

"How many of you want to make it to the NHL?" he asks.

All our hands shoot up.

"That's what I thought," he says.

He talks about sacrificing your body to guard the

slot—the slot's the area in front of the goal. To do that, you need to be diligently working on your dryland muscle work. Otherwise your opponent will simply push you out of the way.

"How many of you have been working on your dryland this summer?"

We all raise our hands.

"Don't lie, because I saw some of your test results," he says. "Most of you did great, but not every single one of you." Nobody puts their hand down.

Then we dress for the ice and begin doing drills. Coach Dusan skates up to me. "Great skating, Conor. Didn't I see you with Ivan one day?"

"Yeah, I just started up with him again," I say eagerly. We all love it when he pays attention to us.

"Good, you doing your push-ups? You're going to need a strong upper body once you advance to bantams next year. I want you to start doing more push-ups. Let's try to get you up to fifty before the end of the season. In fact, start right now. Do fifty." He gives my helmet a couple of almost affectionate thumps, then moves on to talk to Ryan.

I'm glad he talked to me, but I kind of want to

laugh out loud too, 'cause I know exactly how many true push-ups I can do: thirty-three. I manage thirty-five! For a second I think he's glancing my way, though, so I make a big effort to do another. He shouts, "You call that a push-up, Conor?" But he says it like he thinks I'm funny, and then he moves on.

After talking briefly to us individually, Coach Dusan starts the drills. You can feel his eyes boring into you when you skate. It takes a while for me to get used to that, so that I'm focusing on what I'm supposed to be doing instead of focusing on him staring at me. When we mess up, he keeps telling us to act like professionals. "Come on!" he'll yell out. "Is that the way a professional skates?" I'm pretty sure he doesn't even realize we're only eleven and twelve years old.

We're all resigned to getting yelled at. That is, we're resigned and kind of terrified at the same time. Like I've said, almost all my coaches have yelled a lot, but for some reason Coach Dusan's yelling shakes you up more. Like Dad said before, "appropriate fear" is key. It only gets more intense each year, Dad says. He also says most kids quit hockey by bantam, and then a bunch more quit after bantam. There are more injuries in bantam, due to the checking, so that's one reason kids drop out. And the kids who quit aren't only the ones who aren't good enough—some real good players quit as well. Jae-won and I make a pact that we're going to see this thing through to at least eighteen and reevaluate then if we have to.

CHAPTER 33

IN SEPTEMBER WE play four preseason games and win them all. We win by 10–1, 9–3, 13–7, and 6–0. That gets the coaches thinking we might be hockey gods, and Coach Dusan says we should aim high— for the CAHA championship. California Amateur Hockey Association. Every month we have what are called CAHA weekends, which is where you play several other teams, sometimes from Northern California. With preseason games, scrimmages, regular season games, Minnesota and Chicago tournaments, and CAHA weekends, we'll end up playing at least fifty games this season, more if we make the play-offs. But the CAHA games are the only ones that count in the standings.

My speed has gotten me onto the first line for a couple of games. Coach says the lines are temporary while he fiddles around, but my dad is so proud he's been telling total strangers. Like he told a waitress, "He'll take five tacos. He needs a lot of food because he plays first line on a AAA hockey team."

And I have to admit, it's all I can think about. I can't believe I'm AAA this year. I feel like I just made the NHL. Sitting in school is pure torture. Every season the coaches talk about how your GPA is the most important thing in your life. So there's that. But even before I got serious about hockey, I was a below-average student. I used to try hard, but when I still got Cs, I started slacking off a bit. And I still got Cs, except for that one F I got in social studies. Teachers don't like to give out Ds and Fs unless you have a bad attitude in class. All that stuff literally everyone tells parents about GPA being so important is kind of offensive to kids like me, who just can't get good grades even if we try. Teachers think if you're not heading for college, you're not being the best you can be. They always say stuff like that. That's an insult to people like my dad, and sometimes it makes me mad . . . but how did I get on this?

Anyway, school marches on, and I tolerate it. I'm an average, not-special person to my teachers. And you know what? I don't care.

I don't have time to wash cars anymore, but I haven't seen Mr. Reynolds for weeks, so one Sunday I take Sinbad down there just to see what's up. It's about ten in the morning when I knock on his door. I wait for five minutes, 'cause you never know how long it'll take. And sure enough, he finally answers the door. "Conor MacRae!"

"Hi, Mr. Reynolds. Just seeing if you need me to do anything."

"You know what? I'm a little short on cash right now."

"You don't have to pay me!"

He seems annoyed, so I'm just about to tell him forget it when he says, "Oh, all right, come in."

I follow him through the house to the kitchen. It's a mind-bending mess! Gunk encrusted all over the stove, dirty dishes everywhere, and the floor gray with dirt. I think the floor's actually supposed to be white. I try not to show how surprised I am.

"Maybe you could clean up in here," he says. "But I can't pay you this week."

"You don't have to pay me," I say again.

He gestures toward the room. "There you go." Then he leaves.

It's hard to know where to start. I text Dad: *Don't think I can go jogging today. I might be helping Mr. Reynolds for . . .* I think about it, then type in *a few hours.*

On the table are three different bowls partly filled with soup. A half-eaten can of tuna. Three black bananas. A pot with some dried oatmeal. I don't know why, but for a minute I can't get started. I stand there in the middle of all that mess and don't even think. Sinbad nudges me and I look down. "It's a crazy world" is the only thing I can think of to say to him. I know he understands, 'cause he understands everything. And a feeling wells up in me like, *What are we all doing here in this world?* Like seriously, what? Shouldn't this man's niece be here sometimes, cleaning up for him? But she's apparently not, so it's down to me: I get to work.

At my house, we always start with washing dishes before we get to cleaning counters, the floor, the stovetop, etc. There's hardly any dishwashing soap left, but I find some clothes detergent, so I use that. I start soaking all the pots and dishes that need it, then wash and dry the ones that don't. When I open the cabinets to put stuff away, they're all empty—he seems to be using every single dish and pot he owns. So I decide where to put everything, then do the dishes that have been soaking. He actually doesn't have *that* many dishes, so the whole operation takes just a little over an hour. I realize I should have been soaking the stove and start that now, though I'm not optimistic that the stove can be cleaned, ever, no matter how much it soaks.

I sweep the floor and feel pretty shocked over how much dirt, dust, and food bits there are. Mop the floor—turns out it's off-white with flecks of gold. Almost two hours gone; I turn to the stove. No matter how much I scrub, there are places where the gunk just won't come off. I get really involved in one corner, and after I get it clean, the stove looks imbalanced, everything a mess except for that corner.

Hour three. The stove is passable, and Dad has texted me that it's time to come home and eat. So I walk into the hallway calling, "Mr. Reynolds?" He doesn't answer, and I find him in a bedroom, snoring. The bedroom isn't that messy, which kind of relieves me.

Sinbad and I return home, him to dog food with watercress and me to boiled chicken.

"So what was up at Mr. Reynolds's house?" Dad asks.

"I cleaned up his kitchen. I'm not quite done. It was the biggest, dirtiest mess I ever saw."

Dad nods and devours his chicken. Me too. Every meal, we always eat like we're starving, just 'cause we usually are. He cleans up the kitchen to give me a break.

Sinbad seems to feel blah, so I don't take him out again. He had chemo a few days ago, and while he hasn't been awful since then, he's definitely been low energy today. And yet Dr. Pierre keeps saying he's doing well, so I don't know what to think. I wonder if

I'm just being too sensitive to how he feels. I pet him for half an hour, concentrating the whole time on the petting.

So there I am, feeling sad, and all of a sudden Sinbad jumps up and wags his tail! "Are you okay?" I ask, surprised.

He drops his jaw in a smile and slaps his two front paws on the floor, what he does when he wants a walk. "So you were just tired?" I ask.

He slaps his paws on the floor again, so I get up and leash him. "I'm going to take Sinbad for a walk!" I call to my dad. I hear him on the phone talking angrily, so I figure he's speaking to Jenny. At the same time, I don't get why they would be fighting now. I mean, it's been ten or eleven months since she left. But there was a kid at school who said divorce goes on forever sometimes. His mom lost half her hair when she was going through divorce. But when does it end then? Sinbad jumps up, laying his paws on my shoulders, and I try to forget the adult world—I'd rather be in the dog world! But I still feel my dad's argument there, under the surface in my brain.

I bring a flashlight, and we move down the street.

The beam bounces off a cat's eyes in the distance, but Sinbad doesn't notice—he's never had the greatest eyesight. Hope that cat gets inside—you know the coyotes are out. Nighttime's pretty cool in Canyon Country. All of a sudden it seems like you can hear better than you can in the day. And the moon hangs over the hills like it's right there, ten miles away or something.

We take our usual route, down the street and— since he seems to be feeling well—up the path at the hill. It's still kind of spooky since the fire, the way some of the branches still don't have leaves. But there's a *lot* of new growth. At the top, I turn off the light, sit down, and let Sinbad sniff, but I keep him on the leash so he doesn't run off after an animal in the dark. The street below is quiet. I see a huge TV going in a couple of houses. Most of my friends don't watch TV. We're more into our computers or iPads and video games. For a while everybody on last year's team watched *The Walking Dead*, but then we stopped all at once. Jae-won calls it the mind hive when we all do the same thing at the same time.

Sinbad doesn't explore, just lies down, and I think

maybe it was a mistake to bring him up here. Then he lays his head down and closes his eyes, and I know it was a mistake. It just makes me feel like I'm having trouble breathing, like when you get accidentally hit in a hockey game.

I hear a small noise and turn on the light, spotting what looks like a tarantula. Usually they come out when there's been rain, 'cause they love damp conditions. It's bone dry, but there it is anyway. They're not really dangerous to humans, they just look scary. I got nothing against tarantulas. Sinbad spots it and kind of sniffs at the air, but then he's not really interested and closes his eyes again. I don't know what comes over me, but I suddenly stand up and stomp on the tarantula about five times as hard as I can. Afterward I just stand there with my eyes closed. I say, "I'm sorry," out loud. "But I just don't understand why Sinbad has to be sick," I say, opening my eyes and looking up. I vow to double down on my praying. I vow to work harder. I vow to rescue at least twenty dogs when I'm grown up. But I just don't know if anybody's listening to me.

CHAPTER 34

REGULAR SEASON STARTS in October. I start walking Sinbad in the neighborhood instead of up any hills. And the weather cools off, which he seems to like. I'm away a lot for school and hockey, and when I'm home, he's become quite clingy, like he always wants to be touching me. He even scratches at the door when I'm in the bathroom. Then it's finally Saturday, and we have a game Sunday morning. I say some prayers, and I'm in bed by eight.

When the alarm goes off at four a.m., I shoot out of bed and head right to the kitchen to start Dad's coffee. He's still asleep, I guess, 'cause the house is totally quiet. Sinbad doesn't get up either, but I dump a cup of kibble into his bowl. I eat a lot of oatmeal with whole milk and a banana. No sugar. That's my go-to breakfast on game days. Then in the car I'll have a whole-milk yogurt. I force myself not to eat too quickly, but it's hard 'cause I just want to eat and get to the game. The beginning of the regular season always makes me think of the year before, and the year before that, and so on. I mean, I'm only twelve, and here I am doing this memories thing like my grandparents. On the refrigerator, Dad keeps pictures of me in my uniform from every year I played. When I take my bowl back to the kitchen, I pause at the pictures. My hair is down to my shoulders in the first two.

My heart speeds up. Even though I keep saying I want to play in the NHL someday, my real-world goal has always been AAA. I smile and feel really proud. I wonder if I'll be on the first line today. Coach says he doesn't even know who's starting. It'll be a game-time decision.

I wash my bowl and double-check my bag, which I packed last night. I can't find my mouth guard, so I unpack everything. There it is on the bottom of the bag. I repack. I take two big breaths. Then I smile. I love games. I love them!

Dad comes sleepily into the dining room. "What did you eat?" he asks.

"Oatmeal and banana."

He gulps down a banana, pours all the coffee into his big thermos, and we're off.

The game's in Riverside, an hour and a half away. Coach Dusan has told us to get there seventy-five minutes early for every game so we can do some light dryland exercises and still have time to get dressed without a big rush.

When we get to the rink, some of the guys are already standing around in the parking lot. I find out what locker room we're in and rush inside to dump my bag, then join the others. We run a couple of times around the far end of the parking lot, then do some stretching. The sun hasn't risen yet as we stretch on the asphalt. We close our eyes and visualize skating, scoring, winning.

Finally it's time to get dressed. In the locker room, Jeffrey, the second goalie, acts like an idiot per usual. He's telling everyone on D that they better not screw up, 'cause he shouldn't have to cover for our mistakes. He's accusing us of not trying hard enough, and we haven't even done anything yet. When there's an annoying guy on your team, you just have to try to ignore him. Two parents are supposed to keep an eye on the locker room, but they're not around. I stand up and start walking out, and suddenly Jeffrey is right in my face, saying, "You better not screw up." I push him out of the way, 'cause you're allowed when someone's acting like a jerk. Jae-won, Lucas, and I walk out together and sit on the away bench. The warm-up buzzer sounds, and we all skate around carrying a puck. I look over at the opposite team. A couple of them are as big as bantams, but they look slow for this level.

The buzzer sounds again, and Jesus cries out, "One-two-three!"

"GRIZZLIES!"

"One-two-three!"

"GRIZZLIES!"

"Who's gonna win?!"

"GRIZZLIES!"

Matt gets the start, and I can see Jeffrey is upset,

even though he knows he's second goalie. Coach doesn't send me out. I'm disappointed, but I get over it quick. He sends out five guys from his AAA team last year.

Jesus moves across the ice so fast, it's like he's improved by 50 percent since last week. All you can do is admire a guy like that. No jealousy! He loses the puck in a crowd, but Aidan 1 swoops in and picks it off, flicking it back to Jesus, who shoots and misses.

This is my first regular game with Coach Dusan, and he's talking constantly. "Oh, that's great, take a shot lying on the ice. What?! You have got to be kidding me. That's offside! What?! What happened to the playbook? Come on, skate. SKATE, Aidan!" Then forty-five seconds later, I'm out there—second line, not too shabby.

We're in our offensive zone, but Avery loses the puck, so we're on a back-check. I knock a guy kind of hard against the boards, but nobody blows a whistle, so I go after the puck, hacking my stick at his until the puck is loose. I scoop it up and push off hard on my skates.

Then I almost lose the puck for no rational

reason. So I lower my head to get situated, and the next thing I know I'm flying through the air. I land on my head and bang my shoulder to the ice before the rest of me follows. Then I'm in a daze, but I kind of see Jae-won pushing the kid I think hit me. The refs skate in to break it up. I vaguely think to myself that I'm not hurting. But I don't want to get up. I'm really comfortable just lying there. I wonder what's going on in the game. Then Coach Kyle is there, bending over me. "How are you doing?" he asks, and my head clears a bit.

"I'm okay," I answer.

"Do you want to get up?"

"Not really."

Lucas is kneeling beside me, resting his hand on my shoulder. I lie there for a moment while he kneels, the area between his eyes all crinkled up with worry. I become aware that I hurt after all: my shoulder aches. My head doesn't hurt, but it's cloudy.

"I shouldn't have lowered my head," I say, suddenly realizing it.

"You hurting?"

"I don't think so. Is the guy a jerk?"

"I don't think he hit you on purpose," Lucas says. "It looked like he was going for the puck. I think he's sorry. He's in the penalty box. So's Jae-won."

"How's your breathing?" Coach Kyle asks. He looks so serious you'd think I was dying.

"It's kind of hard to breathe," I say.

"Don't worry about it right now. You want to get up?"

So he holds me as I push myself to my feet, and we walk to the bench together. I hear all the players hitting their sticks on the ice and the boards for me. The people in the stands are cheering. Coach Dusan puts his arm around me and helps me to the bench. Then I lean over and throw up.

"I'll get your dad," Coach Kyle says, and he rushes off.

I know that throwing up after a hit like that is a sign that you have a concussion. All the other players leap up while Coach Dusan lays me down on the bench. It seems like only a minute has passed before Dad is leaning over me.

"I called 911," he says. "Just relax."

It's really embarrassing, but I practically shout out, "I don't want to die!"

"You're not going to die," Dad and all three coaches say at the same time. I can hear that the game is continuing. Players are yelling for the puck, and skates are digging into the ice.

I want to keep talking, but at the same time I want to take a nap. In fact, the more I think about it, the better a nap sounds. Like maybe a ten-day nap. That sounds beautiful. I close my eyes, which feels great. Maybe I'm awake, and maybe I'm not. Not sure. But the next thing I know, Dad says, "Wake up, you need to be cleared by a doctor before you sleep." So I force my eyes open until the paramedic arrives.

"Can you hear me?" the guy asks.

For some reason that makes me shoot up so that I'm sitting. Then I barf again. Oatmeal. "Just lie back," the paramedic says.

The two paramedics lift me off the bench and set me on a gurney. As I'm being wheeled out, I wonder idly who's going to clean up the floor where I barfed. My shoulder still hurts, but not a lot, so I think that's okay, nothing broken. I'm more worried about my head. I can't think right. It's like my head is filled with jelly instead of a brain.

As they set me in the ambulance, I open my eyes. "Dad?" I say.

"Right here," he answers.

"Just checking."

He sits there with his hand holding mine. I don't think I've held my dad's hand since I was about seven, but it feels good now. I want to say I quit hockey, but then I think maybe that's premature. I'll see how I feel tomorrow. Right this second, though, I want to quit hockey. It's not worth it. It's just a game, and my brain is, well, it's my brain. It's more important than a game, isn't it? I curse myself for not keeping my head up. The hardest thing about sports is that sometimes things are just plain your fault, your responsibility.

At the hospital, they check my eyes and reflexes, plus ask me a lot of questions. They decide to keep me overnight 'cause I threw up twice. And they're not sure if I lost consciousness. I close my eyes to sleep, thinking my dad will take care of everything.

Sure enough, he does. Because the next time I open my eyes, I'm lying in a hospital bed hooked up

to an IV. That stinks! Dad is sitting next to me reading a golf magazine, even though he doesn't golf.

"Seriously? I need an IV?" I ask.

Dad leaps up. "You okay?"

"Yeah, I'm fine. Do I have to have this thing stuck
in me?"

"Just overnight for observation. And no video
games, computer, or reading when we get home. No
exercise, either. The doctors say you need to rest your
brain and body *both*."

"Who's taking care of Sinbad?" I sit up.

"Lie down. The neighbor's got him."

"Which neighbor?" Some of them are nicer than
others.

"Jack and Susan. Don't worry, they love dogs."

"Then why don't they have any?" I ask reason-
ably, even though they *are* some of the nice ones.

"They like to travel."

"Are they going to make him sleep outside?"

"I didn't ask. Sinbad is going to be fine. This is
your time to relax. In fact, it's important for you to
relax now."

"But Dad, he has cancer."

"He's doing well on his treatment, and he's going to be fine for one night."

"He's not doing *that* well. Can you go home and stay with him?"

"No."

"Dad, please!"

"No. Don't ask again."

"Can you call and ask them to keep him inside their house? He won't understand being put outside." He's never been put outside since I got him. He goes in and out as he pleases. "Do you think it's better for them just to feed him and let him sleep in my room?"

"Is that what you want?"

"Yeah. No. I don't know. What do you think?"

"Actually, that might be best."

So he calls them up and asks if they can feed him but leave him at home. We always leave the back door open, so they'll have no problem getting in. "Now relax," he tells me.

I think about relaxing. That's boring. "What am I supposed to do?"

"You can lie in bed and watch TV. But it's got to

be something quiet—the doctor doesn't want your brain stimulated."

"What time is it?"

"Three p.m."

Three o'clock! Wow, I was really out of it. "Maybe I was sleepy from getting up so early," I say to my dad. I concentrate on how I feel, and I still feel fine.

"Maybe."

"I feel fine. Can't I go home? Sinbad needs me, Dad."

But Dad is worried. That is, he's not frowning or anything, but somehow I can tell how worried he is. "They need to observe you for tonight, because you may have been unconscious. So no, you can't go home."

I become aware that a headache is coming on, completely out of the blue, and I think about that. Minutes pass, and it's still there. "I have a headache."

He calls the nurse, who gives me some kind of pill.

I've only been awake for twenty minutes, and already I'm bored crazy. I'm even more bored thinking about no hockey. Hockey is the whole reason I live. So I ask, "Dad? Seriously? No exercise? For how long?"

"Depends. It could be three weeks, but today some doctors like to get you moving again sooner. In the pros, you'd be back in a week. But you're not in the pros. We'll take it slow."

Three weeks in the middle of the season? That's just nuts. "But Dad, AAA is practically the pros."

Even I know that's a pretty ridiculous thing to say, and he doesn't bother to answer.

"How long with no computer?"

"Same, but they're not sure." I groan. I decide immediately that I'm going to be using my phone instead when Dad's not around.

I see the remote and turn on the television. After switching the channels around, I choose what looks like a horror flick.

"Too stimulating," Dad says. "Try something else."

I end up on a sitcom rerun, even though I never watch sitcoms. I don't understand why people think they're funny. Like now, a character makes what seems to be a joke, and the audience laughs. And I totally don't get the joke. If Dad wants a lack of stimulation, this is perfect. But he laughs, like he gets it.

"Maybe we could get you started on golf," he says suddenly. "That's a nice, safe sport."

And even though earlier I'd thought of quitting hockey, I practically yelp, "I don't want to play golf! Me?! Golf? I'm a hockey player!" I pause. "It's in my blood!"

"There's no such thing." Dad laughs. "I taught you to like hockey, it's not in your blood."

"But you're the one who told me once that it was in my blood," I argue.

He pauses. "Did I say that?" He pauses again. "Oh yeah, I guess I did." He doesn't say more, returning instead to his magazine.

I watch TV for hours, but Dad will only let me watch the super-boring stuff. I fall asleep. When I wake up, and the doctor is leaning over me. Lately everybody's leaning over me. And it's morning! "How's it going, Conor? Did you eat breakfast?"

"He slept through it," Dad tells him. I look over to where he's slumped in a recliner and wonder if that's where he slept.

"Can you sit up?" says the doc.

I sit up.

"How does that feel?"

"Fine. Normal," I say. "But I'm already bored."

"No headache?"

"No."

He nods.

He asks me a few more questions, then talks to Dad about me not exercising or doing anything mentally stimulating, including going to school. Yay! He says research is showing that omega-3 fish oil *may* reduce brain trauma, so why not try it? They talk for a few minutes more, and then the doctor leaves.

Since I don't have street clothes, I put on my hockey jersey over my compression pants. The hospital makes me wear pointy green foam slippers on my feet. I probably look like some kind of hockey elf. Dad's carrying my skates and the rest of my hockey gear. Someone from Transportation takes me out in a wheelchair while Dad walks along in his wrinkly clothes. I think about my expensive hockey bag and $259 stick—even though, like I said, it's lost its pop, it would be expensive to replace. "What about my hockey bag and stick?"

"Jae-won's got your stuff," Dad says. "I'll pick it up eventually."

"Eventually" sounds like about a hundred years. But I guess if I have three weeks, it might as well be a hundred years. Three weeks without hockey.

In the car I ask, "Who won the game?"

"We did."

Yes, I think. But then I think about the next few weeks, and a feeling of frustration washes over me, like I don't understand why I had to get hurt. Why me? Other guys lower their heads and lose focus, and they don't end up with concussions.

So then I think, *Is this just the way it is?* Good stuff happens, bad stuff happens, and you just gotta deal with all of it. And I think about how the whole team was at a fancy hamburger restaurant after a game once, 'cause one of the rich parents took everyone there after a playoff win, since the win happened on his son's birthday. There was a bar, and an old guy was sitting by himself drinking. Dad said that the guy was a really famous actor once, but I had never heard of him. You could just feel how sad and lonely and completely depressed he was. My grandparents on my dad's side are the opposite—they just seem so happy. I mean, they're not happy every single second, but like during Christmas, when they first show me the makeshift rink Grandpa put together for me, they're so happy it's like they can hardly stand it. Even Mr. Reynolds, while definitely lonely, doesn't give off total sadness rays like this old actor did. So. Everybody's got their stuff to deal with. I suddenly feel great to be sitting next to Dad. Whatever happened to that old guy, I know my dad will never let that happen to me. He'll live to be a hundred and ten through sheer willpower, just to take care of me. Won't he?

CHAPTER 35

WE GET HOME, and then . . . nothing. Basically, nothing happens for the first week. Dad won't even let me have visitors. But it's weird, 'cause it's like I don't have any will, which I've heard can happen with a concussion. All I really want to do is sloth around. Sinbad seems curious about why I'm constantly slumped on the couch watching TV. He'll stand in front of me just staring for a minute before lying down again. I can feel my muscles turning into spaghetti, but since I've lost my will, I don't even care.

Dad takes three sick days, and then Aunt Mo takes two. They each walk Sinbad twice a day. Sometimes he goes to the door and whines in the evening, but I give him a bone instead.

Finally, after the following Sunday's game, Jae-won and Lucas come by with the Kang family. I'm sitting in the living room watching TV when they arrive.

Mrs. Kang says, "Oh, you look normal! I happy for you! You okay! Except you gain weight!"

"Mo-*om*," says Jae-won.

"He did. He needed it, too skinny before, like all you boy on team."

Lucas high-fives me. "Hey."

"Hey. Did you win?" I ask.

"Nah," says Jae-won.

"What did Coach Dusan do?"

Jae-won rubs his forehead. "He yelled, and his face got red as tomato sauce," Lucas says. "He said, 'What do you think you were doing out there? I demand an answer!' Then nobody answered, and he randomly looked at Daniel and screamed, 'What were you doing out there?!'"

Jae-won pipes up. "And Daniel said, 'I don't know what happened. I couldn't control the puck today.' He started to cry, and Coach Dusan said, 'Okay, stop crying, you're a good kid. You're all good kids. But we got a *lot* to work on.' Then he walked out."

"Wow, glad I wasn't there," I say.

"So what does it feel like getting a concussion?" Lucas asks. "You okay?"

"It's weird, it's like . . ." Then I lose my train of thought before finding it again. "You kind of lose your will. You don't even feel like thinking. Like you just feel like sitting around, not caring much what you're doing. When I first got it, I had a lot of feelings, but the last week, it's like I don't have any feelings."

"Bizarro," Jae-won says. "Glad you're okay, man. You literally flew up in the air. I wanted to kill that kid."

"He didn't mean it," Lucas says quickly. "I don't believe he did. I talked to him in the parking lot afterward, and he felt bad."

"Really?" I say, interested.

"Yeah, I prayed for him. I prayed for you, too."

"Thanks."

"And your dog. I pray for him every night."

"Wow," I say, surprised. "Thank you."

"How's he doing?"

"Honestly, he's doing so-so."

Lucas looks at me seriously. He hasn't sat down yet. "I'll pray harder, man. I slacked off a couple of days because I was so tired."

He's so earnest, and so worried, and I just think his awesomeness level is off the charts. At school sometimes, the kids who are Christian hang around together, and to be honest, most of the other kids totally ignore them.

Jae-won sits on the floor and starts talking softly to Sinbad, but I can't hear what he's saying. Sinbad loves him. Maybe he can tell that Jae-won wants a dog in the worst way. Jae-won's like me—he's got some lonely stuff inside him, but for different reasons. I guess for him it just comes from being poor and super talented and super guilty at the same time. Also, he has a lot of responsibility, more than me, 'cause of his little brothers wanting to spend every minute with him. I'm surprised they're not here now, since they go to all his games, even the early ones. Then I hear them at the door, Mr. Kang calling out, "How is patient?"

The twins run in, followed by Mr. Kang. He's brought three big bags of McDonald's. Even when I have fast food, I don't eat McDonald's, 'cause there's a rumor at school that their hamburgers never spoil. Don't know if it's true, but why take a chance on eating something that's not actually food? Still, to be nice I say, "Thanks, Mr. Kang!" and take a burger out of the bag he opens in front of me. I have to admit the hamburger tastes good. I'll never eat another one again, but it does taste good.

Mr. Kang and the twins stand right in front of me and stare. "You look good!" Mr. Kang says. "Your brain hurt?"

"Not anymore. It did for a short time. But I don't feel like doing anything at all. I've never been like that before."

"So what are you doing then?" asks one of the twins.

"Nothing, just watching TV."

"All the time?"

"Yeah."

"HOLY COW!!" he exclaims, like I've just said the most amazing thing in history.

We all sit around and talk and eat, and then everybody leaves and I watch TV again. It occurs to me that maybe it's the TV watching and not the concussion that has sapped my will. I get a little scared that maybe my will won't come back. What if I'm just stuck like this forever, watching TV all day, not caring about anything??

On Wednesday, Dad takes me to my doctor, who runs some neurological and cognitive tests. He did the same last week, and I scored okay. But Dad knew and I knew that even though my scores seemed okay, they weren't as good as I would normally have scored. My reflexes, for instance, were average, even though I have really good reflexes. Basically, I had to catch this disk attached to a stick. Dad tried it too, just for a test, and then we all discussed it and felt I was slow for me. We do it again this week, and I ace it. I also have to read some cards with numbers on them, and I do better than last week.

The doc is pretty happy, but he wants me to stay out of hockey for a full three weeks, 'cause why take any chances?

He does make me go to school on Thursday, but I don't get any homework—yay! Nobody comes over after the next game, since it's all the way in Palm Springs, which is two and a half hours from Canyon Country. Turns out they win that game, and lose the next. So we're 2–2. Jae-won and Lucas come by again and talk about how mad Coach Dusan was after the loss. The final score was 7–1, which pretty much means the defense, offense, and goalie all fell apart. Jae-won and Lucas are really glum.

"He made us run around the parking lot in our gear for half an hour. All the parents from the other team were watching us."

"Wow," I say. "Glad I wasn't there!"

Even the twins are glum, like they lost too. Mr. and Mrs. Kang try to keep it cheerful, passing out an extremely spicy meal that Mrs. Kang prepared for us earlier. My mouth burns, and I can tell Lucas's does too. But the Kangs eat like it's nothing. Dad loves spicy food, so he's all good. I'm surprised both Mr. and Mrs. Kang stick around again, 'cause they're usually super busy. Mr. Kang works a lot when Jae-won's not doing hockey, even on weekends. I realize he's just sticking around for me, 'cause I'm Jae-won's best friend and I got hurt. I figure I'll buy them a house too, in the unlikely event that I make it and Jae-won doesn't.

We watch the movie about a tsunami that I've already seen, 'cause though I haven't been cleared for hockey, I *have* been cleared to watch anything I want on TV. When the movie's over and everyone leaves, I go for a short walk with Sinbad. I'm allowed to walk around all I want, just not do anything where I might hit my head.

My will has come back a lot, but not completely. Plus, I've gotten so used to watching TV that I kind of miss it when I slowly stop watching over the rest of the week. But I don't want to get into that, 'cause I just don't have time. Then the doctor clears me completely the Wednesday before our next game. I work out that night, and by morning my muscles are sore.

We have practice Thursday, and when I walk into the locker room, several guys say, "Conor, how's your head?"

"It's okay now. The doctor says I'm back to normal."

"You're lucky you missed our last game. Coach Dusan about killed us," says Avery.

"I heard."

"He said, 'You call yourself AAA?! You're not AAA, you're barely even AA!'"

"But he wasn't mad because we lost, he was mad because we didn't give full effort," Lucas explains. "And we lost focus."

Most of us walk out together. The coaches approach me and say, "How's your head?"

"The doctor says it's fine."

"Great, we need all the help we can get," Coach Dusan says. Then he whistles, and everyone skates as fast as they can to him. He leans over and picks up a puck. "We're starting at square one. This is a hockey puck." He holds up his stick and says, "This is a stick. You hit the puck with the stick. The purpose of hockey is to hit the puck into the net. The only way to do that consistently is through teamwork." He's talking quietly and slowly, then suddenly raises his voice to a shout. "IS THERE ANYONE WHO DOESN'T KNOW WHAT TEAMWORK IS? ANDREW, DO YOU KNOW WHAT TEAMWORK IS?"

"It's when everybody works together!"

"THEN WHY DIDN'T YOU PASS THE PUCK SUNDAY?"

Andrew pauses, starts to speak, pauses, then goes for it. "I forget sometimes. I got selfish."

Coach Dusan seems to like that answer. "I DON'T EVER WANT TO SEE ANYONE BE SELFISH AGAIN! PASS THE FREAKING PUCK!" He nods and says in a normal voice, "Two hard laps around the rink, then we'll do ladders."

He works us hard. I'm out of shape and have to stop twice, looking over both times to see if Coach is going to yell at me. But then when practice is over, he fist-bumps me and says, "Good job, Conor."

In the locker room I become aware of the smell. I've heard a couple of the parents complain about what the locker rooms and the backs of their cars smell like 'cause of all the sweaty gear. But I love the smell of these locker rooms. It's like when I haven't done a good job of washing Sinbad's paws. I actually love the way they smell. I love all these real-life scents. Sometimes I don't give him a bath, 'cause I like the way he smells. And the locker room, it's just really real. A couple of the teachers at school, they don't get sports. They would be happy to see sports wiped off the face of the earth. The smells, the banging around, the speed, the effort, the sweat. The intense coaches. All wiped away.

CHAPTER 36

THE NEXT DAY we take Sinbad to his biweekly appointment. He's been doing great this week! His last chemo, he didn't even seem to notice. Dr. Pierre had said at one visit that a lot of patients actually do feel better during treatment, but that hasn't been the case with Sinbad. I can tell he's not the way he used to be, though this week he seems like 95 percent.

In the waiting room, Dad's on his phone playing spades. I'm kind of surprised—we're here all the time, but today there's something about the lighting that makes me realize he's lost weight in his face. I think back. He seems to be eating the same as usual, but I don't know what he eats at work. He looks thin. But I feel someone's eyes on me and look up.

A woman with a German shepherd sits across the room. She makes me uncomfortable the way she's staring at me. I'm still really aware of my head, even though I'm not having headaches anymore. I know it's my imagination, but it seems like the staring makes my head hurt.

"His face looks fine," she says to me.

What? It's like she read my mind!

"You can tell by their face how they're doing, just like with humans."

"Oh," I say, and realize that she's talking about Sinbad, not my dad. Then I notice that even under all that hair, her dog's face looks pinched and old.

She sees me studying her dog and says, "She's only four. How old is yours?"

"Maybe six, we're not sure."

"Heart dog?"

"I'm sorry?" I ask.

"Heart dog. That's a once-in-a-lifetime soul-mate dog."

"Yeah, he's my soul mate," I answer. "He bit me

once when we first got him, but it wasn't hard, and I didn't give up on him."

She nods, tears falling. "Greta is my heart dog. I've had about a dozen dogs in my life, but none like this."

I'm not sure what to say. I try, "I'm sorry," but I'm not positive that's what I should have said.

She starts crying too hard to answer, and then we get called in to our appointment.

The tech weighs Sinbad—ninety-two pounds—and takes his temperature.

So, every time we go to the oncologist, the doctor looks at Sinbad's weight and examines him, takes his blood, and then they give him the exact amount of chemo that he needs. The doctor is always happy with how he's doing, even when I tell her he's not doing so well.

Today Dr. Pierre enters with a smile. She gives me a quick hug, shakes Dad's hand, then leans over and kisses Sinbad's nose. I like how she's sincere. I've been to a couple of vets who act like they love your dog, but you can tell they're just acting. She feels Sinbad's leg, then all over his body. "He's doing great—he's just doing fantastic! We couldn't ask for more. This is quite literally the best we could have hoped for."

I drop to my knees and hug Sinbad hard. "You're kind of all better!" I look at Dr. Pierre. "Right?"

But Dr. Pierre says, "As I think I told you early on, remission isn't exactly the same as being all better for dogs. In humans, sometimes we can say they're cured. But for dogs, there is no cure." She speaks gently, touches my arm when she sees I'm about to cry. "But he's doing fantastic, basically as well as possible.

"Still, as I told you earlier, we need to continue the full six months of treatment. That's how we do it here, just to make absolutely sure we've destroyed all the cancer cells. But he's doing great!"

"So how long do *you* think he'll be in remission? Five years?"

She pauses. "It's possible, but . . . well, it's possible."

I think hard. "But probably shorter?"

She tilts her head. Frowns. Nods. "Unfortunately, that's true. But he's done fantastic. He's in remission.

Some dogs never go into remission at all. We really don't have exact numbers, unfortunately. Patients always want to know exactly what to expect, but we just can't tell them that."

Dad clears his throat. "So even though he's been in remission for a while, the cost will still be the same as you originally told us, somewhere around seven thousand?"

"Yes, I'm afraid so," Dr. Pierre says.

"All right." He rubs his temples hard. Nobody speaks for a full minute.

We sit in the waiting room while Sinbad gets his chemo. Afterward, like the doctor does every visit, she reminds me, "Make sure you use gloves when you handle the pills."

"I will," I say. "Thank you, Dr. Pierre."

We leave the building and get into the car. Before Dad starts the car, I say, "I'm sorry it costs so much. But don't you think he's worth it, Dad? Don't you?"

"Yeah, yeah, of course I do." He half smiles at me and rubs my head gently. "He's worth any amount, actually."

I know it's a lot of money, but at the same time I

don't have a real clear idea of how much exactly seven thousand dollars is. "So is that an incredible amount of money?" I ask. "Or sort of a lot? Which is it?"

"Ah, somewhere in between maybe," Dad replies. "Can you open up a stick of gum for me?"

I give him gum, then take out my phone and work the calculator. Seven thousand dollars divided by twelve dollars I get for each car wash equals 583.33. If I do an average of three a week, which is the max I'll probably have time for year-round, I can pay for Sinbad's treatment in 3.74 years. *Huh.* I'll be a midget by then. If he's still alive, then it's all good. I think about Dr. Pierre mentioning six months. If the worst happened and he died at six months, and I was still washing cars almost four years later, I wonder if I would become a bitter man. But there's no telling how long Sinbad will live—it could be five years, if I pray a lot. . . . Of course, I don't know if how long matters in terms of how I feel *now*. Now I just feel like I want to spend time with him and soak up his Sinbad-ness for as long as it lasts.

When we reach home, I spot Mr. Reynolds walking slowly back to his house. So I grab Sinbad and catch up with him. "Hi, Mr. Reynolds! Did you want me to finish cleaning up your kitchen?"

"Conor MacRae!" He chuckles. "I think you made it clean enough to last for a few years!"

"Great!" I say, but then think about all the gunk still left on the stove. Dad would have a rare meltdown if I left that kind of gunk on our stove at home. "I can finish with the stove. . . ."

He looks at me suspiciously. "Don't you have grandparents or something?"

"Uh, I do, actually. I'm only friends with my dad's parents, though, not my mom's."

"What?! That's a tragedy! Why aren't you friends with your mom's parents?" His face is suddenly furious. "What's the matter with you? I thought you were a nice boy!"

My mouth falls open, kind of surprised at how angry he looks. Then he ambles off, bitterly muttering, "What's the matter with you?"

I'm still surprised, but I shake off his words so I can take Sinbad for a walk in peace. Afterward I give him his pills with Dad's help, then sit next to him on the bed while he falls asleep. My mind drifts back to

Mr. Reynolds. I start to wonder how clean my mom's parents keep their kitchen. Like do some people just reach a point in life where they don't give a can of beans how much gunk is on their stove? And I think about the way I would know my mom loved me, even if Dad hadn't told me so. Don't ask me how, but I can feel it, even today. I can feel it right now, at this exact moment, if I concentrate.

My mind's a jumble. . . . Sinbad is so still it's scary. So I love Sinbad and he loves me, and my mom loved me, and I still love her. But she's gone, and Sinbad has cancer . . . but he's in remission. So it's all complicated, and it's all a thick jungle in my head. And in my brain I keep seeing Mr. Reynolds's kitchen. Then, just like *that*, the thought pops into my head: my mom would want me to know her parents. 'Cause they raised her, like she would have raised me if she could. 'Cause they're Japanese, and I actually don't know a single Japanese person even though I'm half. 'Cause maybe they're lonely like maybe Mr. Reynolds is lonely. And most especially just 'cause it's the right thing to do. You might not believe it, but there are some cops in the world whose main goal in life is just to do the right thing: That's it.

Even if you don't want to do something, sometimes you just gotta.

CHAPTER 37

OUR GAME SUNDAY is at noon in Simi Valley. I've invited Mr. Reynolds, and he comes, riding in the front seat with Dad, talking about why the blue tarp he bought back in September at a garage sale is better than the one he bought at the store later. It's 'cause every year, they make things cheaper and cheaper. At least that's what he says.

Simi Valley is north of Los Angeles, like we are, so the drive is only half an hour. I listen to Tupac, 'cause even though he probably hated police, he's so real I love him, and that gets me ready for a game. The sky's drizzling, but when we arrive a few minutes late, some of the guys are outside doing light dryland. I rush out, dumping my bag on the asphalt. Dad picks it up and says he'll take it in. Coach Kyle is there, talking to one of the parents. When he spots me, he asks, "How's your brain?" He taps on my head a couple of times. "How many fingers do I have up?" He holds up two fingers.

"Two."

"Wrong." He pokes his fingers toward my eyes, then ruffles my hair.

He takes us through some yoga stretches. Whenever I look up, he seems amused.

"Man, you guys are stiff," he finally says. "I want you to work on your stretching this week, because you're embarrassing me."

In the locker room, I get a sick feeling I don't expect. I've gone back to a previous helmet, one that was uncomfortable but had the highest safety rating of any helmet available—though the reality is none are all that safe. I just feel scared. I feel really scared. I feel dread.

"Glad you're back, man," Jae-won is saying. "Keep your head up out there." He knocks on my helmet. "You in there?"

I try to look calm, and give a fake smile. "Yeah, man, all good."

Ryan tugs at his jersey. "Do you think this jersey is too small?"

Ryan is super picky about his gear. "Looks fine to me," I say.

Then he grimaces as he buckles his helmet. "I think I need a new helmet—this one makes me look like a turtle. But my dad says it fits perfect."

I retighten a lace and head to the rink. The Zamboni is still resurfacing the ice. As soon as it's done, I zoom out and feel the air hitting my face. It feels so good that for a second I forget my fear. I take a couple of fast laps around our half of the rink before grabbing a puck and hitting a slap shot at the net. The other team looks bigger than us, and the fear returns. I don't want to play a big team. Also, I always check stats on Fridays when they're posted, and one of the guys on the other team has the highest penalty minutes in our division. I hate players like that. My future flashes through my mind: Bantam. Checking. Fear. I groan out loud and take another hard slap shot.

When the game starts, the coach doesn't send me

out for the first two shifts; I've been dropped to third line in my absence. That's fair, I don't have a problem with that. I'm playing with Scottie on D. Scottie's one of the best defensemen, so it can't be all bad. I lean over the boards and watch Jae-won on a breakaway— the guy defending him gets caught going for the puck and missing. Jae-won pretends he's going for a wrist shot lower right and instead flicks it left top shelf into the net. A thing of beauty for sure! I pound my stick on the boards for him.

Then I'm out there, and I can't believe how good it feels. I'm skating backward, flying really, for me. I'm really keyed in on my guy. Then I see a weakness and lunge for the puck, but my guy gets by me. I rush to the slot, but it's too late, and he scores. Same mistake Jae-won's defender made. I hear Coach shouting, "Conor, get off the ice!"

I skate to the bench. Coach turns on me and looks like he wants to yell but doesn't.

I slump down, resting the back of my skull on the glass. But there's no room for pouting in hockey, so I get up and hang over the boards again, watching the game. On the good side, getting schooled seems to have knocked the fear out of me—I just want to get out there and school that guy back. And I play great for *most* of the rest of the game. I'm rusty, but I make several excellent stops. There's one point where I'm on their best player. He dekes left, but I'm suddenly so in the zone it's like I'm reading his mind. I stay with him as he resets and pretends he's going left again but goes right. I close in and knock the puck away, and Scottie grabs it and skates off and almost scores. When I get to the bench, Coach Dusan says, "Good work, Conor," and pats my helmet. I feel like I've just won the Lotto, or an Oscar, or something big. The final buzzer sounds.

Unfortunately, bottom line is we lose by one goal—the goal that I gave up. So forget winning the Oscar. In the locker room after the game, Coach Dusan asks me, "Did you read the playbook or what?"

"I did read it," I reply.

"Well, read it again. I don't want you going after pucks you don't have a seventy-five percent chance of getting. All right?"

"All right."

"You played great for someone who's been out three weeks." But because this is hockey, he adds,

"But you need to do better." He takes a big breath and claps his hands once together. All the guys are looking at him. "Tough loss," he says. "I'm not going to yell, because you played pretty good. We still need to work on our forechecks. F2 isn't helping out enough, for one thing. He's just standing there. Hockey is a game of constant motion." Coach Dusan points to his head. "There are a million players with physical skills. In today's game, you need to be smart. The smart players are the ones who are going to make it. All right? Use your brains out there." Then suddenly he does yell: "USE YOUR BRAINS OUT THERE!" He walks out of the locker room.

We all get dressed without the hijinks you would expect if we'd won. Some teams I've been on don't take it hard when they lose, but this team already seems like the opposite. Then Jeffrey says, "Thanks for nothing," to me and turns to leave. Jae-won throws a glove that bonks off the back of Jeffrey's head, and Jeffrey turns on me. "I'm telling the coach you did that!"

"That ain't my glove," I reply. "Tell him anything you want."

Lucas says to me, "You played great, man."

"Thanks." But I get dressed in a hurry and leave.

In the car with Dad, Mr. Reynolds immediately says, "That puck is too small. Why don't they make it bigger so people can see it?"

Nobody answers for a second, and then Dad says, "Yeah, I guess it's pretty small."

"It's too small! Who can I write to to complain?" Then with a big effort, he turns all the way around and says, "You skate fast, young man. I'll bet you play someday in . . . what's it called?"

"The NHL?" I say.

"Wherever they play," he says. "You must work hard. I should have known."

Then we're all quiet for a few minutes. "Wanna talk?" Dad finally asks, but I don't answer. I open the window and let the air hit my face. That wasn't the first guy who's ever scored on me, not by a long shot. It was just that if I hadn't lunged, I could have stopped him. I cost us the game. What if we eventually don't make the play-offs by one game? My fault.

When we're almost home, I ask Dad, "Did you ever make bonehead mistakes?"

"Everyone does," Dad replies. "Everyone. I'm sure

Coach Dusan made bonehead mistakes in his career. I know it's cliché, but you just have to learn from your mistakes. In your case, over time you'll get a better sense of when you should go for the puck. You'll get a better sense of when you can actually get it. These are some talented kids in AAA. You're just as talented, but you're not used to the level of play yet. Don't worry, you'll get used to it. It's like when minor-league base-ball players move up to the bigs, they can't see the fast-balls. The pitches just whiz right by them."

"Really? Coach says I shouldn't go for the puck unless there's a seventy-five percent chance of get-ting it. I remember reading that in the playbook, but how do you know it's seventy-five percent when you make your move?"

"You don't. You just develop a feel for how fast the other guy is moving and how fast you can move. It's not exactly seventy-five percent. It's using your judg-ment. You'll get it."

Mr. Reynolds turns all the way around again. "Did you do something wrong?"

"I let a guy score."

"That's the goalie's responsibility! That's his job!"

"Well, in this case it was actually my fault, not the goalie's."

He turns around again. "You skate faster than I drive, I can tell you that."

I laugh, 'cause he drives so slow, and then I feel a little better. When we drop him off, he says he wants to come to another game someday, but he needs a few weeks to warm up again. Then he asks, "Did you ever talk to your grandparents?"

"I'm going to see them on Thanksgiving."

He smiles with satisfaction. "Always listen to Edwin Reynolds, you won't go wrong."

Dad just looks at me. "I decided," I say, "but I haven't told anyone yet."

He nods. "Good deal," he says. "Very good deal."

As soon as we get home, I put the playbook in my backpack and bike out to the park with Sinbad. He's winded, but I plan on staying for a while, so he'll be able to rest. I stretch out in the grass and read for an hour while Sinbad alternately sleeps and barks at other dogs. Sometimes I read the same sentence over and over, and I still don't get it, even though I got it a couple of months ago. It's so frustrating I could scream. And then I do. I just let it out, halfway between a scream and a yell. As loud as I can. Sinbad sniffs me. "I'm okay," I say.

I bike home, Sinbad loping happily next to me. Dad's left for work, 'cause he took an extra shift this weekend to help pay for the chemo, so I'll be eating my boiled chicken alone. I know Dad would pretty much work round the clock if he could. I rag on the crazed hockey parents sometimes, but the truth is, almost every single one of them is pretty great. There's a small number who are too hard on their kids, and also some who complain about all the time they have to spend at the rink. We only had one bad parent last year. There was a guy on the team with a stepdad who already had two grown kids he was crazy about. He even had grandkids. And you could see he really resented all the time at the rink, all the money. Kind of like Jenny did, though she hardly ever came to the rink. I mean, I know 'cause we were in family therapy that you have to try to be positive about each other, and try to be interested in each other's point of view. But the sad truth is, sometimes the stepparent-stepkid thing works out better than other times. Sometimes it works out great, and sometimes it doesn't, just like anything. The therapist said that there are situations where the best you can hope for is that you all get along. Like forget loving each other, just get along. The guy last year was crying in the locker room one day 'cause he screwed up in a game and knew his stepdad was going to be smoking mad at him. I remember Lucas sitting next to him with his arm around him, not saying anything. That was funny 'cause the guy used to swear a lot, and Lucas never swears and probably never will. So they weren't friends or anything. But there they were, Lucas acting like they were best buds. I guess that's Lucas for you.

CHAPTER 38

THE TEAM WORKS hard, and we win some games, but we can all feel we're not quite coming together. It's nothing personal—most of the guys are nice people—but it's not working yet. Coach Dusan tries changing the lines, tries having individual talks with us all, tries having group talks, tries new drills. It's driving the coaches crazy that we're not living up to our preseason—we lose three of our first seven regular games.

Even though the season is the most important thing, all any of us on the team can think of is our tournament in the Chicago area, coming up in two weeks. It's our chance for redemption! The tournaments are great 'cause they help you see how you stack up against teams from other states. Like if we make finals, we'll almost certainly be playing a team from Michigan called HoneyBaked—HoneyBaked has one of the best clubs in the country, with teams from multiple levels who are ranked high nationally many years. They're legend! When you're not killing it during the season, the chance to win a tournament means a lot, and to be able to play a team from HoneyBaked is pretty much what you dream about when you play kids' hockey. There's just nothing that could happen hockey-wise that would be better, except if we win CAHA.

When the third week of November rolls around, I'm super excited but also really worried about leaving Sinbad for several days. It's like part of me is on a total high, and part of me is on a total low. I feel so guilty about leaving him, it kind of makes me hate myself for being so into hockey. Aunt Mo is coming to stay at the house, and she's been texting, calling, and e-mailing me literally ten times a day to tell me everything is going to be fine. She even sent me flowers!

Like what am I supposed to do with flowers? Like I said, she's great and embarrassing, but mostly great. Then Thursday when it's time to leave for Chicago, a part of me wishes I would catch the flu or something, but I don't. As Dad and I are getting ready to leave, Sinbad's nervous, 'cause he knows what the suitcases mean. I kiss his nose a few times, then remember to brush his teeth, since I don't want to ask Aunt Mo to do it. It takes only a minute.

We decide that he should wait inside while we leave. Aunt Mo waves to us and calls out, "Don't worry, he'll be fine! I swear I will not let him out of this house when I'm not holding his leash. I'll be extremely careful when I open the door!" I trust her a lot, so I feel good about that.

In the car, Dad says, "She's actually the best person I can think of who could possibly take care of him."

"Yeah."

"You okay?"

"Yeah, she's the greatest."

But I don't say much all the way to the airport and even inside LAX.

Every time I get on a plane, I can't believe how

uncomfortable it is. The seats feel like wooden planks covered by cloth, and if the person in front of you reclines, your life just goes down the drain. We sit in the plane on the runway for two hours, and for a second it looks like a fistfight is going to break out when a passenger objects to the guy in front of him reclining. I can tell my dad is hating life. Finally the pilot announces that we're heading for the runway. People applaud. Twenty minutes later we're cleared for liftoff.

Whoa, I'd forgotten how much I hate flying. The plane shakes like it's going to fall apart as we rise through the air. When I think about the possibility of flying several times a week, I question whether I want to be in the NHL. Then we reach cruising altitude, and I feel fine about flying.

There's a movie Dad and I both want to watch, so we don't talk much. We brought sandwiches we bought at the airport, which we eat during the movie. By the time the film ends, the flight is nearly over.

After landing in the late afternoon, we rent a car and drive straight to the arena where the tournament reception is being held. I'm not even sure what town we're in—big tournaments are usually held at different rinks in an area near a city. It's so crowded, you can't move without touching and bumping people. The actual Stanley Cup is here, so we get in a long line to touch it and have pictures taken with it. There's a show going on where someone's talking about hockey equipment, and there are food and equipment booths, as well as reps from prep schools and junior hockey leagues. I figure that including family, players, and coaches, there are about twenty thousand people participating in the tournament. And thousands of them seem to be right here tonight. I keep a close eye on my dad so we don't get separated.

We stand in line to check out some custom sticks. I don't like them; they feel too heavy.

"Are you hungry?" Dad asks, raising his voice above the din.

"Yeah, but look at the lines," I reply.

Every food booth has a long line, and we already spent an hour waiting to touch the Stanley Cup and another hour waiting to look over the sticks. I mean, it's cool that there are this many people, but it's kind of overwhelming, and I have a game at seven a.m.

the next morning. "Can we just go eat somewhere?" I ask, and Dad agrees.

We go outside and cross through the cold parking lot. Man, it's cold in Illinois! We drive toward the hotel. I keep hoping for a Mexican restaurant, but we don't see any, so we decide on a random Chinese place we see. We buy four different dishes and eat every bite. It's actually not that good, don't know why I ate so much!

At the hotel, there are kids from another team talking in the lobby. Their voices have changed, and they're big, and they're all wearing jackets that read CHICAGO MISSION. "Dad!" I hiss. "Do you think that's the bantams?" Chicago Mission almost always has a great bantam club—some people think they have the best team of fourteen-year-olds in the country this season. I can't take my eyes off them. "Do you think that's them?" I say again. "Why are they staying in a hotel if they're local?"

"Looks like it might be them. Let's ask."

"NO, it'll be embarrassing!" I pause. "But do you think that's them?"

"Con, just ask."

It's embarrassing—I don't want to seem like a fanboy—but I have to know. So I casually saunter up and say, "Are you guys bantams?"

They look at me like I'm an ant, and one of them says, "Yeah, bud."

"I'm a peewee. I'll be aging up to bantam next year. Are you going to win nationals in the spring?"

"Yeah," a couple of them say, laughing, and they're friendly now.

"Don't jinx us," one warns the two who said "yeah."

"Cool!" I say. "Wow!" and then I can't think of anything else to say, so I smile stupidly at them before slinking away and going upstairs with Dad.

The hotel is all suites—I take the sofa bed per usual on these trips. "I want you to get a good night's sleep," Dad says, looking a little anxious.

There's a baseball movie on, but baseball being so slow and all, the movie makes me fall asleep, and when I wake up, it's after midnight. The bedroom is dark, so Dad must be asleep. I turn off the TV. And suddenly I feel good. In fact, I feel great! I'm going to be in a *huge* hockey tournament starting tomorrow, and hopefully at the end of the weekend, I'm playing one of the best teams in the country from one of the best clubs in the country. Lucas has been praying that him, Jae-won, and me all score against them. It's gonna be lit! If God's going to listen to anyone, wouldn't it be a great guy like Lucas? Isn't that how it would work? I'm not scared of HoneyBaked!

It seems like for my previous hockey life, I was always chasing something: the chance to be on a better team. I'm still chasing something, but it feels closer now. I'm an elite athlete! Then suddenly I think of Sinbad at home, and it's like someone just poured a bucket of worry over my head. Yet that makes me feel like a professional too. Sometimes in the pros, you probably have to accept missing someone in return for advancing your hockey life. That is, I'll always have Sinbad for as long as he lives, but I'll have to go away a few times now that I'm on a AAA team. So am I sad or happy? My brain is all over the map, like even when I close my eyes, I just see wild shapes and movements.

It's two o'clock before I wind down again, and then I pray for Sinbad, and then I'm asleep.

CHAPTER 39

THE TEAM MEETS for breakfast at four thirty a.m. in the twenty-four-hour restaurant next door. The players eat at several pushed-together tables, while the parents spread out. There are a couple of other teams at the restaurant as well. Coach Dusan sits with us, so there are no food fights or anything like that. Actually, we're all pretty quiet. For my part, I'm nervous, and I expect the other guys feel the same way. This morning I'm feeling more realistic. Considering our record, we probably don't have a chance to get to the finals. But who knows? I remind myself over and over that we have some super-talented kids.

I glance curiously at the other teams also eating at the restaurant. They look like they're midgets—fifteen and up. They seem a little nervous too. The midget games are going to be scouted. That would make me plenty nervous.

Four scrambled eggs, three slices of bacon, and three pieces of toast later, I'm ready to go. Coach tells everyone to drink their orange juice, so I guzzle mine down. Then we head to the rink.

Dad pulls out of the lot, then tells me, "Don't forget, focus. Remember in tryouts how you were holding back during the first shift? Don't let that happen to you today. Head up, but stay low."

"Uh-huh," I say. I don't say more 'cause there are serious butterflies in my stomach, and it's all I can do to keep from grinding my teeth or screaming or *something*. Then I decide to say, "Dad, I'm kind of nervous. Any advice about that?"

Dad nods, as if he's been waiting for me to say this. "I remember an attack of nerves for my first game here too. I played terrible. I lost all my focus. My nerves destroyed me that day. One of the worst games I ever played at any level. That's why I'm reminding you to focus. I don't want the same thing to happen to you."

"Thanks," I say glumly.

"No, I'm not jinxing you or trying to scare you. I just want you to be aware. Don't be so nervous— in the end it's only another game." He nods a couple times, as if I've said something. "You guys are good. And the other team is human, just like you. Just get in the flow. A game's a living thing with its own particular flow."

I stare out the windshield. There's hardly any traffic at this hour, and it's still dark out. I look at the few people in the cars around us and think I'd like to change places with any of them. I would change places with my dad, anyone. I just want to change places. I don't even feel like playing hockey. I wish we could go home. I feel like crap. My stomach is a mess. Breakfast now feels heavy and sour. My heart is fluttery. And it's all 'cause of stupid HoneyBaked.

"You okay?" Dad asks.

"Sure, what do you mean?" I say defensively. "No, not really."

"By the end of the weekend, you're going to be

loving every second, I promise you that. Hang in there today, and you're going to love tomorrow."

"Are you sure? 'Cause I feel like I'm going to hate tomorrow."

"I loved day two," Dad says, patting my shoulder.

So I resolve to love day two. All I have to do is survive day one, which might not happen.

"Don't worry, you're going to survive day one," Dad says, reading my mind.

"I feel like I don't even want to play. Like what's the point?"

"I know, right?" Dad says. "I asked the same question of my dad."

"What did he answer?"

"He got annoyed with me, but don't worry, I'm not going to get annoyed at you. He never went through the same thing, so he didn't get it. I know it seems like a big deal, but really it's just another game."

"I've played lots of games, and none of them felt like this, except maybe my first game ever," I say.

"I know, right?"

I don't answer. The rink is only ten minutes

away, which makes my heart sink. I feel like I need more time, but I plain don't have it. No changing that. After we park, Dad says, "Good luck, Conor. I'll be proud of you no matter what."

"Thanks, Dad," I say. I get out of the car and grab my bag and sticks from the trunk. As we reach the main door, other guys with bags and sticks are trickling in. "Are you sure tomorrow will be fun?" I ask.

"Positive. A hundred percent."

All right, so all I have to do is get through today. I should be able to manage that.

There's a board inside telling players which locker room and rink they're assigned, and whether teams should wear white or dark jerseys. Dad walks me to the locker room and says, "Okay, I'll be in the stands. Good luck. Remember, focus and flow."

"Thanks," I answer unenthusiastically. I go inside the locker room. Aidan 1's boombox is on, and he's dancing. Aidan's been in AAA since he was what's called an atom in Canada, so he never gets nervous. Atoms are nine or ten. Saw some on video on YouTube—the little atom AAAs are *fire*.

"Does someone have some tape I can borrow? I forgot mine," Avery says worriedly. He looks kind of sick today.

"Yeah," we all say at the same time. Someone throws him a roll of black tape, and he starts to tape his stick. Who waits until the last minute to tape his stick?

As I get dressed, more players come in. Usually we have dryland before games, but Coach Dusan decided not to do dryland today 'cause some people flew in kind of late last night. I'm not in the mood for dryland anyway. I get dressed so fast that I'm the first one done. As I wait for everyone else to finish, I decide to break the ice. "Is anyone else nervous?" I ask.

"I am." "Yeah." "Really nervous." "Nah." We all look at Aidan 1, who has said the "Nah."

"What?" he says. "I'm not. I'm excited. I've been waiting for this since summer, man. We're gonna make the finals and give HoneyBaked a beatdown."

"Yeah, but I'm still nervous," I say.

Eric suddenly pukes, and we all jump up. "Man, that's gross!" Aidan 2 shouts. "It's just a freakin' game!" Eric's kind of a nervous guy. I'm not judging him, just commenting.

It smells, so we all hurry out. I'm not sure exactly where the rink is, but I obediently follow the guy in front of me. As we march in our skates, I start to get more of that familiar gladiator feeling. *Gladiator* is the best movie ever made, by the way. It's rated R, but Mr. Kang let us watch it anyway 'cause he's seen it about twelve times and wanted to share it with Jae-won and me. "Look at the floor!" Jae-won says. The soft flooring is new, unlike at our home rink. In fact, the whole rink is pretty spiffy. There are probably twenty or thirty different rinks in the general Chicago area where games are being held today. Got no idea what suburb we're in.

When we reach our rink, we sit on the home bench, since we're white today. Coach is going to wonder where we all went, since he usually gives us a locker-room pep talk before games.

"Man, I can't believe you puked!" Aidan 2 says.

We all laugh. Eric happens to be sitting next to me, so I push him with my shoulder and say, "It's only a game, man. We just gotta get in the flow."

"Yeah, I know. I'm fine now."

The puking turns out to be a good thing, 'cause now the guys are talking and laughing. Jae-won and Ryan are laughing about something. I feel a lot better, like I'm the one who puked and I got something out of my system. "Here comes Coach!" someone says, and we all turn to watch Coach Dusan striding toward us. He doesn't walk, he strides.

"What happened in there?" he asks.

"Eric puked!" Aidan 1 cries out. "Is someone going to clean it up?"

"Yeah, I got someone," Coach says. "So listen up, some of you have a tendency to follow the pass when you're not thinking. So focus out there, follow the player, not the pass. I know that sounds basic, but I also know that some of you may be nervous and might forget some of the basics. And don't try to show off your stick-handling. These guys will make you pay for that. When all else fails, remember the saucer pass. It opens up the ice. Matt is our goalie today. All right, warm-up!"

Jeffrey's face falls, and for a brief moment I feel sorry for him, even though he's kind of the team jerk.

We spill onto the ice, skating a circle around our side of the rink. Someone throws out some pucks, and we practice passing and shooting. Matt seems to be having a bad warm-up. Everything's getting past him. I skate up and pat his shoulder, and he nods.

The buzzer sounds, and we clean up the pucks and huddle around Matt. "Let's win this thing!" Avery shouts. "Grizzlies on three. One-two-three!"

"GRIZZLIES!"

"Who's gonna win?"

"GRIZZLIES!"

And . . . Coach sends me out! I skate to center ice and take my position. The guy standing next to me is a good four inches taller than I am, and I'm one of the taller kids on our team. Great. But maybe he's slow, I tell myself.

"I saw your mom in the parking lot," he says. "She says you suck at hockey."

"I don't have a mom, fool."

"Then how were you born?"

The ref drops the puck, and the game begins!

Jae-won swipes the puck toward me. I can't find the handle. Bad start! I try to steal it back but fail, and my guy gets away. I dig in and skate my fastest as the opposing player is on a breakaway. I almost catch up, but he shoots—AGHH—and misses. Thank you! I'm thinking too much. Focus!

I swoop in for the rebound and send a hard pass to Jae-won. The pass isn't smooth, but he manages to control it. I love Jae-won's hands! I can feel how into the game he is. Then, suddenly, just like that, he passes on his focus to me, like it's contagious. Every time I'm in a fight for the puck I come up with it and flick off a decent pass. I challenge every opposing player trying to skate in for a shot. I stop all except one: he scores. Still, somewhere in the back of my mind I know I'm doing good. I'm not thinking, just feeling my way through the game. It's like a few parts of the playbook are suddenly second nature. And I can see half the ice at a time, sometimes the whole ice. We're all in sync, like Jae-won's focus is so huge it can be used by all of us. We win the game 6–1. That one goal is on me, but overall I played a strong game.

We line up and bump fists with the other team, then head back to the locker room, swaggering triumphantly, totally different people than we were in the locker room before the game.

Coach tells us we did "a pretty good job," but he doesn't want us to get on too big a high, 'cause we have another game tonight. We're on a pretty big high, anyway. We can't help it.

When I leave the locker room, all the parents are waiting. Dad and Mr. Kang are laughing together, Mr. Kang gesturing wildly with his hands whipping through the air. I hurry excitedly up to them and say, "That was so much fun! That was one of my most favorite games ever!"

"You played great," Dad says.

"Everyone play great," Mr. Kang says. "You skate fast today, Conor. You skate five mile an hour faster today."

That's actually not possible for me to have improved that much, but it makes me feel good anyway.

"Even Jae-won skate fast today!" Mr. Kang says as Jae-won walks up. In fact, Jae-won scored a hat trick and was basically the beast to end all beasts today.

Lucas's whole family is here—they always travel together—and they're huddled around him like he's a rock star. He looks kind of embarrassed and pleased at the same time.

The team is going out for pizza. At the team table we roast the other team. "Did you see that big guy? He couldn't even skate." "I can't believe they're a Tier I team. They only got twelve shots on goal." Coach Dusan isn't sitting with us, but I see him look over unhappily; he always says we have to respect the other team.

Then everyone goes their separate ways until the game at seven p.m.

CHAPTER 40

DAD, ME, THE Kangs, and Lucas's family decide to all go to a movie. We have to see a G film, 'cause that's all Lucas is allowed. His two brothers are both older than him, but they don't complain. We end up at a comedy about a spy who goes home for Thanksgiving, and he has to pretend he works as a department store manager. This is probably a goofy thing to say, but Lucas has a really cool laugh. I mean, the movie's pretty average, but he keeps bursting out laughing like it's really fun and funny. It kind of makes me feel good to hear him. In fact, Jae-won and I look at each other and smile about it a few times.

Back at the same rink, there's a lot of chatter as we get our gear on. All the guys are in a good mood.

We're on one of the rink's other sheets of ice for this game, and the surface is a little rougher, but still acceptable. But during the game, it seems like I'm just floating around. Coach can see I'm having a bad game, and he doesn't play me as much as usual. At one point, he even leans over me and asks, "Are you okay?" I don't know what's happened. It's like I've lost my spirit temporarily. One of my issues is that despite how hard I work, sometimes when I play two games in the same day, I don't perform well in the second game. That's a problem, 'cause if we make the finals, we'll be playing three games on Sunday.

I tell Coach I'm fine. We win 7–5.

More than half the team goes to a Denny's, but since the restaurant's not expecting so many people at once, it takes us forever to get our food. We order a ton of stuff to eat, and there's nothing left at the end. All the parents joke with the waiters and waitresses about hungry boys.

It's actually good that the food takes so long, 'cause nobody has a chance to get into any trouble at the hotel when we return. Last year at a tournament in Minnesota, we almost got kicked out of a hotel for stealing all the apples in a Halloween display and throwing them off the roof. Now, when we get to the lobby, there're several kids in hockey jackets getting lectured by a hotel employee.

Jae-won and I are so bloated we're worried we won't be able to sleep. But then when I get to my room, I call Aunt Mo, she tells me Sinbad is doing fantastic, and I collapse. I sleep for thirteen hours. Dad's doing push-ups in the living room when I get up. He makes me do stretching, and then we're off to the rink. Next up, a team from Alaska. We can probably lose and still make the finals, but you never know.

CHAPTER 41

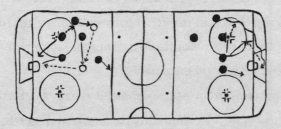

SO WE DO lose our morning game 1–0, but we win our night game 10–0 and come in second in our division with a 3–1 record. We're animals!! I play fantastic!! At our level, there are twenty teams divided into four divisions. HoneyBaked wins their division undefeated, as does the Alaska team that beat us. Then on Sunday, we're in the play-offs: quarterfinals at eight o'clock, semifinals at eleven thirty, and championship at three p.m. All the games kind of blur together, but we get lucky and play two 3–1 teams in the quarters and semis. Bad luck for the Alaska team—they get knocked out by HoneyBaked 5–3. We make the finals!

The whole team's got this major adrenaline thing going, and nobody even feels tired. Per usual, I aced the first game but played so-so in the second game. I've never played three games in a day before, but suddenly I don't feel tired at all.

It's so crazy, 'cause I'm literally right here in my dream. *Right here.* I look up in the locker room after our second game and see Lucas sitting there half-dressed, not moving, just half smiling and staring into space. Jae-won is talking really quickly, like he does when he's excited. "So Aidan's mom went to the HoneyBaked game to scout them—she's going to tell us what they're like—they got scored on three times so they're human—someone pointed out their best goalie to me—he's not that big—I think I can score on him."

I don't answer, 'cause I'm not sure he would even hear me. He's more talking to himself.

The teams have an hour to eat, and like us, HoneyBaked decides to just have pizza at the rink. A couple of them are pretty big, but they're mostly small to average height. Our team becomes kind of quiet, but their team is loud and happy. At one point, they start chanting, "HoneyBaked, HoneyBaked, HoneyBaked!"

So Jesus yells out, "Grizzlies on three, one-two-three!"

"GRIZZLIES!"

It's the worst pizza ever, and then we have to stretch and get dressed again.

In the locker room, Coach has us all sit with our eyes closed and envision winning the game. Envision playing well. Envision us scoring, and scoring again. We keep our eyes closed as he says, "Focus . . . focus . . . ," like he's hypnotizing us. I have my palms on my knees, and I'm leaning slightly forward with my head bowed. Then Coach says loudly, "Matt is the goalie. Let's win this thing!"

Jae-won, Lucas, and I huddle with our eyes closed, then follow everybody else to the ice. On the bench, I close my eyes again and think *Focus . . . focus . . .* Then Coach says, "Warm up!"

I skate onto the ice, feeling like the rink and the other players are somehow not quite real, and I'm the only living thing. I try to shake that out of my head. Usually when I'm on the ice, it all feels so real. I skate around our half of the rink, over and over, as fast as I can. We shoot for a few minutes at Matt. I blast a slap shot past him and figure that's good luck. The buzzer sounds in what seems like half a minute, though I know it's longer.

We huddle. "Let's win this thing! Who's gonna win?!" Aidan 1 shouted.

"GRIZZLIES!"

I'm still on the first line, since I played a super-strong morning game. I skate out. I push the rest of the world out of my head and stare at the puck. At this moment, the puck is the most important thing in the entire world. It's the almighty puck, god of all things.

The ref tells Jae-won he's crowding too much and needs to stand back. Jae-won takes a half step back, but then he's focusing so hard that he moves forward again. The ref gets annoyed and makes him change places with Jesus. That's bad—Jesus is godly, but he's not as good as Jae-won at face-offs.

The ref drops the puck. There's a short struggle, and HoneyBaked gets the puck and makes three quick, perfect passes to move close to our net. They've got a guy who just explodes off his first step. Lucas anticipates a pass and manages to get a piece of the puck.

Jae-won bats it to me, and I skate off, my feet flying. It's a three on two. I pass to Jae-won, who passes back to me, and then I pass across the ice to Jesus, who passes to Jae-won. Jae-won scores! We score first!

We jump into each other's arms like we just won the Stanley Cup, but then we immediately realize we're acting like idiots and skate back to the bench. The rest of the period is just bruising hockey. Totally intense defense on both sides, and nobody scores. We're all fighting for the puck so hard, I can tell everyone's gonna be battered and sore later.

To open the second period, Jae-won loses the face-off, but I go right to where I somehow know my guy is going to be, and I bat the puck away. I feel a rush of happiness, but I push emotions out of my mind. My emotions don't matter. Only the puck matters.

But it's too late. I lost focus for a second, and my guy gets around me. I blaze after him, but he's got a head start and makes a wicked backhand into the net. I immediately skate up and slap Matt's helmet and say, "Sorry!"

Back on the bench, I feel like crap, and suddenly I'm kind of tired. I need to close my eyes to find my focus again. HoneyBaked scores again with a series of awesome passes, but then Avery slips the puck through in a crowded struggle in front of the net. 2–2.

In the huddle before the third period, Coach Dusan says, "We need another. Come on, guys, let's get that puck in the net." He looks right at me. "Defense, Conor! They're getting too many shots!"

Back on the ice, the ref drops the puck. The other center hits it, but it flies to the boards, where I swoop down on it and immediately pass to Jae-won across the ice. I'm already flying, and then I make a bonehead play. The puck always needs to enter your offensive zone before any of your players, and I skate into the zone before the puck gets there. The ref whistles. "Offside!" he calls out. Truly, truly unbelievable. I haven't been called offside all season. So the puck moves to our defensive zone.

I wait to be taken out of the game, but Coach

keeps me in. But I hear him laughing that maniac laugh he reserves for when we're driving him crazy during a game. He bellows, "Wake up, Conor!"

There's some back and forth while nobody can control the puck. Then it's time for a line change, and I skate to the bench and lean forward on the boards.

Nobody can score.

Then I'm on the ice again, and I'm moving like something liquid as I skate between the opposing players. None of this is in the playbook—we're beyond that now. Even though I'm D, Jae-won and I are on a breakaway, passing the puck back and forth as we fly. Near the net I think about shooting, but instead I pass to Jae-won, who passes to Jesus coming out of nowhere. Jesus scores! We hop into each other's arms, and this time we don't care if we're idiots. Jesus has been in a slump this tournament, so it's especially sweet. But then we get right back into the game. The HoneyBaked goalie swings his stick hard against a post, and it splinters. So we all wait while he changes sticks.

3–2. There're only thirty seconds left, and I can already feel the win. Jae-won and Lucas are laughing together. I laugh for no reason but get serious for the face-off, which we lose.

My guy ends up with the puck near the boards, but I chop my stick hard on the ice around his blade. I feel like an animal. I get the puck and mean to pass to Jae-won. I'm half smiling. Then somehow the puck slips off the end of my stick as Jae-won waits for it across the ice. AHGGGGH! Lucas swoops in and grabs it. He passes toward Jae-won, but it goes off the end of *Lucas's* stick and dribbles off to the HoneyBaked center . . . who immediately passes to one of his guys, who's already sprinting down the ice. He yells out, "Sebastian!" Sebastian catches the pass, flicks it softly into the net as the final buzzer sounds.

They jump into the air while we stand staring. The tournament doesn't have overtime. They do shootouts instead for some reason. We're kind of dazed as the shootout starts right away. Sebastian starts, and scores. Jae-won's first up for us. I'm clutching my stick so hard it hurts. He skates left slowly, picks up speed, leans hard right. And flips the puck into the post, making a *ping*. He falls to the ice and just lies there facedown while HoneyBaked celebrates. I skate out to stand next to him, but he won't get up until the handshake begins.

Shaking hands after a big loss is one of the hardest things about hockey. But we all man up, then stand there while the medallions are handed out. After that, we watch as HoneyBaked takes the banner and skates around the ice with it. Finally we're allowed to leave as they're still celebrating.

We trudge to our locker room, my skates heavy on my feet. We all sit down next to our bags, but nobody starts getting undressed. I lean forward, elbows on my knees, face in my hands. I don't feel like crying exactly. As a matter of fact, I can't even remember the last time I cried. I just can't believe I lost that puck—and Jae-won was wide open! I try to think about how that happened, but I can't figure it out. Dad will have to tell me later what I did wrong. Usually I can remember every little detail, but somehow I'm drawing a blank on this. I'm a screwup! If that puck had reached Jae-won, we'd have won the game. That's on me. Then somebody *is* crying. I don't look up; I know it's Lucas. Finally I look up and see his head hanging down, snot falling to the ground.

"It's on me, Lucas," I say loudly. "I screwed up." He keeps crying, and I realize he's thinking it's all his fault.

Coach Dusan comes in holding his clipboard. We look at him, waiting to get yelled at.

He nods his head at us, then says, "That was some of the best hockey you guys have played all year. I couldn't be more proud of you. You held your own against one of the best peewee AAA teams in the nation. They're ranked third in the country. Think about that. And you played them even for three full periods. That game could've gone either way. You're one of the strongest peewee teams I've ever coached. And we're going to go home and get even better, and if you keep playing the way you played today, we're going deep into the state play-offs. So hold your heads high when you walk out of this locker room." He pauses, eyes Lucas, who's still crying. "Great game, Lukie, I mean it, you played amazing. All of you, great game." Then he walks out.

It's not like that makes us feel good exactly, but you can feel the mood has shifted. Third in the nation . . . game could have gone either way . . . deep into the state play-offs. We all get dressed, and it's hard but we *do* hold our heads high as we walk out.

The parents are out there waiting. They don't applaud the way they do when you win a big game. They all wear exactly the same look. I've seen it before. It's like, *Aw, my boy feels bad.* Dad puts an arm around me, and as we head out of the rink, he says, "I'm so proud of you. So proud."

In the parking lot, I see Jae-won and Mr. Kang walking toward their rental. I don't shout out, 'cause sometimes after a loss you really don't feel like socializing. Then, out of total left field, a feeling of *anger* washes over me, like I'm not going to let this loss get me down. I mean, I still feel like crap, but I also feel like I'm right exactly in the center of where I should be at this moment in my life. I just played freaking HoneyBaked. If they're number three in the nation, maybe we're number four. Maybe!

CHAPTER 42

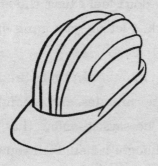

WE CHECKED OUT of the hotel when we left for the first game, so we head right to the airport. At first we're quiet in the car. Then I say, "How did I lose that puck? I thought I had it."

"Hit it off the end of your blade instead of the middle."

"But how?"

"It's just poise. They were an incredibly poised team for a bunch of young kids. You guys will learn. Don't worry. By the time you're all bantams, you'll be making those mistakes less and less. Don't get me wrong, you'll always make mistakes, that's just sports. But less and less. Definitely less and less."

But we just played seven games in three days, and I suddenly don't feel I have the energy to even open my mouth. I let my jaw hang open and stop thinking.

Once we get into the air, Dad's tired too. He naps for thirty or forty minutes, and when he wakes up, the first thing he says is, "Now that your tournament's over, I thought I should tell you something."

It's like he's been waiting to say this. That sounds bad for some reason! So I kind of don't want to know what he's talking about. But I can tell he's waiting for me to ask, so I do. "What is it, Dad?"

"I'm going to be changing jobs."

"What?" I look into his face to see if he's kidding. I just think of him as a police officer. It's what he does; it's who he is.

"I'm tired," he says. "I'm tired of being a cop."

"But Dad! You're a good cop, I know you are. The world needs good cops."

"Over the past year, I just realized, this isn't what I want to do anymore. I'm going to work at my friend's construction firm. I'm really looking forward to it.

He understands that I've got to take you to hockey, and we're going to work around that."

I try to think what I should say and blurt out, "I want you to be happy. I don't want you to cry anymore."

He nods. "Yeah, I know. I won't. I'm okay now."

I feel like . . . I feel like I gotta take care of him at this moment, and that maybe he wants to talk, so I say, "Actually, that's great news. I mean, you're a great cop, but you'll be great at anything you do. I—" But he's leaning back and closing his eyes like he's exhausted, probably 'cause, let's face it, raising a hockey kid probably *is* pretty exhausting. So I just say, "Thanks, Dad," but he doesn't answer. I look out the window at the lights below. We're in flyover country, where I once lived, and where Dad once played hockey back when he thought he'd be an NHL star someday. And now here he is. My dad.

CHAPTER 43

BACK AT HOME, Sinbad squeals like a puppy when he sees me. He jumps up and nips at my forehead, just like he used to when we first got him and he was excited. I think he actually breaks skin. I touch my forehead, and there's blood. But I'm so happy to see him that I say, "Good boy!" I hug him close, which makes him so still I can't even feel him breathe.

Then I hug my aunt. "Thanks, Aunt Mo. I really appreciate it."

"I know you do, hon. It was fun. He's a great dog."

"Where did he sleep?"

"By the front door, actually."

"Every night?"

"Every night."

I kneel in front of Sinbad, show him the second-place medallion I won.

"Did you come in first?" Aunt Mo asks.

"Nah, second. It was a lot of fun, though. I mean, it kind of sucked when we lost, but overall it was fun. I guess you could say I screwed up toward the end. We could have won. I had the whole game in my hands there for a second, and I blew it." I put out my hands and look at them, like I still can't believe it.

She shakes her head. "Oh, honey, no no no no no, a game is three periods, no one person is at fault. You didn't screw up!"

"I did, actually. But it's okay. Next time I won't."

"He played great," Dad says. "Really, really great. The best I ever saw him play."

"Thanks," I say. "Maybe this'll turn our season around." Sinbad is pressing his whole body into my side, so I slide down and hold him with my eyes closed.

"Thanks, Mo," Dad says. "I owe you."

"No, you don't. I'm your sister, you don't owe me anything." I stand up, and she kisses my cheek.

"Okay, I better get going, I've got work tomorrow. See you on Thanksgiving."

That makes my insides wrench: my grandparents—Aunt Mo asked me to call them before I left. I go into my room. Two phone numbers are scribbled on a slip of paper. My grandparents' home number—they don't have a cell—and their hotel number. They're probably still at home, so I dial their number, and someone picks up on the first ring.

"Hello?" a man says.

"Hi, this is Conor."

"Conor!"

I just blurt it out. "I just wanted to say I hope to see you at my aunt's house on Thanksgiving." There's a silence that goes on so long I say, "Hello?"

"Hello, yes, we'll see you there. Thank you. Thank you."

"My pleasure." I wait. I remember Dad telling me about the long silences that could happen sometimes with them. "I look forward to seeing you."

"All right, bye."

He hangs up abruptly, and I just look at my phone for a moment. "Bye," I murmur to nobody.

Since I took Thursday and Friday off the previous week, I've got schoolwork to do. I'm awake until midnight working.

At school the next day, everybody's in a good mood 'cause it's a short week. Monday and Tuesday I'm sleepy both days. The junior high holds a special assembly on Thanksgivings, where kids in chorus and dance perform. The elementary kids are here too. So the last thing we do Wednesday is watch the show. It's pretty entertaining, with two or three standouts like every year. There's a boy whose voice fills up the entire auditorium, and a break-dancing group with two amazing athletes. I'm so used to being out there in front of people playing hockey, it feels kind of unusual to be watching other kids perform. It's really cool.

CHAPTER 44

ON THANKSGIVING I decide to wear my only button-up shirt. Dad gets me a new one every year. Otherwise I only wear T-shirts, with a hoodie if it's cold. I put Sinbad's special red-and-green Christmas collar on—the one that Aunt Mo got him one year— and he looks all dressed up. He can feel something special in the air, 'cause when we get to the front yard, he's pulling so hard I decide to unleash him. He runs circles over and over around the yard while we wait for him to calm down. Dad and I watch, amused. When he settles, we get in the car.

Suddenly I'm so nervous about seeing my

grandparents that there's a part of me that just wants to stay home, and hear the coyotes yipping and howling and the wind blowing through the hills. Home. I wonder if I'll ever feel the same about any home again in my life. If I make the NHL, maybe I'll have a fancy house, a house like Ryan's. But it won't be the same. It'll never be the same. My dad won't be there. Sinbad won't be there.

"You okay?" Dad says as we drive off.

"Yeah."

I keep my head turned away 'cause for some reason I've started crying. I think Dad knows I'm crying, but he doesn't say anything. And, you know, it feels good. I cry almost all the way to Long Beach, and I'm not even thinking about anything specific. Maybe Sinbad. Maybe the game I blew. Maybe who knows what. I'm just crying.

"Something I never mentioned to you," Dad suddenly says when we're almost there. "I never told this to anybody. But right around the time your mother was dying, I saw her face as clear as day. I was in Nebraska for a game, and I was taking a nap at the motel. I was dreaming, but I wasn't dreaming. She told me to take care of you, and then I woke up and knew she was dead before anybody called me with the news." He pauses and adds, "I'm just telling you because I want you to see how when you love someone, you're really connected to them in ways that I don't think anybody comprehends. I want you to understand all that when you see your grandparents. They were really connected to your mother. So . . . you should keep this in mind tonight, that's all."

I'm not sure what he's saying, but I answer, "Okay, Dad." I dry off my face on my shirt.

When we get to Aunt Mo's house, my heart is beating hard. I close my eyes and focus on being normal.

We let ourselves in like we do when we know Aunt Mo is home, and my grandparents are sitting at the dining room table. They both quickly stand up, their mouths dropping open, like they're literally flabbergasted to see me. I don't move until Dad gently pushes me forward. I guess I'm supposed to hug them, so I do. Then Grandma Toshi stands there staring at me with the back of her hand against her mouth. Her round face . . . she looks so much like my mother it's shocking. I almost cry again. Grandpa Takao takes my hand, and for a second I think he's going to say, "Nice to meet you." Instead he says, "Sit down and talk to us. You're big!" They both sit down, and so do I.

Grandpa is not much taller than me, and you can see his face is old, but all his hair isn't gray yet. They're somewhere in their late sixties, I think. Grandma is small too and looks like she weighs maybe ninety-five pounds, if that.

"Aren't you tall for your age?" Grandma asks.

"Uh-huh—I mean, I'm not the tallest kid on my team, but I'm one of the taller ones."

"Hockey, yes?" she asks.

"Right."

"Do you enjoy that?"

"Yes, I spend a lot of time at it. I want to be a professional hockey player one day."

"Ohhh," they both say, glancing at each other with no particular expression.

Grandpa suddenly seems to remember something, stands up, and holds his hand out to Dad. "Keith . . . Keith." They do a quick man-hug. Then

Grandpa's face kind of contorts before becoming calm again as he says, "You're a good man." They hug again, less quickly.

They ask me a lot of questions about school and almost none about hockey and none at all about Sinbad. That's 'cause they don't know me. But they're cool; they remind me of my other grandparents in that they seem to have lots of stories about their lives. Like about how they were hippies during the sixties, which is hard to picture, and how Grandma was told she couldn't have kids, and then she had my mom.

Aunt Mo sets all the food on the table, and I suddenly decide to say a prayer. "Thank you for this food, and for my aunt and dad and Sinbad and all my grandparents." I hesitate. "And thank you for my mother." I hesitate again, then finish: "That's it, thank you very much."

Even after the long talk with my grandparents, I can't deny that dinner's a little awkward. It seems like nobody ever quite relaxes. But I eat about half a pound of turkey stuffing, which is one of my favorite foods, and afterward we all watch *Happy Gilmore*. Dad and I watch it with Aunt Mo every

Thanksgiving—it's rated PG-13—'cause it's basically the funniest, most totally ridiculous sports movie ever made. The grandparents are not amused!

Before Grandpa and Grandma leave, Grandpa invites me to play miniature golf the next day, and I say sure even though I'm really too old for that. I also hate miniature golf 'cause the turf is always uneven, and I'm so competitive I hate feeling like I can't really use my coordination to control where the ball goes. That doesn't mean I'm not happy to do it, 'cause I am. When we all say good-bye for the night, they study my face, like they're looking for my mom. Grandma reaches out and touches my cheek like she's amazed. "Your mother was a wonderful girl," she says. "And you're just like her." I don't know what to say to that. I guess it makes me feel surprised, 'cause I always assume I'm just like my dad. She and Grandpa leave then without saying anything more, not even "bye."

"She looks like Mom," I say.

"I know," Dad answers.

Aunt Mo packs leftover food for Dad, me, and Sinbad. "So what did you think?" she asks as she hands over the food.

"It's all good," I say simply.

"Do you like them?"

"Yeah, I liked them a lot. It did feel kind of strange. But they're—they seem like really good people."

"They were devastated when your mother died. She *was* a wonderful girl, and you *are* just like her." She musses my hair.

Embarrassing. But mostly great.

Later, at home, I take a plate of leftovers down to Mr. Reynolds. He's not around, even though I wait for ten minutes. This is good—hopefully, it means he's with relatives. When I return, Dad is in his room watching TV. I sit out front with Sinbad and hear a coyote howling in the distance. I think about processing the night, but my mind's not working that well for some reason. Sinbad's happy, but I can see he's tired. There's a look in his face, like maybe just being alive is a bit of a strain tonight. I remember the lady at the oncologist saying you can see how sick they are from their faces. I think of how hard the past few months have been for him. And I suddenly, totally understand that he's got two years, tops, probably less, no matter how much I pray. 'Cause if there's a God, that's not what he is. He doesn't just give you anything you beg him for. If that's the way it worked, every single person in the world would be a Christian. And I guess I learned something these past few weeks from Lucas and the way he acts. You just gotta be a good person. But your dog's gonna die when he's gonna die. I'll keep praying, though, 'cause it's important to believe.

My mind drifts back to earlier tonight. I think about Grandpa and Grandma's expressions when they first saw me. I think about Aunt Mo and how much she loves me. Something occurs to me that I never thought of before: if I live a happy life, I'll make everybody happy. I'll make my dad, my aunt, and my grandparents—both sets of grandparents—happy. Even just being happy now, that'll make a difference to them all. It's like I always wanted to be happy for myself, but now I see it as kind of a responsibility, too. So I gotta grow up and have a good life. Maybe I even need to work harder in school to make sure I have a decent backup. I'll get Cs whether I work hard or not, but that's no reason not to work hard.

Sinbad howls at the coyotes, which he does once

in a while. He's not as energetic as usual, but he's so *passionate* when he howls. *Owooooo!* Someday, when I see his electricity in the room or he comes to me in a dream, I just feel like at that exact second I won't be a kid anymore. It's like that's when I'll change into a grown man, even if I'm only thirteen or fourteen. I'll be in bantams, I'll be checking, and I'll say my last good-bye to my dog. I decide right then that I want to scatter his ashes in the hills of Canyon Country. Right where he belongs, and where I'll always belong.

For now, I want to be right here, in the moment, the way Sinbad always is. *Owooooo!*

Acknowledgments

Thank you as always to my stupendously talented and stupendously patient editor, Caitlyn Dlouhy, who has to take so very much abuse from me!! And I can never adequately express my appreciation for Russell Gordon—it brings actual tears to my eyes because I love his work so much. Deepest appreciation as well to the incomparable Justin Chanda and Jon Anderson. And I'm just so fortunate to have had Jeannie Ng watching my back all these years with Atheneum—I've loved every copy editor I've ever worked with, but she is my favorite for sure. And Alex Borbolla rocks as well!

I would also like to thank David Rolston; George Miyamoto; Kimberly Freeman, DVM, DACVIM (Oncology); Christopher M. Fulkerson, DVM, MS, DACVIM (Oncology); Tina Stevens; Trifun Zivanovic; Todd Peterson; and Julie Ho. Any mistakes in the story about canine cancer treatment are most assuredly my errors and not errors on the part of either Dr. Fulkerson or Dr. Freeman. (That said, being two different people, they obviously do things somewhat differently, so I used what seemed to me to fit the story best, and also did some things they would probably both disapprove of, like having the main character take a shower with his postsurgery dog, letting a twelve-year-old boy pill his dog, etc.)

And of course thank you to my favorite hockey boy, Sammy!!

A Reading Group Guide for *Checked* by Cynthia Kadohata

About the Book

Three things matter most to Conor: his dad, his dog, and hockey. Conor and his dad, once a pro hockey player, spend long hours at the rink and on the road for tournaments, aiming for Conor to go pro someday. When Conor's not skating, he hangs out with his beloved dog, Sinbad. But then Sinbad gets cancer, and treatment costs thousands of dollars. Conor must confront a choice between his extra hockey lessons and helping Sinbad live a few more years—at most. It's only when Conor's out on the ice that he can leave his troubles behind and get in the zone—with the best team he's ever been on!

Discussion Questions

1. Think about the book's title. What are different meanings for the word *checked*? Why do you think the author chose it? How does it reflect important elements of the novel?

2. What kind of a person is Conor? What are some things he's concerned with, and what gives him happiness? Consider how he changes in the course of the book, and what brings about those changes.

3. What is Conor's father like? How does he treat Conor? What is their everyday life like together? What do they have in common that's important to both of them?

4. Think about why Conor's father cries, and whether you think that will change in the future. Judging from Mr. MacRae's life, why is being a police officer difficult? When it comes to his father, why does Conor say, "I gotta take care of him"?

5. Describe Sinbad, his personality, and his role in Conor's life. Why do you think they are so close? How does Sinbad's illness affect Conor? Near the end of the book, Conor says he wants to be "right here, in the moment, the way Sinbad always is." What does he mean by that?

6. Think about the importance of hockey in

Conor's life. Why does it matter so much to him? What are some of the benefits of playing hockey? What are some of the drawbacks? Do you think it's a good choice for him to pursue hockey so intensely?

7. Describe the house and the neighborhood where Conor lives. On the last page, Conor says that the hills of Canyon Country are "where I'll always belong." Why does this location matter so much to him?

8. Point to some of the ways in which Conor helps Mr. Reynolds. What do these interactions show about Conor's character and his upbringing? Does Mr. Reynolds help Conor at all?

9. More than once, Conor describes his aunt Mo as "great and embarrassing, but mostly great." What's her relationship like with Conor and his father? What does Conor like about her? How does she embarrass him?

10. Conor says of Coach Dusan: "He's literally the only person I know who I never see

standing around looking at his phone." What does that tell you about the coach? Why does Conor want to be on Coach Dusan's team? How does the coach treat his players?

11. Why do you think the author closed the book with the chapter about Thanksgiving and Conor meeting his grandparents? Why did he decide at first not to see them? Why did he change his mind? Describe their meeting and his reaction to his grandparents.

12. Conor makes observations about the different kinds of parents who attend their kids' hockey practices and games. Find examples from the novel and talk about them. What are some of the characteristics that parents display that are good for the athletes? What actions present problems for the child and the coach?

13. Describe Jae-won and his family. Consider Conor's friendship with him and his relationship with Jae-won's family. What

activities and feelings do the boys share? How are they different?

14. Describe Lucas's personality. In what ways is his family life different from Conor's? Why does Conor feel grateful for Lucas, and what does he learn from him?

15. This is a novel about hard choices. Identify some of the hard choices that Conor, his father, and others make in the book, and what Conor has to say about those choices. How does dealing with hard choices change some of the characters and their lives?

16. Conor's father says, "having a life you're passionate about is the only thing that's worth a can of beans in this world." What does he mean? What prompts him to say it? Who in the book has such a passion, and how has it affected his or her life?

17. Conor thinks about the importance of moving on from mistakes or disappointments, saying, "It's just like a tree getting burned down. Then you regenerate." What does he mean by that? What problems is he facing?

What are different ways he and Sinbad regenerate in the novel?

Turn the page for a sneak peek at
A Place to Belong.

THIS WAS THE secret thing Hanako felt about old people: she really didn't understand them. It seemed like they just sat there and didn't do much. Sometimes they were rude to you, and yet you had to be extremely, extremely polite to them. And when they were nice to you, they asked you lots and lots of questions. Lots!

Her mother's parents were both dead—Grandpa from being run over with a tractor while he was drunk, and Grandma from drowning in a giant wave off the coast of Hawaii. They had already passed away when Japan bombed Pearl Harbor. But when

Hanako had worked in her family's restaurant, she'd encountered many old people with their families for dinner. Mostly, as said, they just sat there.

And now her family was on this gigantic ship, going across the ocean to live with her father's elderly parents in Japan.

This was the thing about Japan: she had never been there. Her parents had told her for her entire life that it was important to be American. It was important to talk just a little more loudly than some of the girls who were being raised to be more Japanese. It was important to make eye contact and not cover your mouth when you laughed, like some of the more Japanese girls did. Basically, the way to be Japanese in America was to be more American than the Americans. And now she was being told she would need to learn to be more Japanese.

Her family had been imprisoned for almost four years—since she was eight—so as she stood here now, sometimes she felt like her insides were quivering, not with excitement but with fear. She did not know what was out there in the world, in the future. She had no idea. She knew that at this exact moment her family still didn't have any choices about what they could do with their lives, but from now on, and maybe forever, she would never be in jail and nobody would ever point a gun at her again.

"Hanako, do you have any candy left?" Hanako turned to look at her brother, who was standing in his underwear, his pajamas in his hands. He had pale eyebrows and a ton of black hair, with a big wine stain covering the skin around his right eye and beyond, like a pirate's patch. She kissed his stain the way she liked to do, because it was so beautiful. It was shaped like Australia, except sideways.

Reaching into her pocket, she pretended to be searching, though her fingers were already clutching a candy. "Hmm, I don't . . . oh, wait, I do!" She pulled the candy out and held it up triumphantly. Akira grinned and took it from her. She liked to make him grin—some days it was all she lived for, really. The candy was a butterscotch, his favorite. They had bought a bag of it a few weeks ago at one of the co-op stores in Tule Lake, where they'd last been imprisoned. Tule Lake was a high-security segregation center with almost 19,000 inmates. Each of the three camps where they'd been imprisoned had been different, all awful, but not in exactly the same ways. Plus, there was a different prison where her father had been held for almost a year. That was the most serious prison of all—even though he had been an American citizen, and even though he'd broken no law, he'd been housed with enemy prisoners of war from other countries in the freezing cold of North Dakota. Probably that prison was the most awful! She had never been freezing, but in Tule Lake she had been very cold for several days at a time, and she did not like it at all. Papa said that when you were freezing, your feet started to hurt a lot.

"Mmm, butterscotch!" Akira said, holding it up like he was looking at a marble.

Akira had a teensy, squeaky voice—sometimes Hanako thought he sounded like he would fit in your hand. She had to admit he was a strange little creature, with his squeaky voice and with Australia on his eye and with the way he was several inches shorter than other five-year-old boys. But it seemed as though their parents didn't even notice that he was different. They had always treated him just like they treated her. They acted like he didn't sometimes cry himself to sleep at night, even though you could hear him. When he was only a baby, Mama had said, "He was born sad." She had rarely spoken of it again, but Hanako had not forgotten it. She was always looking for signs of sadness in his face, and she often found such signs. Sometimes, even when nothing bad had happened, he looked like he wanted to cry from something—maybe loneliness?

After Akira put the candy in his mouth, she put his pajamas on him, sneaking a look toward her mom, who she knew didn't like her to baby him. But she didn't see Mama anywhere.

"What if we sink?" he asked suddenly.

Hanako tried to think of something comforting to say to her brother. It was hard, because she didn't know how something as big as this ship *could* stop itself from sinking. "It's impossible for us to sink," was what she came up with. "It's a US Navy vessel. It's probably one of the best ships in the world." The ship they were on was called the USS *Gordon*, and it was about two football fields long. She didn't understand how airplanes flew, and she didn't understand how ships floated. She'd been quite scared about that. But at this point, who even cared? They were on the ship, and they weren't getting off. Life was a tunnel; there was only one direction they could go.

Akira grabbed her hand and started digging into it with his nails. Hanako always cut his nails into sharp spikes, because he liked them like that. He said he needed to protect himself from . . . he could never say what. Hanako tried to wriggle her hand free. In response, he dug in harder.

She concentrated on keeping her voice calm like she (almost) always did with him. "Akira, can you hold on to my sleeve instead, *please*?"

"All right," he said, grabbing her purple coat and pulling at it. She didn't like him to pull on her purple coat—it was her favorite thing, and it was from a store instead of sewn by her mother. But she didn't scold him, though that took a heap of self-control. She didn't want him to say what he'd said to her twice in the past: "You like your coat more than you like me!"

She looked around but didn't see where their

mother had gone off to. Mama always liked to know what was going on. In camp she used to go out every morning after breakfast and just talk and talk to people. That's what Hanako had heard, anyway; she was at school. Mama was obsessed about *what was going on*. It was like she was desperate to know more. Always *more*. Mama used to be a calm person—serene, even. She never used to care that much about what was happening in the outside world. But in camp, her eyes became filled with a hunger to know things.

Hanako looked around, wondering if anybody here actually knew anything about what was going on. How would anyone know? It was very crowded here in the sleeping quarters, and you couldn't see much because the aisles—the space between each set of bunks—was maybe two feet. So mostly all you could see were the people in the two feet of space near you.

She scrambled up to the top bunk, looking around and seeing . . . more bunks. But not that many. Sixty? In stacks of four. So two hundred and forty people sleeping here. Supposedly there were thousands of Nikkei being sent to Japan on this very ship. Nikkei were people of Japanese descent, whether they were citizens of America, Japan, or in any other country. Only women and children were in this room, but she didn't see Mama. It was strange how quiet the whole crowd was; she heard not a single word, except from themselves. Then Akira whimpered, "Hanako, I'm scared. Why do we have to go on this ship?"

She tried to get quickly down, tumbling to the floor and then immediately dusting off her coat. "Because we don't belong in America anymore," she said as she dusted.

Akira closed his right eye and tilted his head. That's what he did sometimes when he was trying to decide something. "I think I do. I do belong in America."

Hanako thought this over. That was a hard one, because she wasn't sure about it. "Belonging" was a difficult concept at the moment. Really, for the people on this ship, they "belonged" with their families, if they had them. Where else was there to belong at this point?

It was a complicated and confusing story, why they had to be on this ship. So she always just told Akira, "We have to go to Japan because Papa and Mama say so." There was no way to think about it and have it make sense. First, Japan had bombed Pearl Harbor, Hawaii, in early December 1941, a little more than four years ago. Second, that caused America to enter World War II. And third, more than 110,000 Nikkei—mostly American citizens—living on the West Coast had been imprisoned in ten different places for no good reason. And then about 6,000 more had been born in the camps! What had Hanako's family done wrong that they had to be held captive for almost *four* entire years? They ran a restaurant in Little Tokyo in Los Angeles! They were sent to a temporary camp nearby, then a permanent one in Jerome, Arkansas. Jerome was a bad camp, because the director was really tough and made some of the inmates cut down trees for the whole camp for heat in the winter. Logging was one of the most deadly professions in America. Papa said that at Jerome, it was grueling work with old equipment. The men—like Papa—who worked as loggers there had no prior experience, so Hanako was always worried that someone would get killed. The other camps were provided with coal, but Jerome's director, Mr. Taylor, wouldn't stand for that. He was only thirty-four, and Papa said he did not have the least idea of what the difference was between right and wrong. But, still, he insisted Hanako and Akira call him "Mr." She called him "Taylor" once, and Papa reprimanded her for being rude. "But he didn't hear me, he's not even here," she had replied. Her father hadn't answered, just frowned at her.

One time she had complained to Akira, "I don't know why we have to call him 'Mr.'" And Akira had said patiently to her, "Because he's the *boss man*, Hana." And he was only three years old when he said that! Actually, Hanako had realized she agreed with him, because that's the way she was raised: She could not stand the idea of not showing a grown-up respect. Even if it made her angry and sometimes made her cry, she could not stand it. Even if it ripped her whole heart out, she could not have stood it. So she always called him Mr. Taylor after that. She also hated him.